About the

Otto's fascination with horror started from a young age with television series such as the *Addams Family*, the *Munsters* and the *Twilight Zone*. He sought out horror and gothic literature classics writers, such as Mary Shelley, Bram Stoker, H P Lovecraft and Edgar Allen Poe and developed a love for the classic Hammer Horror and B-movies of the 1960s and 1970s. Otto revelled in the dark and strange worlds created by Wes Craven, Jess

Franco and Jean Rolling and the charismatic acting of Christopher Lee, Peter Cushing and Vincent Price. Finally, during the COVID lockdown he decided to turn his hand to writing horror stories of his own. Otto lives in the beautiful Hampshire countryside alongside his many loyal cats.

THE VAMPIRE OF PORTSMOUTH

Otto Redman

THE VAMPIRE OF PORTSMOUTH

Otto Redman

Vanguard Press

Dedication

For my loving brother

Acknowledgements

I would like to thank my GCSE English teacher David, for giving me a lifelong interest in literature; and my brother for repeatedly reading through my story.

Prologue

'And every spirit that confeseth not that
Jesus Christ is come in the flesh is not from
God: andthis is that spirit of the antichrist,
whereof ye have heard that it should come;
and even now already is it in the world'

John 4:3

(King James version)

A smartly dressed man in his forties made his way at a fast pace through the dark back streets of the more dubious side of York, his expensive finery concealed beneath the folds of a large and tatty cloak. He was a tall, thin man with light blue eyes and a meticulously sculpted beard that further added to his appearance of nobility. He had left his family's manor a short while ago, growing fed up with the 'high society' party that was being held there tonight. He found these sorts of events so desperately boring, completely lacking in excitement and stimulation, driving him to the brink of wanting to kill either the guests or himself. As he had become talented at playing several musical instruments over the years, his mother would always make him perform, and he hated it. To her it was a moment of pride, for him it was a cruel and unnecessary punishment, worse than any humiliation that they could bestow. To sit there pouring all his heart and emotions into his music to a roomful of aristocratic fools with the musical ability of an ass was degrading. He liked his position in society and accepted that it came with certain responsibilities that needed to be fulfilled, but that request was a step too far, and one that they did not deserve. His music was to be appreciated and not just a showpiece to uphold family egos or as a background filler to drunken behaviour. He could have accepted the drunkenness more if there had been a few pretty young ladies present at the event to dance with and have fun around; a pretty face would always cheer up a dull party, but most of his father's guests were much older, and about as attractive as a wild boar. He wanted some real drinks and good available women, like that of Lord Walton's gentleman's club, which he had had the pleasure of attending on several occasions. By the end of the night at those events the girls were always easily available, and fun could be had until the morning.

He had no particular destination in mind when he had set out, and wandered around the streets aimlessly, looking for a tavern where he could perhaps pick up a couple of whores for the night. In a strange way, he enjoyed the randomness of just wandering down the streets looking for new ventures, as there were always new places and pretty faces to discover. His parents hated his night-time activities, and on several occasions had been forced to buy off a young girl's father in order to keep his reputation in a suitable condition for the family's status; but he had always enjoyed the thrill of running from a girl's chambers whilst her father chased him with a pitchfork — it made him feel alive and free from responsibility.

The moon was high tonight, and cast an unnatural light across the streets, throwing an almost blue shimmer onto the cobblestones, and creating long well-defined shadows. He was not a timid man, and had been jailed several times for fighting, once for assaulting a girl's father after he caught them together in a back alley, and several times for settling disputes surrounding gambling with his fists; but he was not stupid either, and knew that these streets could be dangerous to a gentleman of his standing, but the shabby cape that covered his fine clothes and hiding his brightly coloured garments helped disguise his true identity, and besides, he was a good fighter and more than capable of defending himself, and if there was a serious problem from more professional ruffians, he kept a selection of blades concealed around his person, just in case they were needed. He was good with these weapons and had spent many hours practising throwing them as a youth and become quite an expert over the years.

He passed a small tavern called the 'Blood of the King', where the smell of mead and music drifted onto the street. He was about to go in on hearing the musical chime of women's voices and the potential of fun, when he noticed the shape of a pale young lady down the alleyway beside the free house, and she seemed to be beckoning to him. This spiked his curiosity as well as his loins, and he made his way towards her.

'*Come,*' she seemed to say to him with her eyes. '*Come, I will make you happy. I understand your needs and can fulfil them, tonight, come...*' — and she backed away, always keeping a short distance ahead of him, dancing and skipping quickly, then turning and beckoning again, allowing him to catch up, before racing off again, teasing him. She was a fine young girl of about twenty, with a very pale complexion and intense blue eyes. Oh, those eyes! They seemed to burn with a passionate fire that drew him on. It was electric, and he just couldn't seem to help himself.

Her blonde hair was so fair it was almost white and was tied up in a series of complicated plaits. She wore a red silk gown, which plunged low at the front, exposing her white, almost see-through bodice, which amplified her plentiful cleavage in all the right places. It tapered in at her shapely waist and then flowered outwards in many pleats, revealing the quality of its workmanship. She was truly a stunner, and seemed very well off; surely, she wasn't the daughter of any of the pathetic peasants in this town, or a common whore after a trick? Not that it would have bothered him, but this girl was bewitching, she was truly something special, and he desired, no had to know more about her.

Eventually, once they had reached the outskirts of the woods, she finally allowed him to catch up with her, and she turned to face him. Her smile was intoxicating, making his head swim and his feet unsteady. The whiteness of her teeth was dazzling and made him feel self-conscious about his own slightly yellow and crooked ones. She reached out to him with one hand and with the other lifted her skirt to well above her knee, revealing the pale porcelain-coloured skin of her leg and some of her many multi-coloured petticoats. He had been with many women, but the sight bewitched him more than ever before.

'*Come to me, Adam,*' she said seductively. '*Become one with me and we can run this godforsaken area together as it should be.*'

'How do you know my name?' he stuttered. Was this a trap to embroil him in a scandal?

'*I have watched you by night for weeks, Mr Decker.*' She hoiked her skirts higher, revealing far more than just her leg this time. '*I am Countess Rebecca Gunther of noble blood from Germany, and you will be mine,*' she whispered, '*forever...*' — and it sounded more of a statement of fact than a suggestive idea, although she was now unlacing the top of her bodice, setting his heart pounding. He could now detect the German tinge to her pronunciation of certain words, and she was beginning to move closer towards him, swaying her hips as she walked. He desired her, there was no doubt about that, and he pulled her closer to him roughly, feeling her leg from the knee right the way up to her hip. She giggled musically, and put her arms around him, pulling his head closer to hers, and she leaned right in and bit his neck. At first this shocked him, but instead of pain as he had expected, he felt such pleasure, and he pulled her even closer to him, realising that she felt so cold to the touch, and desired to warm her up. They both sank to the ground embracing, and when he awoke, she was gone, and the sun was beginning to rise in the morning sky, beginning to cast its warmth onto the grass.

From that day on, he returned to that very spot every night to meet with the mysterious and beautiful young lady, engaging in both passion and blood drinking. He loved her both physically and mentally, for she had no equal. Her mind was like one that had lived for hundreds of years gaining wisdom and experience, and he found that he loved her, and finally pledged his soul to her shortly before his unexpected death on 5th March 1720 at the age of just forty, leaving strict instructions about his funeral arrangements, and that under no circumstances should he be burnt. It was said in gossip around the town that he had been drained of blood, and his complexion at his funeral was completely white like a swan's feathers, or that he had sold his soul to the devil, but no one could prove the rumours' validity as his body was kept at his parents' estate in the family crypt as requested, and therefore unreachable, for it was guarded against such desecration.

His parents took his death badly, and were distraught at the passing of their only son, and no longer took guests or held parties as they had previously, and instead, withdrew from society until they died together a year later on 15th November 1721 and were laid to rest in the crypt alongside their son's body. The procedures and inheritance of the estate were taken care of the very next day by a mysterious relative who was just returning from his travels around Europe. He looked a distinguished man who bore an almost exact likeness to their son, so his claim to the estate was never even questioned due to the family resemblance. He had returned from his travels with an amazingly beautiful and astonishingly blonde, almost white-haired wife, Rebecca, whose startling beauty was the talk for miles around. Their movements were eccentric, like most well-off gentry, and they were typically only ever seen after dark, where they held extravagant parties, inviting guests from far and wide, and Lord James and Lady Rebecca Decker's events gradually became legendary throughout the whole of England, gaining them the nickname of the 'twilight couple'.

The Decker family were not just loved by the wealthy, academic and Bohemian artists, but gained an improved popularity with the people of the village when they provided the opportunity for over a hundred jobs through their massive redesigning and landscaping of the estate's large gardens, which also included the building of an improved and extra-secure family crypt and vaults that extended from the manor house for miles, if the rumours were correct. Many more people moved into the area to cope with all the work, and the Deckers even provided funds for a school to be built to manage their children's education, and funded a yearly feast for the whole village, including dances, games and a competition to name the year's village beauty, which became a very popular and well-attended event that ran from dusk to dawn, with the Lord and Lady leading the first and last dance of the night. Their dancing was the most elegant and accomplished York had seen; as the twilight couple spun around the ballroom, the sequins and gems on their clothes sparkled under the candlelight. They made an elegant couple, and the villagers were always mesmerised by their occasional appearances, and their ease at interactions made everyone feel welcome and important.

A fascination for the village teens and children were the exotic animals that the Deckers kept. They had many large wolves that they took with them when hunting at night, their howls audible for miles around, and they could just be spotted roaming the grounds when a brave teen dared to peer over the walls. They also had several large aviaries containing bats and crows rather than birds of prey, which was the fashion of the time, although the keen of eye could possibly have noticed that they were being used for the same hunting purposes, released from gloved hands and sent to attack small birds and mice, returning to their keeper with a whistle.

Rumours also spread that the Lord and Lady Decker were the area's hosts of the only ever whispered about hellfire club meetings, and heads of the 'Order of Darkness' secret society. Tales spread in the taverns late at night when tongues were loosened by alcohol, of many light pyres being visible at night, along with naked dancers and huge blood orgies visible under the moon, but as with any gossip from locals, much was put down to rumours and fanciful imaginations. It did not become known for many years how many of the village's young men and women actually attended these hushed events, and how many of them didn't ever remember going, bearing two marks on their throat, which rumours suggested were the trademark of a secret society.

Strangely, as is often found when things are in plain sight, the Lord and Lady's lack of ageing over the years was never questioned by the villagers! For those that saw them on the public engagements that they made, their skin remained unlined, their hair free from grey, and their eyes never lost that burning intensity.

Chapter 1
The Train, Interview and a Night Out

'Wherefore, as by one man sin entered
Into the world , and death by sin; and
so death passed upon all men,
for that all have sinned:'
Romans 5:12
(King James Version)

In the darkness of an early dawn in the first week of November, a dirty blue VW Golf headed up the A3 at a point roughly level with Drift Road in Clanfield, breaking the stillness of the day with a noise typically associated with a hole in the exhaust pipe. Hellen was running late again and was in considerable danger of missing her train to London Waterloo. This should have come as no real surprise for her, as she was usually unintentionally late for almost everything, no matter how hard she tried. Today she had hoped would be different, and had even left home early as a precaution, and now she couldn't really figure out how this could be happening to her despite her extensive efforts to be early. She smiled as she remembered what her father told her when she was sixteen: 'You'll be late for your own funeral one day,' he had joked after she had managed to turn up over an hour late for her own birthday party. She missed her father dearly and had never quite come to terms with his tragic death in an unexpected accident two years ago, just a month before her fortieth birthday, which she thought to herself completed a really shitty year, coinciding with the break-up of her relationship with John, and the subsequent diagnosis of her mother's terminal illness.

She checked her watch again as she finally pulled into Petersfield station and hunted around desperately for a parking place. Most people these days had forsaken watches in favour of their mobile phone, but she remained old fashioned in this respect and always wore her small gold watch with the thin black leather strap. Ever since her mother had given it to her as a Christmas present over thirty years ago, she had never gone out without it. *'Why at five in the morning can't I find a bloody space?'* she thought to herself, a strange phenomenon that never ceased to amaze her, and should probably have its own ties within chaos theory, and after several further circles of the car park she finally gave up and drove the short distance into town and parked in the car park behind the supermarket. Frantically she rummaged through her handbag for enough change to pay; she was sure that she had put enough money in there yesterday, it ought to be in there, as it was damn well heavy enough. There was no way she was going to risk getting her details cloned by some spotty punk by using her card in the machine's unguarded chip and pin mechanism, which was something that had happened to her mother ten years ago. 'Why couldn't they just use contactless?' she mumbled to herself and the small number of pigeons that had bothered to come out early looking for food. The birds were cautiously edging towards her to catch the many crumbs dropping onto the floor from her bag. Eventually, after chipping a nail and getting an unknown sticky substance under another, she had found enough change to pay, spent what seemed like too much valuable time feeding it into the slot, and was finally able to collect the ticket, which she chucked onto the dashboard, hastily locked her car and set off walking up Lavant Street towards the station, her heels' gentle click following her in the dark of the morning.

It was at this point that there was a rumble across the sky, and it started to rain, just small droplets to start with speckling her face like her freckles, but as she hurried along, they became more frequent, and got larger and heavier.

For the first time on travelling up to London, Hellen had been efficient and actually bought her ticket in advance and was able to just step onto the train at the very moment that the guard blew his whistle and the doors closed behind her with a squeak. Before finding a seat, which she knew wasn't going to be a problem until at least Haslemere, she walked down the carriages until she found the toilet, and went in. She pushed the button and waited until the door rolled shut with its distinctive trundling sound that reminded her of those old

American detective shows where the prison door slammed shut. She hated that noise and especially those doors, and always took extra care that it was locked after an incident the previous year when one had actually opened on her, exposing her squatting on the loo with her knickers around her ankles, to a crowded carriage of rather embarrassed commuters, who she bet were not as embarrassed as she was, and she remembered turning as red as her hair. Why the door mechanism had to be on the opposite wall to the toilet she could not fathom but felt sure that it had been designed by a man, who at least had the ability to turn his back to the door, whereas she had had to face them, and would have had to stand up to shut it, if a kindly older woman hadn't pushed the close button on the outside.

Using the large and well-lit mirror above the sink, she tidied up her long, slightly curly red hair which had become blown around and wet on the walk from the car to the station and took a minute to check her appearance in the mirror. She didn't like to think of herself as vain, but always liked to be smart in her appearance, something her mother had installed in her from a young age, saying, 'Always look as smart as you are intelligent, Hellen; look like you mean business', along with the slightly less useful advice of 'Always wear clean knickers in case you have an accident and get taken to hospital' — but she had to admit, she had always followed it. Her mother had always been inventive with memorable sayings, which she swore had been passed down from her mother, and by God did she miss them now that she wasn't here. For forty-two years old, Hellen was still very pleased with her appearance, and was often mistaken for thirty. Her fiery hair did not display any greys as yet, and her face was remarkably line-free. She required no make-up, and actually chose not to wear much anyway, as she felt that the small scattering of freckles covering her face made her look cute, which, of course, they did. She smoothed out her tweed skirt which hung just above her knee, and brushed the excess water from her jacket, wishing that she had brought a coat. It was heading towards winter, after all, and they never got the weather right — sunshine indeed, that had been highly optimistic. A piece of seaweed hung up on a washing line could have proved more accurate with its predictions.

Annoyingly, her white blouse was now uncomfortably damp, and she checked carefully that it had not become too transparent, embarrassingly noting that it was at that point of turning. She was proud of her trim and firm body, with her small, pert breasts, and was grateful that neither had as yet thrown their hand in and given way to gravity. Hellen would not normally have worried as she always wore sensible underwear, but she desperately didn't want to give the wrong impression at her interview: she desperately needed this job. She felt sure that for a lecturing position, a visible pink bra and nipples winking at you through the lace would not send the message that she wanted. 'Why didn't I wear the black one?' she said to herself, rather annoyed with her decision and almost stamped her foot, a habit from her childhood. 'What was I thinking of?' She had worked hard over the years to get where she was, and although she could potentially swing an interview easily on her looks, as she had before when applying for temporary work whilst an undergraduate, but she wanted to get this job on her abilities, and not on whether the panel wanted to fuck her.

Once finished, she made her way to the nearest seat and spent the journey on her laptop, making small tweaks and corrections to her presentation for the Head of Chemistry position at King's College. If this went well, she planned to move to London for a fresh start after the death of her mother in the summer. Hellen's attention was only distracted when the train began to pass through the outskirts of London, and an arch of lightning made its way across the sky with a crack and the heavens opened up with torrential rain. Sighing, she checked just to make sure her umbrella was still in her bag; she felt sure that she had put it in when she had also squeezed in her laptop. It wasn't. 'Damn,' she mouthed to herself as the thunder rumbled outside and the rain began pounding the glass of the window next to her, and she remembered that it was probably still sitting on the bed with the other things that she had meant to bring along with her but had forgotten, including her diary and spare panties, another of her mum's requirements for a sensible woman's handbag. '*Well*,' she thought miserably, '*here's to another victory for sod's law.*'

For the first time that she could remember from her many trips to London over the years, the train actually arrived at Waterloo station on time, and after getting through the ticket gates, which, as usual, wouldn't accept her ticket and she had to wait for a less than enthusiastic station hand to slowly walk over and let her through, eyeing her with suspicion as if she was trying to avoid paying her fare, she stepped out onto the main station. Hellen then had to make her way across Waterloo Bridge in the torrential rain, a not unsubstantial distance in the open, with little in the way of cover. Running wasn't really preventing her from getting wet, but she was pleased that she could still run in heels without falling over, and she couldn't remember the last time that she had done that. Having had to give up her job at Portsmouth University due to caring for her mother in the last months of her life, she was now running short of money and couldn't afford the price of getting a taxi, given how long it would take to get through the traffic. Hellen always tried to look for the positive in events and thought to herself that at least her make-up couldn't run. Finally, dripping wet, she entered King's College and made her way to the toilets to see if she could use the hand drier to dry off; it had worked before on many occasions when she was an undergraduate and might save her today.

* * *

It was five in the evening and darkness was falling quickly. Hellen was tucked into a corner table in a small independent coffee shop off Camden High Street, nursing her fifth Americano. She hadn't been able to face going home yet, and was still crying about the day's events, and her eyes had become red and the skin around them puffy. Everything that could possibly have gone wrong, had done. 'Bastards,' she muttered to herself whilst tracing the outside edge of her mobile phone for no real reason other than because she was stressed. Despite dripping water on the floor throughout the interview, which no one appeared to notice or care about, her laptop had refused to talk to the projector halfway through her presentation and the interview panel had been made up mostly of women who seemed to spend most of their time focusing on a male candidate called Aaron, making it obvious to her that he was an internal candidate and the fact that the job had been advertised at all was only to fulfil legal requirements, and was already decided. The rest of their time was engaged in critiquing her at any possible opportunity, far more visibly than she thought an 'impartial' panel was legally allowed to do. They didn't quite make it obvious, but their faces showed it, along with the snide comments and the put-downs that they kept dropping in about the standards of Portsmouth University and the quality of its research. They were unfair academic

27

snobs, and most of it was untrue. She had worked hard there and produced many internationally well-received papers, and if she hadn't been upset enough, her bra had been showing through her blouse, as one of the panel had sneeringly pointed out after informing her of the panel's decision, with a superior look on her face, using that new quite horrible form of passive aggression. At which point she had pulled her jacket tightly around herself, grabbed her bag and stormed off. She would have liked to have really given it to that bitch, but she had already felt the tears coming, and didn't want to give them the satisfaction of seeing that they had got to her. She typically liked to hide her emotions and deal with them herself in private and had only on a few occasions broken down in public, her father's death being one of them.

After several hours wandering aimlessly around central London, she had made her way to Camden and had lunch in the 'Worlds End' pub opposite the underground station. She had always liked the place since first visiting it as a teenager and felt that there was something other worldly about it, sort of like the 'Prancing Pony' in Tolkien's *Lord of the Rings*. After enjoying a trip down memory lane wandering around the huge variety of stalls and shops, Hellen had bought a cheap coat in the market to keep warm; not an expense that she had wanted, but it was cold and on top of everything she did not want to catch a cold.

'*What do I do now?*' she thought, taking a bite out of the chocolate muffin that she had been nibbling on for the last hour or so. She didn't want to stay in Portsmouth as it held too many bad memories for her now, and she needed to move on and start fresh somewhere else. She came to the decision to apply for some of the other lectureships that she had seen advertised further afield tomorrow, and concluded that as she was in London already, she might for the first time in a year enjoy a night out, and just add it on the credit card, '*Yes,*' she thought, '*she — Dr Hellen Oswold — was going to be reckless.*' She was usually against such behaviour, but this was an exception and she needed cheering up, by God did she need cheering up! So, she finished her coffee, wrapped the remains of her muffin into a napkin, stuffing it into her bag to crumble and become forgotten about until a later date. She dried her eyes with her fancy silk handkerchief that her friend Sophie had given her when at school, with 'Tough Bitch' embroidered onto it, and headed back out into Camden, although this time she looked more confident than when she had walked into the coffee shop two hours earlier.

Hellen managed to get a returned ticket at the box office and enjoyed watching the evening production of Andrew Lloyd Webber's *Phantom of the Opera*. She had always loved the bit when she stepped through the mirror as the phantom enticed the heroine on and wondered why she had not listened to it for so long. She made her way back up to Camden's Underworld so that she could see a band that she had seen advertised in the 'Worlds End' called 'The Devil's Rejects', one that she had not listened to since she was twenty, shortly after their original singer had committed suicide in a highly publicised event where he was found hanging off London Bridge from a rope which went into his mouth, through his digestive system and out of his ass. No one had managed to establish how this was possible, and to some extent how it had actually even been classified as suicide. She shuddered at the thought, as she had a crush on him for a year or two, and had once even tried to get to see him by going around to his tour bus at the end of a show in Southampton, but his crew had turned her away fearing that she was under age, for she had always looked younger than her years. Whilst this was annoying when trying to get a drink at eighteen, she felt that it proved an advantage now that she was older. Once the headliner took the stage, she let the music wash over her and began to feel like a teenager again, hopping up and down to the thumping beat of the double-kick drum, and from nowhere managed to sing along to most of the songs, the lyrics just popping back into her mind. The only difference she could see from when she was younger was that she looked rather silly head-banging in a tweed suit, but what the hell, it had been a bad day and she felt young and carefree again, even if it only lasted for a short while.

The new singer was pretty good, and the set included all their favourites such as 'Frankenstein is my Bitch', 'Dracula was a Pussy' and 'Necrophilia is Cool', ending with their famous track 'I was Fucked by a Werewolf and had Pups', and as Hellen headed up the old rickety stairs to exit the venue, she checked the time on her watch and realised that it had stopped. 'Hey, what's the time?' she had to shout at the burly security guard, fighting to be heard over the music.

'It's midnight, ginger dear,' he replied, whilst suddenly having to prevent a large aggressive-looking bald guy with a huge beard getting into the venue without a wristband.

'Oh shit, I've missed my last train,' she thought, beginning to panic. She certainly did not have the money to get a hotel for the night, even if she could find an available room, and she didn't want to spend the night wandering around the town on her own in the dark. *'Calm down, Hellen,'* she told herself. *'You're not a kid, you're not going to get mugged or raped on just one occasion; you did it many times when younger, you just slept on a bench at the station.'* Having said that, she remembered that she had always been with Sophie or Ben, and two kids were safer together than one, especially as Ben was quite big, and she thought to herself *'You'll just have to find somewhere safe to kill time, until the first train of the morning.'*

Whilst standing in the warmth of the doorway of the kebab shop opposite the Underworld, her mind raced as to where she could go that would be relatively safe. She didn't fancy a night club, unless it was a last resort, because as a single woman on her own, she would have to spend the night turning down propositions from random drunk men, and that always presented the chance that things could get nasty, as drunk men never liked being turned down. Besides, she was really a bit old for clubbing. God, she hated admitting to that, it made her sound middle-aged, which, depressingly, it dawned on her that she was. Middle-aged, single and unlikely now to have children. Shit, there was a downer. A gay club could be a possibility, but she didn't fancy the loud noise and really needed somewhere to sit down, as she was feeling tired. Helen then remembered that the legendary Ronnie Scott's Jazz Club often did a late set that ran on well into the early hours, perhaps even two or three in the morning, which would cover a couple of hours until she had time to think of what to do until the first train of the morning; so, she hurried down the stairs to the underground and headed for Tottenham Court Road and Frith Street. Once inside, she was warm and comfortable sitting on the nice, padded seats and able to get a drink and listen to the smooth jazz playing on the stage, a marked difference to the Underworld, and she was pleased to note that she had listened to a stage musical, death metal and jazz all in one night. 'Live it up, girl' came to mind — that's what Sophie would say. She didn't know the group that was playing, but they weren't bad, and in a short while her eyelids began to droop and she drifted off to sleep, protectively clutching her handbag to her chest.

* * *

'Hello.'

There came a distant voice.

'Are you all right?'

Hellen nodded awake to find a rather handsome man trying to talk to her. She blinked.

'Sorry, what were you saying?' She blinked again to make her eyes adjust to the dim light.

'Beg your pardon, my lady, I was just asking if you were all right? This club will be shutting soon, and I noticed you from the stage,' said the stranger.

Hellen smiled and involuntarily blinked her large green eyes for effect. On glancing over him again, she thought that he was very well dressed, if not slightly old-fashioned for a man of his age, which she reckoned must have been about mid-thirties; but musicians tended to want to make fashion statements, and hey, what the hell, she wouldn't expect anyone to judge her on what she was wearing. He was dressed in a dark green smoking jacket, long enough to be a Victorian frock coat, a ruffle shirt and dark round glasses which hid his eyes. His face was clean-shaven, his skin so very pale and she noticed slightly drawn in, probably caused by the night-based lifestyle musicians tended to have, and

33

more importantly, no wedding ring, although there was a mark where one had been. She quickly rebuked herself for this thought as he was much too young for her, and then she realised that he was still waiting for a reply.

'Oh,' she said, stammering, 'sorry! Miles away there. I'm all right, just a very long and tiring day. Thanks for waking me. I'm Hellen, by the way.' She extended her hand towards him, offering to shake hands, but he instead took her hand and kissed it gently with dry and slightly cracked lips, which sent tremors through her body. '*How quaintly old-fashioned,*' she thought, '*but cute; well, perhaps creepily cute. Did anyone actually do that any more?*' She had certainly not come across it; she had had her ass pinched on several occasions, been whistled at, and on one occasion even had her boobs grabbed, but not that. Hand kissing was surely *Jane Eyre* territory!

'What a lovely name, my dear, as in the Greek mythology' he replied, his voice musical and almost hypnotic. 'Mine is Adam, and I am at your service.'

He sat down opposite her. 'I play sax in the band, my lady, and I couldn't help but see you nodding off at the back. I hope I wasn't too boring? My solos can go on a bit, but when you're in the zone, you're aware of nothing else.' He said this with a smile and Hellen flushed a dark shade of scarlet at having been spotted sleeping.

'No, no, I was just up at four a.m. this morning. Er, sorry, I probably mean yesterday morning now, and I just dropped off. Nothing to do with your playing, honestly.'

She felt that this sounded shallow, but it was the truth; there was no point in lying, and hey, she didn't know him, but he did seem nice.

'I'm only joking,' he said. 'Any excuse to have a drink with a pretty young lady and talk to someone other than another jazzer. I have heard their stories so many times and it becomes so tiring.'

Hellen inwardly cringed at what was probably the worst chat-up line she had heard since college, when a scruffy lad in caterpillar boots and a Metallica t-shirt had come up to her and declared, 'Nice legs, darling, what time do they open?' and had gained himself a sore face and her a sore hand from her replying slap. But she was also somehow drawn to this stranger. He had removed his glasses now to reveal his intense pale blue eyes, which seemed to also be burning red at the same time, but that couldn't be right, it must be the lighting in the club. As she looked into them, she began to get the feeling that he might be far older than his appearance portrayed. There was just something about him — what was it? Age, sadness, maybe regret, but defiant determination, and a little worryingly, anger, which made her shiver despite the warmth of the club. She felt the hairs on her neck rise for no reason, along with a strange tingling through her body as she looked into those eyes. With an effort, she pulled her gaze away, which seemed to leave her with a sudden emptiness, and a strong desire to look back. She felt the immediate need for some fresh air and stood up suddenly, knocking her bag off the table.

'I'm... I'm very... very sorry, but I'd... better... I'd better go, I have to get... somewhere. I have to get to the... er... to the station.' She struggled to pick up her bag from the floor, and almost rushed the words out, stumbling and repeating herself. He said some pleasantries, but she didn't really hear them; her head was now swimming, his words unintelligible, and she made her way to the door, a humming sound penetrating her head, echoing around, getting louder and louder, causing her to stumble, which was when everything went black.

* * *

Lights flashed all around, and she didn't know if she was standing, lying or flying. Blood seemed to rush to every part of her body, internal and external, causing pleasure and pain to merge and exist together in every one of her nerve endings, while her head seemed to swim through murky water that was thicker than a soup. Two white peaks began to circle around her vision to a background of blurred colours, like two coins in a lava lamp. Her hair suddenly stood erect, as did her nipples, whilst shots of pain flashed through her from her neck to her feet, like the lightning she had seen the day before. Then there was a rushing, like a dam had opened, a rush of open-headed emptiness typically associated with either passing out or an orgasm, and then...

Hellen woke with a gasp, sucking in air as if she had been drowning under water. When her eyes finally focused enough to see, she found herself in a gloomy backstreet, laid curled up amongst the rubbish bags on the floor and the litter that was piled up by the wall. At the end of the street a drug addict lay in the corner, while a drunk shuffled around on unsteady feet, pissing by his feet, droplets springing back up from the floor and speckling his shoes. '*My god*,' she thought as her head cleared, '*that bastard raped me, he drugged my drink and raped me.*' She had read all about date-rape drugs in scientific journals and seen the tragic results on the news. She frantically felt herself over, but nothing seemed to be wrong; there was nothing out of place, no cuts, no blood, no bruises, all her clothes were untorn, even her tights — which usually took any opportunity to ladder or tear — were fully intact, and she still had her handbag with her cards and money, so a mugging was out of the question. The drunk at the end of the alley viewed her frantic movements suspiciously, and he shuffled off after taking the drug addict's shoes. Her blouse was the only article of her clothes that seemed disturbed, which was now unbuttoned down to her navel, but all the buttons were intact.

It was now heading towards dawn; she judged about five or six in the morning, as it was still very quiet, and despite wracking her memories she could remember nothing of what happened since speaking to Adam at the club, and she remembered that face very clearly. She clambered up and out of the pile of bags and staggered out of the alley as her legs protested at the effort. Hellen turned out to be in a small road just off the building works where Duke Street was. She checked herself over again, and after still finding no signs of abuse, she made her way towards the underground station, where she bumped into a police woman, who seemed to be finishing for the night and was just getting into her car with a large cup of coffee and a sandwich that was so large that no normal human could possibly consume it, and half fell onto the panda car's bonnet.

Several hours later, Hellen was in a soft chair in the police station, drinking a rather dilute coffee from a mug stating to the world 'Best cop ever', whilst waiting for something to happen. It had been over an hour since she had last spoken to anyone, and she decided that the cup would have been better off saying 'Slowest cop ever'. Following standard procedure, she had been taken to hospital and examined intimately by the doctors, which, despite being hugely embarrassing, was a success for her mother's sayings, and she was relieved that she had new panties on. It had only revealed what she was already sure of, that she had not been drugged or raped; her blood pressure was a bit too high, even taking the night's events into account, and they felt that she might be anaemic, as she was very pale, and might well just have fainted when coming out of the club into the cold air of the night.

After a further half an hour wait, an overweight and rather red-faced detective with thinning hair came into the room and sat down next to her and introduced himself as Detective James Dick.

'Well, Miss Oswold.'

'Er, Doctor,' she corrected him kindly. She hadn't spent all her life working to gain that prestigious title without using it.

'Dr Oswold, the bloods run at the hospital showed no sign of any known date-rape drugs or other narcotics in your system, and you were not sexually assaulted as there was no bruising, tears, bleeding, residues of semen or any typical signs of sexual assault, so this is a bit of a mystery. If you would follow me, please.' He led her to another room filled with TV screens and computers and pointed to one particular screen with a frozen image of an alley on it. 'We looked up the street's CCTV, one of the reasons everything took a while — we weren't just keeping you waiting for nothing — and found little that was of use, just what you see here.' He clicked 'play' on the computer and the image began to move. In it, Hellen walked very slowly, almost unnaturally slowly into the alley, where she then stood still almost in direct view of the camera, unbuttoned her blouse down to her belly button piercing, and then very strangely lent her head to one side. She stood like that for several minutes, until she finally seemed to float a couple of inches into the air and fly backwards into the rubbish bags, where she remained crumpled up and unmoving. All the time there was an annoying fuzz present that seemed to follow her image on the screen until the point at which she flew backwards, when it flashed off the screen in the other direction.

Hellen involuntarily rubbed her neck at the place that had been exposed in the video. 'Ouch,' she said, realising that she had two small puncture marks on her neck: her fingers could distinctly make the swellings out, and the movement started them bleeding. 'What's that?' she said, as she tried to look at them in the small mirror that she kept in her bag. The policeman lent towards her and seeming rather embarrassed looked at her neck, and sure enough there were two small marks there.

'It looks like a love bite, Miss! Did you forget to mention something to us about earlier in the evening or perhaps at home, an over-friendly boyfriend?'

'No, I told you who I spoke to, and what happened, and what was that on the video?' she said angrily. The policeman looked at the screen again.

'Most likely dirt on the camera lens, I'm afraid. We will endeavour to get it cleaned; they don't get used much in piss alley. As for the marks, I don't think it was from that incident; there's a lot of odd folk around here, but no one that would just bite a pretty girl like you without taking it further down the criminal route, if you know what I mean, and the doctors said that's not the case. Maybe they might have been distracted and run off before they were ready, but no one else is shown on any of the surrounding cameras, and we did look at all of them following your walk from Ronnie Scott's to the alley. We also checked out the band you told us about, and there was no one in the band called Adam. They didn't even have a saxophone player! They were just keys, bass and drums. The club's CCTV shows nothing either, just you talking to yourself and leaving the venue on your own. It could be stress or exhaustion, or as the doctor said, anaemia. Go home, have a rest, and we will keep looking into it; the case will remain open, but I don't know if we will find anything.' With this, he took some pictures of the puncture marks for the file, and the tiny amount of blood that on her closer examination was found on her right breast and spotted onto the edge of the lace on her bra, which she and apparently the doctors and police had at first missed and told her she was free to go. That, so to speak, was it, she thought: another open case to be filed at a later date as a case of a middle-aged woman's excessive night out who was bitten by a stripper, or she thought it would say something like that. *'So much for a night out to enjoy myself,'* she chided. *'You flunked the interview, went around London like an*

41

out-of-control teen, and almost got into real trouble. You were lucky this time and you must be careful in future; you were lucky this time,' she repeated as if to convince herself.

Chapter 2
Home, Dreams and Walks

'Ye shall not fear them:
For the Lord your God
He shall fight for you'
Deuteronomy 3:22
(King James version)

Hellen's day did not get any better, as she ended up having to buy a new rail ticket at Waterloo Station to get her home, as the previous return had become invalid at midnight, and on returning to her car she found it had a parking ticket on it. Some days were unquestionably complete bastards, she thought, as she struggled to peel the ominous yellow plastic from her windscreen, checked out the reprimanding tone of the ticket and that if she played it quickly online it would be half the price, which she placed on her mental 'to do' list, and sank into her car, finally laddering her tights. She drove home in silence, without the radio on. She usually liked to listen to audio books, but just didn't feel like it today; she had the feeling that her privacy had been violated and just couldn't shake it off, and it was making her feel sick at the bottom of her stomach.

She pulled into her parking space on automatic pilot, walked up the stairs to her flat and went to bed fully dressed. Her flat was not very big, consisting of only four rooms, a living area, a small kitchen diner, a bathroom and a bedroom, but she had done her best to make it homely. She did have an inheritance coming from her mother's will, but probate was taking a painfully long time, and as she had been caring for her mum and not working, readily available cash was now in short supply. She woke up at eight in the evening, stripped off her stale and crumpled clothes and had a long deserved hot shower. She couldn't help but notice as the hot water flowed over her that there was a stinging pain from the puncture marks on her neck, which seemed to penetrate deep into her muscles, as if trying to work its way towards her bones. They also started bleeding again, like an insect bite which stopped the blood clotting. The thought crossed her mind that it might have been a greedy horsefly that had fed on her whilst she was lying in the rubbish and it had just bitten her twice, but she wasn't really very convinced by this argument. She had experienced a few of those bites as a child, and none of them had felt like this, and one of them had got infected as well. But back then she had her parents to kiss it better and tell her that everything would be all right; now she was on her own.

She didn't bother to get dressed as it was so late in the evening, and instead opted just to wear her dressing gown. After eating a simple and easily prepared tea of a microwave vegetarian curry, she settled into the comfort of her sofa and fell asleep whilst watching the TV. Although science had been her life for so long now, and that she had chosen to dedicate herself to research over personal relationships for years, that Professor with all the hair had the tone of voice that just made her drift off, even though she did find him sort of sexy for a physicist.

Through misty, damp and dark air she pushed, desperately trying to find an area where she could see clearly to find out where she was, but it was like wading through a swamp. Wolf-like howls were hidden somewhere in the distance and flapping noises seemed to follow her whichever direction she headed. It was not the noise of birds though, as the sound was leathery and scratchy. Then there were the shadows. Continually altering shapes that remained just out of sight at the edge of her vision, but were there nonetheless, moving around and disappearing whenever she tried to look at them. The feeling of being watched was unbearable. She ran cold and naked through the forest, trying to escape the eyes, but they were always watching, and their eyes followed her every move. Claws scratched at her back, and when she turned around...

Hellen jerked awake as she fell off the sofa and hit the laminate floor with a thud. 'Damn it!' she said aloud as she sat up and scraped her fear-dampened hair from her face. In the morning light, she could hear her neighbour's dog howling away, so she figured it must be after seven in the morning as the damn thing always barked for at least an hour straight after its owners left, before it supposedly gave up on their return and settled down, only to start again at ten when the postman usually came, and it decided to find good sport in trying to take the man's fingers off. It was only a matter of time before it succeeded, she reckoned. She pulled herself up, slipped into some leggings and a sweatshirt, tied her hair back and set off on her morning run. Maybe some air would get rid of that horrid feeling which sometimes lingered after nightmares, although that was usually when it was still dark, not during daylight. After only two miles she turned back and headed home; for reasons that she could not explain, the chill from that nightmare would not leave her, and the puncture marks on her neck had suddenly started bleeding again, and the blood was beginning to trickle down from her throat and into her cleavage, not a good look when out, and she was beginning to feel faint again. Points of light were beginning to appear in front of her eyes, and the patches of light remained on closing them. As she approached her door, she felt that it was defiantly going to be a migraine, or she was going to turn around and pass out.

Once showered, Hellen was pleased to note that the lights had gone and went to see her GP off the Cosham High Street. The walk-in clinic service that they provided always had a big queue, but as she had possibly passed out the night before and almost fainted this morning, she decided that she had better persevere with the trial of getting an appointment. After taking a deep breath, she approached the receptionist at the counter, a large, sullen-looking woman who would not have seemed out of place on the defence line-up of an American Football team. After a curt exchange which reminded her of the 'computer says no' sketch from *Little Britain*, she had to use the practised look that she gave her most difficult students to break down their resistance, and it eventually worked, and she managed to get an appointment, and went to sit down, mentally preparing herself for the long wait. After the expected hour and a half wait, she finally got to meet the doctor, a small grey man who looked like he needed to see a medic himself. Bloods were taken, her neck wound was prodded and her blood pressure taken.

'Yes, yes, I know!' she replied as the result came back high, and she was told to phone back for the results of the bloods in a couple of days. As she had expected, he had no idea what the marks were and told her to take an antihistamine in case she was allergic to an insect that might have bitten her, although he had to admit that he had not seen anything quite like them before, not as a pair, and asked her if she was sure it wasn't a love bite as the marks were about the distance apart of human canines, to which she smiled and told him in her most sarcastic voice that she thought she might just have remembered being bitten, and she didn't think that an imaginary boyfriend would quite have been able to produce the same marks.

She decided to make use of what remained of the day by sorting out her applications to the several University posts remaining advertised — Nottingham, Durham, Bristol and Surrey — hoping that she would have better luck this time if any of them went to interview. Sophie Jenner, an old friend of hers from childhood, school and college, and who had worked in the Library at Portsmouth University when she was there, called to find out how the King's job interview had gone. Her cheery voice managed to brighten Hellen's mood, and by the end of the call both women were laughing about the absurdity of the events, and she promised to pop around in a couple of weeks when she could get out of work-based commitments and they would share a pizza and a rom com.

That night Hellen slept better, and didn't have any dreams, although she did wake up in the armchair in her living room, and she felt sure that she definitely remembered going to bed; even her book and reading glasses were on her bedside table. Hellen thought that this was strange, but better than the dreams, and set about getting dressed and preparing for her run by stretching out and warming up.

Hellen got out into the fresh air and instantly felt more refreshed as the crisp autumn air filled her lungs, far better than she had been the other day, and set out on her run, making for the Hambledon Road. She had opted for her maroon bra top as it provided good support and running shorts, along with a hair tie that sported several fluffy creatures with swirling eyes that Sophie had given her as a joke last Hallowe'en. The cold finished waking her up, as her exposed skin lightly shivered, rising into Goosebumps, but she would warm up as the run went on, and by the end she would probably feel too hot. Her muscles felt tight and sluggish today, and complained heavily when she started out, making it an effort to place one foot in front of the other; but by the time she got half a mile down the road and passed the BP petrol station they were beginning to come alive, her speed picked up and her Goosebumps had smoothed out and subsided. She picked up her rhythm, listening only to the rhythmic pounding of her feet on the ground backed up by her heart's thump, and the steady noise of her breath, which made little plumbs of mist which looked like cigarette smoke as it exited her lungs.

She cleared Denmead village in just under her normal time and was beginning to head down Southwick Road when Matt Boone joined her from Ashling Park Road. He was instantly recognisable with a quick glance by his bright red sleeveless vest and overly revealing Lycra shorts. '*God, who designed those things for men?*' she thought as she glanced over her shoulder at his approach — they were practically indecent. Matt worked at the same Tesco that she did, although only in a part-time capacity, as he was obsessed with his fitness, what she considered a

terminal condition called a 'sports fantasist'. He had
dreams of running professionally but was one of those
people who didn't really have the commitment to do
what was necessary to achieve the goal; he just liked
posing and was really too old to become a professional.
His running routes unfortunately on occasion coincided
with hers, and he would always insist on running with
her, which usually consisted of actually running behind
her and staring at her ass — she could always feel his
eyes on her. It always sent a shudder through her that
ran down her spine when this happened. Jill Connor also
sometimes joined them on a run as well, and it was Jill
that had told her what he was up to when they were
having a drink.

'You are so naïve, Hellen,' she had said whilst
sipping her vodka and tonic, smiling. 'He runs behind
you fixated on your ass. You have a fine tush there, girl,
and he's watching it jiggle. You should hear him big it
up with his mates talking about it; he's a slimeball. He
used to ogle my ass until I told his wife. Never ran on
his own with me again after that,' she had said with
distinct satisfaction.

He was fixed in the belief that anyone female would
just adore him, and he still kept trying to get her to go
out with him for drinks, despite her refusals and the fact
he was married, yuck. He wasn't her type, and she
definitely knew that hell could freeze over and leave
Satan ice skating before that would happen, and just to
make sure she would happily buy the coal for hell's

boilers herself. Matt was a complete jerk, with no redeemable features that she could think of. Confidence was attractive, not arrogance.

'Hello, Hellen,' he called out in his annoying way, as if he was talking to a child, and she couldn't help herself from counting the seconds before he mentioned himself. 'I'm running the London Marathon this year, it will be fantastic, you should do it as well.' Well, that was a record, under two seconds. Why did he always think that everyone should want to do the same things as him? Such an ego.

'Morning, Matt,' she said sweetly, 'some of us just don't have the time, you know, or your level of commitment. I'll have to leave that sort of thing to you!' How she kept a straight face saying that she didn't know, but he wasn't good at picking up on sarcasm, and would probably see it as a compliment. She slowed down her pace, letting him pass, and then pretended to stumble, and stopped, looking at her shoes accusingly.

'Keep going,' she called after him, 'my legs are cramping. I'll catch you up.' And, as she expected, he kept going. '*Phew,*' she thought. '*Not in the mood for him this morning.*' Hellen started running again, and turned left, cutting down Ashling Close and into the park, deciding to do a few laps of the field, just to make sure that she wouldn't catch up with him and he was well out of the way. She preferred running on her own as it gave her time to relax.

After her third lap of the field, she began to feel a prickle at the back of her neck, as her hairs began standing on end and she had the feeling that she was being watched. She stopped running and looked around her, but couldn't see anyone at all, not even in the distance. There were only the birds on the railings, but no, it couldn't be them! That was silly. Hellen turned around and headed back the way that she had come, deciding to keep her run to the main roads so that she wasn't on her own. What she didn't see was one large crow leap into flight and follow her down the road at a distance, perching on lamp posts to let her get ahead, and then flying on, almost like a plain-clothed policeman following a suspect.

She didn't feel faint, which was positive, but the bites on her neck were swollen and bleeding again, which she had annoyingly failed to notice earlier, and they had run and stained the elastic around the neck of her top. She would have to find where she had put that old Stain Devil she had bought last year; it might just get it out if she tackled it soon enough. She knew that she still had it somewhere, it just didn't mean that she would be able to find it; once put away, it was as if they entered a different dimension, and vanished. Hellen glanced at her watch as she slowed to open her block's door and realised that she was late for work. 'Damn, not again!' She had already been given one warning for lateness and didn't want another. The note in her file she couldn't care less about, but the condescending 'chat' she could really do without.

The store's manager, and her friend Tim, was away on holiday this week with his wife in Greece, and Olivia Marcus had been put in charge. She was tall and thin and would have been a good-looking lady if she could have stopped herself frowning all the time, Hellen thought as she listened to one of her long-winded lectures about timekeeping.

'I'm very sorry, Olivia, I will make sure that it doesn't happen again,' she said when Olivia had finally paused for a moment, trying to sound both sorry and convincing, shifting her feet around like a naughty schoolgirl waiting to see the headmaster. After all, her being on time was probably never going to happen, they both knew that really, and she always made the time up. It was just Olivia exerting her authority as Tim was out. If only she would recognise that she wasn't a threat to her promotion: there was no way she was going to do this forever and would not be trying to move up within the company.

'You just need to keep to a schedule; if you did that it would be so much easier,' she said, eyebrows twitching, trying to form a different expression but failing and returning to their default setting, a frown.

'Will do,' said Hellen, and quickly slipped out of the office and to her till, before Olivia got started again. The skill, she thought, was to slide out when she was distracted and hopefully, she wouldn't notice, and typically she would be too lazy to track you down later.

The shift was long, boring and completely uneventful. The only excitement was security catching a shoplifter with a bottle of scotch shoved down his pants, and Hellen wondered how he had managed to walk with it in there; plenty of space, she supposed, allowing herself a smile at her observation. By the time she got home at half past eight, Hellen was feeling shattered, but was pleased to note not faint, making a whole day of reasonable health: '*Score me*,' she thought. Slipping into her most comfortable nightdress, she curled up on the sofa to watch the soaps with a blanket, and promptly drifted off to sleep.

* * *

Tap...

　Tap... tap...

She opened her eyes and looked around, what the hell was that noise? [*Tap... tap...*] the noise repeated itself, and she got up and started looking around to see where it was coming from. The bathroom and kitchen taps were off, the radiators were on and working, hot at the top and bottom so no trapped air. [*Tap...*] She looked up at the window and heard that it was coming from there. She peeked out of the curtains and saw that a large crow was perched on the sill, and was tapping on the glass with its beak, and as she looked at it, the bird tilted its head sideways as if eyeing her up, dandiest thing that she had ever seen. She pulled the curtains tightly and headed to bed; she was on early shift in the morning and needed to get some rest. If she had remained at the window for a moment longer, she might have noticed a shadow move from the treeline watching her window, and a dog-like shape disappear into the woods.

She was in the forest, and looking around for something, but couldn't remember what it was. Her feet were bare, and she could feel the crunch of the leaves on the floor. On looking down, she saw that she was naked, and started to run; she had to find something to cover herself up with. There was a loud breathing behind her... She ran faster...

Hellen writhed on the bed, forming shapes beneath the covers, her eyes moving rapidly under her closed lids. She awoke with a start, and frantically felt herself to check that she was dressed, which she was, and realised that it had been a dream. 'Shit!' It had been so vivid. She never usually had nightmares and could only put it down to her traumatic experience in London. She didn't really like nightmares as they made her feel out of control, and she had always worked hard to ensure that she was empowered in every aspect of her life and everything was ordered; but lately, since her mother's death, that concept had turned to shit, as she had no academic job, was working in a supermarket at the bottom of the staff pile and she was beginning to feel really lonely, wondering if she should have made a better effort with the few relationships that she had. Who was she kidding? None of them had been what you would class as serious, and even fewer had even reached sleeping together. There was just something missing from them, that connection she needed to feel loved and to be comfortable. Science was so much simpler, but sadly, science couldn't love you.

That week turned out to be rather depressing, as she received three job rejections in as many days, with Surrey, Bristol and Durham all sending her e-mails confirming that she hadn't made it to interview. They had, of course, been politely worded, saying, 'We're sorry but we had so many applications, etc, etc'; but it still meant the same thing: no interviews, and therefore no hope of a lectureship. Shit! With only Nottingham left to respond, she used her day off to trail through all the job pages, but no more were advertised yet, just her luck. Hellen couldn't be bothered to take a run today and opted for a soak in the bath instead. Her neck was hurting, and she hoped that the warm water might relax her muscles as they seemed so tense at the moment and were getting to the point of hurting. She put Radio Three on in the background, which was playing a pleasant but somewhat unmemorable Baroque symphony and dropped a 'deep relax' bath bomb that Sophie had bought for her into the steaming water, and climbed in, letting the bubbles tease her skin and the warmth work its wonders, as she closed her eyes and dropped off to sleep.

'Go to London, Hellen...'

'Come to me, my child...'

'Come to London...'

'You desire me... You long to be with me... Come...'

She spluttered, flailing her arms around in desperation as her head slipped under the water, feet thrashing in the air, and her mouth filled with water as she screamed. Within ten seconds her head exploded from the water as she gasped for air, sucking the warm damp bathroom air into her lungs, her body shaking with fear.

'Shit, that was close,' she thought. *'Mum always warned me not to fall asleep in the bath; now I know why.'* Her chest was heaving as if she had been holding her breath for far longer than she actually had, and she had to make a conscious effort to slow her breathing. Hellen quickly stood up, wrapped a towel around her wet body and stepped out of the bath carefully so as not to slip over. Someone had been calling her, she thought, telling her to go to London, or was it just the water in her ears? Hard to tell, she thought, shivering as the colder air of her bedroom hit her as she chose some clothes to put on.

Hellen was distracted by the phone ringing and dashed barefoot into the kitchen to grab her mobile from her bag. It was the doctor's surgery with her blood results, all of which had turned out to be fine, except her iron levels, which were very low, and they suggested that she started to take iron supplements.

That evening, Hellen spent her time trying to improve her CV for when another job was advertised, but she couldn't really focus on the task and opted to go in early. To her surprise, she awoke standing up looking out of the bedroom window. She had somehow taken her nightie off without knowing it and could see her naked reflection looking back at her in the glass. Thankfully, there was no one walking outside, but the crow was back again, seemingly staring at her, making her feel really uncomfortable. As she looked down at the bird staring at her, she made to cover her breasts with her arm and noticed a trickle of blood running down from the puncture wounds on her neck. It had made its path all the way down between her cleavage to her belly ring and was just beginning to circle around the metal bar, and she watched it for a minute, mesmerised. She quickly pulled the curtains closed, feeling self-conscious, and used a tissue to mop up the blood. '*Why won't these damn things heal up?*' she thought, putting a plaster over the punctures in her skin and pulling her nightie back on. She tried to force the event to the back of her mind, and attempted to go back to sleep, where the dream she had experienced the previous night repeated itself again.

Chapter 3
Bad Dreams, Good News,
Unusual Behaviour

'When thou liest down, thou shall not be afraid:
Yea, thou shalt lie down, and thy sleep shall be sweet.'
Proverbs 3:24
(King James version)

Hellen was running through the woods, and the fog was catching her up, but she knew that she had to keep ahead of it, she had to run. Her feet hurt and bled from the brambles, and her naked body was covered in cuts and tears. Tears stung her eyes, but the fog still got closer, its tendrils reaching out, trying to grab her, but she kept running, she had to... All around her a voice echoed...

'Come...'
'Come to me...'

She awoke in the living room chair, sitting bolt upright — she had sleepwalked again. This was getting more frequent now, and she hated the lack of control. She got up stiffly and stretched out, thinking to herself that she must have been there a while as her back hurt. She made her way over to the table and checked the job pages. Six new posts had gone up overnight, and she quickly sent applications to all of them: Cardiff, Hull, Sheffield, Plymouth, Bournemouth and Loughborough. Not particularly where she wanted to live, but she needed to get out of here, and anywhere at present would be better than this place. She needed a break, she decided, and any one of these jobs would be a step in the right direction.

By the time she had eaten breakfast, Hellen was beginning to feel better, and as that week she was working nights, she decided that she would go down to Portsmouth and do some shopping early in the day, and that would allow her time to have a quick snooze before work started at eight. It had the desired effect and lifted her mood. She had started her trip by having a nice coffee and a shortbread in the bookshop, and had then managed to get herself a pretty leather skirt in a deep scarlet, and a couple of new white blouses made of a thicker fabric, as she wasn't going to be caught out again as in her previous interview. She also noticed a lovely coat, but that would have to wait until she was paid in a couple of days' time; they had plenty of them.

Her week of nights went very slowly, and she wished that just one of the applications that she had submitted would turn into an interview. She needed to get back to science and her research as soon as possible; she was at her happiest doing that, it was her comfort area, and besides, it was her life and she missed it. For the second time in a while, she felt really lonely; it would have been good to have talked through her job woes and her dreams with, well, a partner, and it resided as a pain deep in her chest. She sighed as if trying to get rid of the feeling. Oh well, too late for regrets now; at least Sophie was due around soon, only a couple of days' time — she would understand. No one had known her longer than Sophie, and although brash and to some rude, she was so confident, and Hellen wished that she had less self-doubt as far as men were concerned.

She was running again; faster and faster she went and the trees flew by her, but it was still gaining, getting closer. The fog was spreading around her and the howls were getting nearer. She tried to run faster but it began to surround her, its substance-less tendrils closing in. Its touch was moist and chilly on her skin, and sent tingles through her body, arousing her. Hellen tripped and fell to the floor face first with a crash, tasting the sour earth in her mouth. She turned over as the howls approached... It was upon her... And she screamed...

Hellen awoke screaming, flailing her limbs around, violently fighting off an unseen creature's vicious attack. Then she fell off the kitchen stool, crashing onto the hard kitchen floor winding herself. 'Fucking shit,' she moaned, as pain seared through her body, and she arched her back in pain as her muscles stiffened, and then shuddered, making her shake for a minute. With an effort, she clambered to her feet, using the work surface to help pull herself up. Hobbling through to the bedroom, she sat on the end of the bed until she had regained her breath, and rubbed her arm, which was now developing a large bruise. 'Damn sleepwalking,' she mumbled. 'If this goes on much longer, I'll have to see the doctor again. Ouch, my ass hurts.'

Hellen looked at the time, realised that she had a few hours of sleep left, and rolled onto her side, curling up into a ball under the sheets of her bed, tucking her hands between her legs; but the normally soft cotton of the sheets was brushing harshly against her skin, annoying her, as she drifted into a half-sleep.

It was eight in the evening, and it now seemed that the three weeks had passed quickly since Sophie had called. The doorbell chimed, sounding the arrival of the pizza. The events that Hellen had experienced in London were beginning to fade, but she still had constant reminders of that 'bad day', as she referred to it. She kept seeing, or perhaps more accurately felt eyes watching her in her sleep, along with a faint voice that kept telling her to come to London, finding herself in different rooms upon waking up; but worst of all, the nightmares still lingered and were getting worse. Damn odd, but dreams were meant to be weird. She would have looked up the meaning in Sigmund Freud's work which she had purchased several years back on a fancy and never read but felt sure that it would present her with something even weirder, most likely something referring to her childhood and sexual frustration. It always related to points like that.

So far, Hellen and Sophie had enjoyed a good evening catching up over a bottle of wine, and were ready to start the film, although they had always had the unspoken rule that the film did not go on until the food had arrived, and now it had. Sophie was three years younger than Hellen but didn't look it. She had dark hair and the physique of a sports woman. In her youth, she had been a semi-professional, winning international judo competitions in her teens and kickboxing trophies in her twenties. This endeavour had resulted in the end of her career in sport when she had injured her knee, and had retired whilst she could still walk, and, as she put it, 'quit whilst I am still able to kneel down with my future children'; but life never worked out as expected and she had not as yet found the right man.

Both women had gone for the comfort of jog pants and jumpers, as Sophie had decided to stay the night so she could drink and would go on to work from Hellen's. They had settled for *Bridget Jones*, which Netflix was happy to provide. They had seen it many times before but opted for its well-known comfort. Both women fell asleep before the end of the film, sharing the sofa as they had as children, with Hellen being shorter, resting her head on her friend's hips.

When Sophie woke up it had gone eleven, and Hellen was just stood in front of her, just looking at her, although that was impossible as her eyes were closed, but it made Sophie shiver — it reminded her of something out of *Paranormal Activity*, and that had given her sleepless nights for days. Not a good film to watch when you're on your own afterwards. Having heard something on the TV about not waking sleepwalkers as it could traumatise them, she carefully guided Hellen back to the bedroom slowly and helped her lie down, gently pulling the cover up to her breasts, before returning to the couch. '*Creepy*,' she thought, before turning over and returning to sleep.

Hellen was standing alone in the fog. The darkness seemed to be wrapping itself around her, pushing in with crushing force, before forcing its way into every orifice and pore in her body, pushing deeper and deeper inside her, until it hurt. She tried to gasp but she couldn't breathe; her chest was being crushed tighter and tighter. Her body burnt as her nerves screamed, as the white points appeared again and got closer and closer until they disappeared and were replaced by two burning red orbs. She screamed...

Sophie jumped from the couch at the sound of a scream and ran into the bedroom, only to find Hellen was not there. Her clothes were, but there was no sign of their owner. She ran around the flat to see if she was in the bathroom, but found the front door open, and she dashed outside and followed the footprints in the slightly frosty grass, wincing at the cold on her bare feet.

Hellen awoke to find herself stood in the forest behind her home, shivering violently. On dreamily looking around, she realised that she was completely naked, with Goosebumps all over her body. She had a painful crick in her neck, her nipples were so hard they hurt, and her crutch was sticky.

'Hellen,' a voice called dreamily somewhere far off in the distance.

'Hellen,' it called again, this time more clearly, and loud enough to cut through the fog in her mind.

'S… Sop… Sophie…' she said quietly, the word feeling strange as it came out of her mouth, then louder, filled with fear and panic, 'Sophie!'

'Hellen,' the voice called again, and she turned around, trying to cover her modesty with her trembling hands. 'What on earth are you doing?' Sophie said as she approached, pulling off her jumper and helping Hellen put it on, leaving herself now shivering in just her bra and jog pants.

'I d-d-d… don't k-k-k-k… know,' stuttered Hellen between her teeth chattering and frightful shivering, and they both started heading back to the flat, with Hellen using Sophie for support and guidance, as her friend still seemed not quite with it, and her eyes were unfocused. Once inside, Sophie closed the door as a rather surprised paperboy gasped at an adolescent's dream come true, and she helped Hellen get into something warm.

'I'm so sorry,' Hellen stuttered. 'I've been having these dreams for several weeks now, but I've never, well, you know, done that. I'm not the type to wander around like that, you know that don't you? I just don't know what's happening to me.'

Sophie offered reassuring words as she made them both a hot drink.

'You're bleeding,' she said, pointing to Hellen's neck, where the two piercings were dribbling blood and looked frightfully inflamed. After cleaning the wound again, using copious quantities of antiseptic, Sophie put a dressing over the top, and felt Hellen's head. 'You look really pale, Hellen,' she said as she finished off. 'You need to see another doctor; you don't look well. That incident in London has left you unwell; maybe you've caught something?'

'I know,' Hellen replied. 'I'll ring the surgery again later and see if my new results are back yet. The previous ones were all right, but they suggested running them again, and they haven't phoned me yet; they're crap like that. Something might have shown up on them.' With that, she got up to go to the loo and the world spun around her, a curtain of sparkling lights came down across her vision and she passed out, her hands frantically trying to grab Sophie as she collapsed. Sophie just managed to stop her friend's head hitting the floor, and with a struggle, managed to get her back onto the bed. Thank God she still did some weightlifting — not that Hellen was that heavy, and she felt sure that she has lost weight.

When Hellen came around, the grey-looking GP was standing over her talking to Sophie. His name badge informed her that his name was actually Dr Andrew Jefferies. She had seen him many times before and had never known his name.

'I've not come across this before,' he was saying. 'She is extremely anaemic; signs don't often come on this quickly without previous warnings though. It's like she's actually lost a lot of blood. She hasn't donated or anything, has she?' Sophie shook her head. 'Give her these iron tablets for now and we will have to monitor it closely and see if it gets worse. If it does, she will have to go into hospital for tests and perhaps even have a blood transfusion.'

'Oh, shit, that's a bit extreme, isn't it?' Hellen said, drawing both of their attention to the fact she had woken up. 'I feel somewhat better now, just hungry. I'll be fine, honestly.' With which she sat up, pulling the sheets higher to fully cover herself to the shoulders.

'Well, take it easy,' the doctor said. 'I still want you to talk to a friend of mine about those bite marks. He's an expert in tropical diseases and might be able to help identify the insect that must have caused them. He's a real boffin on all that sort of thing, and he will get in touch with you shortly. He's due back from abroad in a couple of days, and I will speak to you later as well.' He turned and left the room, leaving both women looking rather worried.

Sophie had to leave due to her work commitments the next morning, and she bade Hellen farewell, feeling bad about having to leave her friend so soon after she had collapsed.

'Look, Hellen, I don't like to leave you like this, but I just can't get any more leave from work. I had to take too much earlier in the year when I had that stomach bug. But I just don't want to leave you on your own. If I had known you were having problems I would have tried to have got over here sooner, but you didn't say.'

'I know, Soph, I'll be OK. I'll phone out for food and watch the TV.'

'But what if you wander again? You'll either catch your death in this cold weather, or worse case you could get raped. You were well out of it — I don't even know if you would not have wandered further if my shouting hadn't woken you up.' Sophie was close to tears and was desperately considering how she could shift things around at work so that she could watch over her friend. 'If you passed out again you could hit your head. I…'

'Soph.'

'But if I hadn't caught you, Hellen?'

'Don't worry, you'll have me crying in a minute. To play safe I'll put the chain on the door and also lock my bedroom door. I doubt that if I'm sleeping I would be able to open both of those. I have trouble with the deadlock as it is; that's why I never use the bloody thing

— managed to lock myself in for hours until the locksmith could come out.'

'But, Hellen, you managed to get outside completely naked. You're not at university any more.'

'I know, I know. I never did that then, mind you. Perhaps I was traumatised after London; these things sometimes take a while to come on, so they say. I will be fine, don't worry.' She said this with a voice of certainty that she was most definitely not feeling. Inside, her heart was pounding, echoing within her chest, and a sense of panic was beginning to develop. 'Now go. Go! You've been good enough to me as it is. I don't want to be responsible for you losing your job. Go home and I will be fine. I feel better now, I promise.'

'I suppose… You will call me if you need to? Any time, no matter what hour. You promise?'

'I promise, Sophie. Now get yourself off — Alfie will be getting hungry by now.'

'Oh my god, the dog!' Sophie exclaimed. 'Poor Alfie, I forgot all about him! I hope he hasn't eaten the chair or torn anything up — he seems to like soft furnishing. All right, all right, I'll go, but you must promise to phone me before you go to bed, all right?'

Hellen promised and reluctantly Sophie left, getting into her old and battered seventies Beetle and with a copious cloud of blue smoke she disappeared up the road. It was only three in the afternoon, but the clouds had drawn across and the sky and it was already very dark. The rain that the over-cheery weather girl had predicted might actually be correct. Hellen shivered involuntarily and tried to keep her fears about the night under control. She hadn't really wanted Sophie to leave, but it would have been wrong to keep her. Helen quickly shut the door, getting the feeling that she was being watched again, and went up to her flat, and for the first time since trapping herself in that time, she locked the door's deadlock.

The rain did arrive at five as promised, and it was heavy, with the wind picking up and making the windows rattle. Hellen looked gloomily out of the window, watching the trees bend backwards and forwards in the wind. For a reason that she couldn't place, she felt that many eyes were watching her from all angles. Gazing around, she couldn't make anyone out, but the feeling was still there. No houses overlooked her flat, just the trees in the car park, and then the woods, and her eyes kept being drawn in their direction. The hypnotic swaying of the branches, the red lights, the leaves rustling. Her mind took a minute to process that thought. There were no red lights in that direction; she had lived here for years, and there were no lights. She looked again more carefully and could just make out row upon row of large black crows lined up on the branches, and they all seemed to be looking at her. She was sure crows didn't gather in large numbers; somewhere in the back of her mind she remembered reading that a group of crows was called a 'murder', for they would rarely group together, and on those few occasions they would kill one member of the group, as a form of capital punishment, but that must be superstition, along with them being an omen of bad news! She reprimanded herself for that thought, blinked, and looked again more carefully. To her horror, all the birds slowly turned their heads to face her, and then bang! She jumped back as a large bat hit the glass of the window and fell down dead onto the path by the ground-floor flat. 'Shit,' she gasped, breathing heavily, and she quickly pulled the frayed curtains together, and shakenly returned to the couch, turning on the TV to provide another human voice in the room. It was Bradley Walsh on *The Chase*. She had always enjoyed the show and had soon managed to distract herself with its unique form of casual entertainment. She could always score quite well if no art and artistic questions were asked. Unseen by Hellen, more crows joined the gathering, all watching her window avidly.

By the time it got to eight o'clock, Hellen had calmed her nerves and her thoughts turned to dinner. She decided that given her new-found anaemia, her waistline could afford to take another pizza. You had to be careful at her age — as the saying went, 'a minute on the lips, a lifetime on the hips' — and shortly after her call she was facing an exquisite-looking stuffed crust veggie feast, garlic bread and salad. She had even managed to find a bottle of red wine left in the cupboard. She would have to remember to go shopping in the morning, assuming she didn't do it naked in her sleep, the thought of which managed to provide her a small smile. Nothing would surprise her after yesterday. The only sign of nerves that she had shown was that when the delivery driver rang the door, she used the spy hole to check who it was, something that she had never done before, as the previous owner had stupidly put the thing too low down, and all you got was a good view of any caller's chest, unless they were vertically challenged, but thankfully he had the company's name embroidered on his jacket and it had actually been of some use.

After eating, she felt a bit queasy and kept tasting garlic in the back of her throat. She had never had a problem with it before — it had been a favourite — and she put it down to being greedy and having eaten the whole lot. '*I'll pay for that later,*' she thought. '*I'll have to quit chocolate for a week to let my calories catch up, or I suppose I could run a bit further, providing I stop feeling like I want to faint.*' She fulfilled her promise to Sophie and called her at ten, saying that she was fine, and was going to go to bed early. This was actually a small lie, as sleeping was far from her mind, as she was worried about what might happen whilst asleep and intended to stay up as long as possible. Once finished talking on the phone, she picked up her laptop and went through her e-mails. The last one was from Nottingham University's Department of Chemistry offering her an interview, and it had been sent by a Professor Ben Harwood. 'Yes!' she called out aloud. 'Thank God!' If it was who she was thinking of, he had been a handsome, but slightly overweight friend of hers that had always sat next to her during all of their chemistry lectures ever since she was a fresher at Southampton University. In fact, that would have been somewhat reductive: they had become completely inseparable and excellent friends over the following years.

Now this was good news. Ben was a really nice guy and had always been very kind, and thinking about it now, she realised that he used to have a big-time crush on her from the moment they had met, which she had sort of helped fuel by drunkenly kissing him at the Christmas ball, before falling asleep on the floor. She had always been thankful that he had not been like many of the other guys she had come to know, and had treated her with complete respect, calling a cab, and not just dumping her in it, but had actually escorted her back to her student flat and made sure that she was inside, and on the bed, before declining her drunken advances and leaving. There were times when she thought that somehow, she had managed to let the good one get away and felt guilty about how they had lost contact. They had been so close; why had she not called him? And for the first time in a while, she felt a strange tingle deep in her body thinking about him, the type you get when about to kiss a date for the first time. She had not had many boyfriends over the years, as she had always put her work first, and they usually got bored and left her, which is what had happened with John. It had only got to six months, and poof, it was all over. But why did she get that tingle for Ben now? She had known him for three years and they had been inseparable friends, but not romantic; she couldn't think why not, but... She looked up his university profile, just to check what he was up to now, and couldn't help but smile at his picture; it was a little dated, but he looked good, and it brought back some wonderful memories for her. How she had always gone shopping with him, and he had patiently waited and never failed to compliment her; their trips to several music festivals where she had even asked him to share her tent without ever feeling uncomfortable about him; and she again wondered, *'Why didn't I make a move on him?'* Do we only get the one chance to find true love? God, she sounded like a teenager — but what if it was him and she had missed her chance?

'Never mind,' she thought, closing her computer and making her way to the bedroom. She locked the door behind her, putting the key in the pocket of her jacket to add a layer of difficulty in getting out if she did sleepwalk. Might burn to death if there was a fire, but hopefully not caught outside like she was before, which was why she also chose to wear leggings under her seventies-style dungarees; she had trouble getting out of those at the best of times, let alone if she was asleep. With this comforting thought, she sat up in the bed, put on her glasses and started reading. Ironically, with the situations that she had been finding herself in lately, *One Flew over the Cuckoo's Nest* seemed somewhat

appropriate, but she had decided to work her way through the list of a hundred best books, and she was now about half way through, although she chose not to read them in order, but by how she felt at the time of selection. She was almost finished with this, and it would be *Dracula* next, one that that she had always meant to read but never got around to, like *War and Peace*, which she had almost held a party once she actually finished it, saying that it was good for her soul. As the hours drifted by, her head began to nod, until, despite her worries, the book fell from her hand, and she passed into the realms of sleep. If she had been less tired or managed to hold back sleep for a little longer, she might have noticed the shadows that kept interrupting the thin beam of moonlight that had now begun to shine through the gap in the curtains. She also might have heard a deep, quiet growling from the other side of her bedroom wall, coming from the neighbour's dog, until it was silenced by its owners.

Chapter 4
Feeling Better, Strange Tastes, The Visitor

'Then when lust hath conceived,
it bringeth forth sin:
and sin, when it is finished,
bringeth forth death'
James 1:15
(King James version)

'*Hellen...*'

A voice whispered to her as she slept and she turned over.

'*Come to me, Hellen, come.*'

'*It is your desire.*'

'*You feel it... Need it... Long for it...*'

'*Come.*'

She groaned, rolling onto her other side, her hand feeling her throat.

'*Your body craves me... Your blood flows for me...*'

'*You belong to me...*'

She ran her hands down her body, sliding into her leggings and coming to rest between her legs.

'*Come...*'

'*Come...*'

'*Come...*'

The voice faded and grew quieter, still continuing to beckon until it had completely faded and disappeared.

It was almost light when Hellen woke up, which was to her pleasure actually in her own bed. She had not seemed to go walkabouts, and on a quick check was still dressed. The only bad thing was that her glasses lay squashed out of shape under her book, which she must have rolled onto during the night, and she had no memory of her dreams, and this pleased her no end. There was a desperate dash to the loo, made even more urgent as she had to find where she had put the key to unlock the bedroom door, and then she had to fight with the buckles on her dungarees. Maybe she would go without those next time. Today she felt fantastic. She had a quick breakfast of wholemeal toast and peanut butter, which she felt would help provide her body with some extra protein to build her up, and then headed out for her run. As she jogged down the old London Road towards Cowplain, she realised that as the sun rose her eyes felt sore and she had to resort to putting her sunglasses on. Now there was a first for December, she thought, but it was bright and the sun was low in the sky at this time of year, and she picked up her speed and thought no more of it.

Hellen had always enjoyed running on winter mornings: the feel of the warm sun on her face, the crunch of the frost under her feet, the slight tingle that the cold gave her skin. Things were looking up. She had a job interview, she had survived the night with no dreams and not unwillingly flashed the world. Yes, things were going to be fine. Well, at least she could dare to hope.

By the time she returned home, she had exceeded her ten-mile target by two miles and felt great for it. She was super-charged, and for the first time in over twenty years had a craving for some crispy smoked bacon, which was strange as she had turned vegetarian long ago and had not felt that way for years. But no. She would not give way; she didn't want the death of anything on her conscience. It was not that she was a hippie or had strong feelings about what anyone else was eating — they could do what they liked — but she did like to think of her body as a temple, and she was going to do her best to look after it without resulting to murder.

Hellen checked the date of her interview, which was two weeks away, and headed over to the Tesco's in Havant. Her journey had two main purposes. One was to get some food in, and the other was to speak to Tim Allwright, the shop's manager, and her boss. To keep enough money coming in to manage, she had been forced to take this job in the store until a university post presented itself and given the problems she'd experienced over the last couple of days, she had forgotten to call and explain. Strange they hadn't called her, but she thought that she had better see if she still had a job to return to, something best done in person.

'Hi, Tim,' she said once inside his small and untidy office that smelt of hot cross buns, which had been stored there until its conversion into his office after the fire in his previous one, which she suspected was caused by him trying to sneak in a crafty fag; but hey, he was actually a really good guy, and she was friends with his wife Becca, and had been for over ten years. Tim was in his late thirties, slightly overweight, and no matter how hard he tried always looked unkempt. He had sandy-coloured hair and grey eyes that were set a little too wide, which were over-emphasised by the large glasses that he chose to wear, and she felt that contacts would have suited him better. On the other hand, Becca was in her late twenties, a physiotherapist, who had the looks of a film star with her perfect hourglass figure, long legs and even longer blonde hair. How on earth they came to be together, gave Hellen's enquiring mind a full work-out to try and contemplate. Her only assumption was that Becca was a complete control freak, which she knew to be a fact, and needed someone like Tim who she could boss around, which, she had to admit, he seemed very comfortable with. Maybe she was an absolute demon in bed and the sex made up for the continual control she exerted over him.

'Hellen, I was going to phone you,' he said sheepishly whilst trying to clear some space on his desk, 'but the systems went down with all the staff timetables and I thought you might have been on holiday.'

'Er, not quite,' she replied. This was just like him: Tim had huge problems with the computer systems, and the shop's IT support were constantly having to support him. From what she had seen, he was actually reasonable on a computer — it was just that they seemed to hate him, and would produce brand new errors to torture him — but on this occasion the computer system might have helped her out. 'I was ill, and I'm afraid I forgot to call you. I'm very sorry. Is my job still, OK? I don't want to make things bad for you or anything; you can put them down as holiday if that helps.'

'No, no, it's fine. Start back tonight if you like; it would really help me out if you could.'

'Of course I will, Tim. I owe you one,' Hellen said, pleased with the result. She would have money for the month after all. 'I'll be there. What are the hours tonight, then, eight to six?'

'No, not that late this time,' Tim said. 'It's five until midnight. Look, thanks for helping out, and it's good to hear you're all right. See you tonight.'

'See you later, then, Tim,' said Hellen, smiling. She really did like Tim. Almost completely hopeless in everything he did, but well meaning, a wife well above his league and he was one of those rare people that was actually happy with his lot in life.

Hellen spent over an hour in the shop getting food as she couldn't really settle on what she wanted. Her thoughts kept turning to meat, which she guessed must be the anaemia. Her body's way of trying to get her to eat what she needed. Well, she thought defiantly, I have the iron pills and that will have to do, so she paid and set off to have something to eat before having to return for work. Her drive back was uneventful, and she was able to stop off at the opticians on her way to get her reading glasses straightened. If she got time before work, she might make a push and try to get her book finished.

As she pulled into her flat's driveway, she noticed that there were a large number of insects gathering around where her kitchen window was. She involuntarily pulled the face of disgust that all people pull when seeing a distasteful parasite or something else horrible and made a note to herself to get hold of the block's handyman to spray them or something. She never liked speaking to creepy Gary. Everyone in the six flats that were contained in the block she lived in could tell many a story about him. Most came about his laziness, or his habit of talking as if breaking the fourth wall of a book, but if you asked any of the female residents, they all suspected that he was the block's 'phantom knicker snatcher' and felt uneasy with the way he would look at them, as if undressing them with his pale watery eyes. Hellen herself had mysteriously lost an expensive pair of lace panties and her favourite M&S bra from her balcony whilst drying them. It was more than just suspicious that he had been around cleaning the windows at the time. She wished that the block's lease owner would hire someone else, but nonetheless, before she forgot, she called his number. Thankfully, she got put through to voicemail, and left a message.

* * *

Midnight approached, and Hellen had almost finished on the till, when she was greeted by the chirpy voice of Jasmine Fuller, who lived in the block next to hers. Like Hellen, she was single, and they had struck up a friendship almost six months ago when, not knowing that they lived right by each other, Hellen had met her at the florist when arranging flowers for her mother's funeral. It turned out that she owned the small shop and very kindly sorted out a beautiful display for her. She was in her sixties, and her husband had died from a heart attack three months before her mother's death. She had three children, a son of forty who was an accountant who lived in London with his partner James, a daughter of thirty-eight, who was divorced with three children herself and based miles away in Bristol, and her youngest son, who was twenty-five, serving in the army and currently posted in Iraq, so she had no one at home, and they had enjoyed going to the cinema together through their mutual love of horror films; plus, if there was any gossip going around their area and probably everywhere in the whole country, she knew it. There was never a possibility of Jasmine keeping a secret:

whatever you told her would be out there quicker than a post by a celebrity.

'Oooh, Hellen dear,' she said, placing her shopping on the checkout, 'are you feeling better? I heard you took a bad turn and was out running around late at night! Fever, was it?'

'I'm much better, thanks,' Hellen replied, smiling. Fever, she thought, she'd extracted the gossip from that bloody paperboy, she thought, and was just trying to validate it and get more info. No one could hold out against her questioning for very long — she would have made a good interrogator if she had the will and perhaps been a bit younger. 'It was sleep walking actually, or so the doctor reckons. Stress and all that.'

'Well, you be careful, dear, you'll not only get a cold, but get all the wrong sort of attention round here. Mind, once you hit menopause, those hot flushes will make you want to run out in the snow naked just to cool down. Anyway, did you hear about Gary? It was horrible, you know.'

'No, I called him earlier to fix some insects around my window.'

'Well, he won't be doing that. Not now. He won't be doing anything any more.'

'*My god, he is the Phantom Knicker Snatcher*,' Hellen thought to herself. '*He's either been arrested with a pile of stolen panties or found dead, hung by a rope in his cupboard wanking off in his stolen items.*'

Then she frowned as the words sank in. 'Why not?' she said slowly.

'He's dead. An accident, so they say. It was me who found him, you know, four hours ago now I think, dead as anything. His flat's door was open as I passed, and I went in — well, you know, someone had to check that he wasn't being broken into, and I am a member of Neighbourhood Watch — and there he was, lying on the floor. Completely white he was, like a sheet. He had bite marks all over what was left of him. They reckon some wild dogs got in there, the police said. They called out animal control and everything but didn't find nothing. It had me all of a wobble it did. There was blood everywhere: walls, floor, ceiling, everywhere. Didn't look like he had put up any resistance. It was horrible, never seen anything like it in my life.'

'Oh my God. I'm glad I locked up well last night,' Hellen said, and to herself thanked God that she had not gone sleepwalking. 'That must have been terrible for you!'

'When you get to my age, nothing shocks you, not after seeing yourself in the mirror in the morning and having three children, but I'm still getting over it now. The police have put notes in everyone's doors, and there's a residents' meeting tomorrow night. He had CCTV in his house, you know, and they are going to check that and give us advice. You should be there, and then we could treat ourselves to a nice cake or something, and it would be good to catch up. I haven't seen you in over a week.'

Hellen promised that she would, put her store's staff food discount onto Jasmine's shopping and closed her till. For some reason, the puncture wounds on her neck that had not bothered her all day began to throb. Time for home, she thought.

Hellen was not a coward and prided herself on her independence. She had studied Karate for years as a child as her parents wanted her to be able to defend herself if required, and she had delivered a few very painful cock shots with her boot as a student, but tonight, after Jasmine's news, she had an unsettled feeling, which combined with her sense of being watched. The police were still there when she parked up, with their yellow 'don't cross' crime-scene tape and blue flashing lights. She didn't hang around outside, and quickly made her way inside. To her surprise, she almost got bitten by the neighbour's dog when it shot out of nowhere and tried to get through the gate at her. Its lips were pulled back, baring its small teeth as spittle shot everywhere. Damn thing was a nuisance with its barking, but it had never tried to bite her. What the fuck had rattled its cage? Once inside, she locked the door and pulled the curtains.

Twenty minutes later she was undressed, washed and tucked up in bed with a cocoa and a bar of Jamaican rum chocolate. Double chocolate — you could never go wrong with that. She hated late-night shifts. It wasn't the work but coming back that late. As she got older, she tended to worry about things more. Soon, she thought. If I get that job, it will be back to normal hours and anything late night would be able to be done at home. She liked writing up research papers and making grant applications. '*God, how sad am I?*' she thought as she turned the light off.

She was woken at two in the morning by a scratching noise at the window. She found that all her hairs were standing up on end as if charged, her neck throbbed, and she had a hot ache running through her body. She got out of bed and reluctantly made her way over to the curtains, steeling her nerves to open them. The closer she got, the more it seemed like she was pushing through a static field, somewhat like a Van de Graaff generator, that got harder to move through the closer she got. Her nipples bulged, and she ached, as if coming to a climax. She reached out her hand so slowly it was like moving through treacle, and then she quickly pulled the fabric back. Just as she did so, the door's intercom phone rang, and she let out a squeak of fear as she fell over, landing heavily on her ass. As she stood up rubbing her bottom, her fear didn't reduce, but kept building. Who would be at her door in the early hours? Was it the police? She didn't think so. Her mind created images of Gary's flabby body, covered in bites and tears, completely bloodless. The ache in her body got stronger still, and her thighs began to tremble, and she picked up the phone with a shaking hand.

'Hello,' she said in an incredibly unstable voice, 'who's there?' At first there was no answer, only static. She was about to put the receiver down when a familiar voice replied.

'*Hellen.*'

She squeaked. 'Who are you?' she said after gathering her nerve, her voice cracking and higher than it usually was, making her sound like a little girl.

'*Let me in, Hellen. You must let me in.*'

She knew the voice from her dreams, and its mesmerising quality, and its owner's face appeared in her mind, blurred and not quite visible.

'*You will let me in. I can't come and see you if you don't let me in.*'

Although her body ached with unwanted sexual pleasure, she was terrified. It was Adam. She trembled as she fought back what was an irresistible urge to just say 'Come in', and to be with him. It took all her concentration not to beg him to come in, to come in and take her right there in the hall. But something surprising helped save her. The small cross that she had inherited from her mother, the one that had remained in her drawer for months until she had got home that very night and had felt the urge to put it on. It started to feel hot against her chest where it hung. Its burning against her skin broke through Adam's voice and his hypnotic requests to be let in. 'Ouch,' she said in return, and as her mind suddenly became clear for a second with the smell of burning flesh, 'Fuck off, you bastard!' she shouted into the receiver and slammed it down. She had been so close to saying 'Come in', it terrified her. The static electricity seemed to vanish as quickly as it came, leaving her standing in the dark, silently shaking as sticky beads ran down her inner thighs. Then there was a banging at the door. Hellen flinched at the sound, backing into the kitchen door with a bang as if she had been slapped, which made her jump again, but she managed to pick up the receiver, which now had a crack in it, and gasp, 'What?' It was all her constricted throat would allow her to vocalise.

'You all right, Miss?' a clear but unknown voice shouted from outside. 'It's the police. I thought I saw something by your door, a shadow. By the time I came running over, it had disappeared. Just seemed to vanish into thin air.'

'I'm OK,' Hellen said, composing herself, whilst using the door handle for support, her small hand gripping it tightly. 'Just managed to spook myself. I'll be fine.'

'If you're sure, Miss?' he replied. 'If you need me, I expect to be guarding the crime scene until the morning; just give me a call. I'm PC Tom Hawthorne if you need to talk to me.'

Relaxing, she said in a steadier voice, 'Thanks, PC Hawthorne, I might take you up on that kind offer.' With a sigh, she looked out of the window just to check it actually was the police and watched the policeman heading back towards Gary's flat. It was still dark as it was only three in the morning, but she could just make out his rough shape as he walked back to Gary's house, and the birds in the trees seemed to watch him. She blinked and looked again, and now found that their beady malevolent eyes were now locked onto her. She took a step back and they seemed to call out, 'Mine... Mine...'

Chapter 5
New Friends, The Meeting, Accident

'In the multitude of my thoughts within me
Thy comforts delight my soul'
Psalm 94:19
(King James version)

Helen woke early, despite having worked late and her fright in the early hours. She had decided to take the policeman from the previous night a cup of coffee, as she felt that she might have been a bit abrupt when speaking to him, but she had been terrified at the time, and she thought if that wasn't an excuse, nothing was. But still. She didn't like being rude to people, so she quickly brushed her hair, and was just putting on her best silk dressing gown when she noticed a red mark on her throat, just behind her crucifix pendant. On closer inspection, as she pulled the cross to one side, she could see that it was a faint burn mark. And strangely it was in the shape of the cross, which was very odd, given that she had only put it on last night. She shrugged it off, assuming that she had just slept on it, digging it into her skin and she poured out the hot water into a mug, and quickly trotted out to find the pleasant policeman.

PC Hawthorne was just packing things into his car's boot when she sauntered up behind him. 'Morning,' she said, as she approached in the walk that she always unwittingly put on when approaching men. He jumped, and on realising that it was the woman that he had talked to during the night, turned and sat on the edge of the patrol car's boot. Tom was in his late forties with a muscular physique. He had kind brown eyes and short hair that was beginning to turn grey; she felt that the term was salt and pepper, or something like that.

'Morning, Miss,' he said kindly. 'Sorry about disturbing you last night. I must have been seeing things myself after being with the body all day and that, but given that a potential murder had occurred, I had to check out anything suspicious.' He tried hard to prevent his gaze from drifting down to her rather exposed breasts with their delicate speckling of freckles, which were distractingly visible where her gown had parted during her jog over.

'No, it was very kind of you, really. Someone was asking me to open the door just before you spoke to me. It was really creeping me out, and you must have seen them off, as I wasn't disturbed again, thank you. I didn't mean to be rude or anything, I was just a bit shaken up. I brought you a coffee!' And she offered him the mug.

'Thanks very much, Miss. Haven't had a chance to stop yet; forensics have been working to pick up what evidence they can and that isn't much.' '*Damn,*' he thought to himself, '*she's got nice hips.*'

'Are you allowed to tell me what killed him?' Hellen asked, feeling his gaze on her, and a heat spread around her shoulders and down her spine.

'Don't really know that yet, Miss. Should be able to tell you more tonight once we have extracted the CCTV and had a chance to look through it. His place was absolutely filled with cameras. Not just a couple; I mean, they were everywhere, outside as well as inside. Suspicious someone should have that many for personal safety, but on the positive side they should reveal what happened to him. Though he must have either been a very paranoid or a very scared man, maybe both.'

'You're doing the meeting tonight, then?'

'Yes, Miss. It will be at the start of my shift. You should come, you know. I'll know more by then, I hope.' And he handed the cup back to her. 'Thanks for the coffee.'

'I'll be there,' she said, and jogged back to her flat quickly as she was beginning to feel cold. As Tom watched her go, he just couldn't help himself watching her slender figure shifting under the thin white silk as she went. Once inside, Hellen started getting ready for work. A quick cold shower refreshed her, as she was still flushed after her talk with Tom, and then on with her work clothes. She had to skip breakfast and head straight in for seven. Without thinking about it further, or realising that it was still on, she did not take the cross off.

By the time five came, Hellen was feeling tired. It had been a long, busy day with a lot of bad-tempered customers, a seasonal problem when Christmas approached. Bring on a return to academia, she thought, as she walked to her car whilst trying to fish the keys out of her bag. '*Shit*,' she thought as she remembered that the neighbourhood meeting was only a couple of hours away. Just enough time to eat, before having to go out again. She started the car, put on the lights as it was getting dark, and pulled out of Tesco's car park and onto Park Road South. The traffic was heavy, as usual, due to there being so many traffic lights in a short stretch of road, and whilst waiting for them to change, out of the corner of her vision she saw a man dressed in black with a wide-brimmed hat standing on the corner of the pavement looking at her. It was Adam, she was sure of it. It made her shiver; his eyes were so intense! But when she turned around in her seat to look again, no one was there. She was jolted back to facing front when the lights changed and the car behind her hooted. She stuck up her middle finger and moved on.

Despite carefully preparing dinner, she didn't feel hungry, and seemed not to be able to taste the food, despite the spices, herbs and garlic that she had added. Pushing it around her plate, Hellen noticed again that the garlic gave a tingle in her throat as she ate it, but she kept pushing on with the endeavour of eating, as on looking in the mirror when she had got home, she felt that she looked pale and thin, despite physically feeling good. Giving up on the last few mouthfuls, she tidied up, and picked out a warm coat for the meeting. The community centre where it was being held was only a short walk up the road, but it was cold, and there was going to be heavy rain tonight. She picked up a torch for the way back and slid the Taser that her father had bought for her into her bag. 'Just in case,' he had said as she set off on her own for the first time to university. That 'just in case' hadn't occurred at university, or up to this very point in time. The only occasion she could have done with it was that time at home, but she didn't like to think about that, bad memories.

The community hall was busy, with familiar faces all around the room and the slight stagnant smell the building had always had since it was built due to its incorrectly fitted damp course. At the front by the stage, the Neighbourhood Watch representative James and the Policeman Tom were getting ready to get started. The first half of the meeting turned out to be rather boring, giving general information on making sure that doors and windows were locked, etc. In the second half, a few more facts became apparent about Gary's death. For one, although being called an accident, which was a little far-fetched, the CCTV footage had apparently shown animals pouring through the open door and attacking him, and no reason for this was ever presented; and secondly, they had found out that Gary had been filming the comings and goings of all the residents from his cameras outside his flat, and many stolen items of clothing were found in his possession. No surprises there, she thought, and on looking around she could see the knowing nods from other female residents. As everyone began to disperse, eager to get home for dinner, Hellen sought out Tom, who was packing his stuff away into a large plastic box and was preparing to leave.

'Tom,' she said, touching his arm, 'is that all those cameras really showed?'

'Hello, Miss,' he said, turning. 'Well, not completely. I am going to need to speak to you, if that's all right? Would you care to come to the station now and we can have a talk and get the process done?'

'Have I done something wrong?' Hellen asked, rather confused.

'No, Miss, not at all. There was just footage of you found on Mr Macdonald's CCTV that we felt you ought to see.'

Hellen followed Tom out to his car and he held the door open for her to get in. Once inside, she blurted out the thought that had kept running through her mind since the talk: 'Was he filming me?' If he had cameras all round his house, God knows where else he had put them up and what he had filmed. She shuddered as she remembered that he had been in her flat and fixed her shower a couple of months back. Had he been watching her wash? Even worse, had he posted them up online? Her mind raced and her lip trembled a little at the potential invasion in her home.

'Not exactly, Miss. I think I know what you're guessing and worried about, but he hadn't been using them for voyeuristic purposes. Nothing was found that showed that. You were just indirectly caught on several of his outdoor cameras on a couple of occasions, and I felt that you should see what they show.'

'*Oh God*,' she thought as she realised the state she might have been caught filmed in, depending on how many weeks he had gone back, and she changed the subject as her cheeks flushed red and burnt with embarrassment. 'Surely there must have been something more on his death. What you said in there was very improbable.'

'We have to use our discretion on what we reveal at public meetings, Miss Oswold. There were some points that we just couldn't say. It was a brutal crime scene, you know, and I think that Mrs Fuller might have been blotting out a lot of what she actually saw. She was very shaken when she called us out, and almost in shock by the time I arrived. In fact, I'm not sure why I'm telling you this, but it was weird and it does relate to you. The overall account is what I said in there. I wasn't lying. It's just that at the start of the footage the door was closed, and then it just opened.'

'Opened, by itself?'

'Yeah, it just slowly swung open and revealed a dark shadow standing outside, but it did not enter. Then all these animals came rushing in and tore the poor bastard to pieces. He didn't stand a chance, they swarmed all over him. But it was the shadow that spooked me. I've seen animal attacks before and although horrible, I don't know, there was just something about it. The shape though was like the one that I saw at your door. That's why I looked through all the footage from his cameras facing you for several weeks, and I saw it again.'

Hellen gasped, as they pulled into the station.

'It will be simpler if I just show you,' he said, and led her inside.

Tom led her through a maze of corridors until they reached an interview room and led her to a laptop that had been set up there, along with two cups of coffee.

'I can't show you the murder footage, as it's very graphic, and not so important to you. I can only show you the images that relate directly to yourself.' He started the first clip running. The image started moving and just showed her block's front door. At first, nothing seemed to be happening as the time counter moved on.

'What am I looking for?' she asked, peering at the screen.

'This is from last night, when you said that someone rang your door. Now watch.'

The time counter moved on, and then she saw a shadow, or fog perhaps, appear by the door, and it stayed there by the push button caller to the different flats. She gasped. Although indistinct, there was definitely something there, and human-shaped. Then it appeared to look up and she was sure that she could make out two red eyes, before it suddenly vanished as Tom came into frame, pointing his torch.

'I thought initially that I was seeing things when I went to your door last night,' he said, 'but I've watched it several times now, and wondered if it was some kind of interference or something. So, I decided to watch the previous week's footage from that camera to see if it was an effect of the lighting or something like that, when I came across something odd.'

Hellen turned a deep shade of red. 'Look, I was unwell and tired. I didn't even know that I was sleepwalking. We don't need to watch that one; watch that one on your own.' Oh God, did she just say that? This was turning out to be very embarrassing.

'Look, I know it's you, and yes you were naked, but I wasn't watching for that. What you get up to in your own time is your own business, although if someone made a complaint about your nudity offending them, it could be a problem,' he said, trying to sound convincing. 'Honestly, I wasn't looking at you.' Now he was the one blushing, or was he just flushed with excitement about his discovery? It was difficult to tell.

'Just watch,' he said. And with that, he started playing the video. As before, it started with a view of the door, lit just by the flickering light above. Then it opened really slowly, and Hellen appeared walking out as if in a haze, or one of those tacky 1970s porn films. As she knew already, she appeared completely naked, and the image was clear enough that she could see the

Goosebumps all over her body. She slowly walked along the path and to her horror she could see something behind her. Seeing herself nude seemed creepy enough when observing it on CCTV in a police station interview room with a policeman watching, but the shadow following her made her stomach turn and she had to stifle a retch.

'Shit,' she whispered as her lips went dry.

'I know, it's there again. Keep watching,' he said.

It was the strange shadow that had been on the footage of the door and it was following along behind her, just like on the night at Ronnie Scott's as well, she thought. Tom then switched to a different camera view as her image vanished from view, and this angle showed her from behind walking onto the grass as the frost crackled under her feet. Her firm ass and long wavy hair flowing down her back were partially obscured by the shadow as it ominously followed, getting closer and closer behind her. It then seemed to begin shifting form, until it looked almost human in shape, and it seemed to move the hair from her shoulder and tilt her head to one side. It moved in closer to her neck, touching the skin on her back, and then the image of her suddenly screamed. The shadow vanished from view and a couple of seconds later Sophie came into view, pulling her jumper off, at which point Tom stopped the video. Hellen shuddered, and suddenly vomited into the bin in the corner of the room. For a moment she felt completely exposed and vulnerable, involuntarily pulling her coat tight around her as if to ward off unseeing eyes looking at her.

'I just don't know what to say,' he said after checking that she was all right. 'Not about you, I mean, but I just can't explain it; there was someone or something there, but... I looked you up on the police system, and it showed the footage you didn't tell me about in London, and it's the same, just weeks earlier.' He tailed off. 'As the police, there's just nothing we can specifically do. No one would believe it, despite having it on film. I suppose Gary could have been playing with and altering the images, but that just doesn't strike me as plausible, given the London footage. I just felt you should see for yourself. I don't know what I'm asking, or actually expecting you to do, but, well... Have you sleepwalked again since?'

'No,' Hellen said. 'I locked myself in my bedroom last night, the only other thing you saw yourself. I suppose Gary must have been killed the next night then, despite Jasmine reporting it during the day.'

'Yes,' he said, rubbing his hand through his hair. 'Look, I don't want you to think that I'm chatting you up or anything, not that I wouldn't or anything, but I'm not going to be on nights again until the end of next week, and I am now really worried about you. My job's been everything to me since I joined the force after leaving the army, and when I joined to protect people, I meant it. I'm sorry, I'm sometimes clumsy talking to people, but I want you to have my mobile number, not to be friends, but... There's too much that I don't know here. My gut feelings are usually right, and my gut is telling me you're in danger.' He couldn't help flashing a guilty smile. 'Of course, call the police if you can if there is trouble, but just in case, just if you don't have enough time or anything. I only live the other side of the town centre and can be with you quickly, within five minutes. If there is anything you need, anything that worries you, you know, trouble-wise, call and I'll be there.'

Hellen took his number, and he drove her home. This had to be the strangest way that she had got a man's number yet, but she felt that he really did mean well and genuinely seemed worried himself. Given how nervous she was feeling, you never knew what might prove helpful, and she felt that she could well like him. Much to his embarrassment, she kissed him on the cheek before heading indoors quickly, noting to herself that it looked like there was going to be a storm.

As she disappeared inside, Tom remained watching her until the door shut and her legs disappeared up the stairs. It was now midnight, and he had the rest of the night to go until getting off shift. She was one beautiful woman, that was without doubt, and he felt guilty about having seen the footage of her in a compromised position. He hoped that she didn't feel that he was taking advantage. Perhaps after all this was over, he might ask her out; the worst that could happen is that she could say no. Looking out of the car window, his eyes were drawn to the trees at the edge of the forest, and he noticed that there were loads of crows beginning to line up on the branches, and they were all looking at her window. 'Well, I'll be damned,' he said aloud. He had seen almost everything there was to see, from his time in the army and the police force, but there was always something that would come along and shock him. He decided that something was going on here, and he had better do a drive-by in a couple of hours' time, just in case. As he pulled out, he failed to notice the birds all turn their heads and watch him until he was out of view.

Hellen watched him drive off from her window, before pulling the curtains and going around checking that everything was locked up. She slid into her nightdress and headed to bed. It was late and she suddenly felt very tired, so very, very tired. She had a headache forming that was tightening like a band around her head, and she had a pressure building up behind her eyes. She fell asleep shortly after curling up in bed, forgetting to lock her bedroom door.

Bang...

Bang... Bang...

The noise repeated itself...

'Hellen...' [No]

'Come to me, Hellen...' [Fuck, no]

She was desperately trying to resist that voice, but it was getting so hard... [Please no, she muttered to herself.]

Hellen rose from her bed and walked to the door, trying the handle — it was unlocked. He was calling her... Calling, and she had to obey...

She opened the door, despite trying to resist, and headed outside into the pouring rain. Although she could feel the static charge again, her hair and nightdress were rapidly plastered to her body by the heavy rain as she headed into the woods... The crows silently watching her every movement. [I must stop, please God, I must stop...] But her feet kept moving, ignoring her requests.

She walked to him, the dark shape standing tall with his arms held out welcoming her... [No, no...]

He whispered something and she slowly undid her thin nightdress [No...] and let it slide from her wet body. She opened her arms to him, offering herself, although she was still inwardly fighting to resist his commands, her lips continually mouthing the word 'No!'

The form, Adam, approached and took her hair in one hand and pulled her head to the side roughly. She could feel the soft velvet of his jacket brush against her erect nipples, and then... [No, not like this, no!]

He held her left breast tightly with one hand and gripped her sex with the other, and his teeth sank slowly into her neck. [No... I don't... want to...]

She felt it as a sting in her neck, and a whoosh as her blood flowed up and out; the feeling was orgasmic and she began to tremble violently.

There was a sudden horrible hiss, like a deflating truck tyre, and then an awful gagging noise and it... he was gone. The sudden removal of its presence hit her like jumping into arctic water. With no energy left, her wet and naked body crumpled to the floor, leaving her small frame exposed, vulnerable and bleeding. Her cross, however, shone out despite the darkness, appearing to smoke gently, as two small trickles of blood ran down her neck and dripped onto the floor.

Chapter 6
The Rounds, Discovery and Forebodings

'And fear not them which kill the body,
But are not able to kill the soul:
But rather fear him which is able
To destroy both soul and body in hell'
Matthew 10:28
(King James version)

He was in Year 11, and the GCSEs were approaching fast, and, shit, he was going to do badly. Tom had always had trouble concentrating in school, apart from the amount of time that he spent in detention and excluded for fighting. The unfairness of most of the punishments was that he was usually defending himself from bullying, or on many occasions trying to stop others being picked on; but he had always been rather blunt in his approach, and his large stature at that age tended to typecast him as 'trouble', and he always got caught. It was after a particularly nasty confrontation with Jeff and Colin, where he had laid them both on their ass for smacking around one of the nerdy boys in his class, and he was now walking home with him to ensure that they caused him no further problems, when they were jumped from behind. Colin had produced a knife and stabbed both of them, running off and leaving them bleeding on the floor. Tom, who had been the luckier of the two, had taken the knife in the thigh due to his height, but the nerd, Joe, got stabbed in the stomach and was bleeding heavily. Tom had managed to carry him into the town centre before running out of strength, and they were lucky in that a pair of cops had been passing and saw them, and both had been treated and survived. It was after this encounter that Tom had focused his attention on joining the army and cleaned up his act. He had improved his work ethic, leading to middle-of-the-road results, avoided trouble and spent his spare time at the gym building up his fitness. From that point on, his life had picked up, and he had become a good soldier, and earned several awards for bravery. It was not until his mid-twenties that he heard that Jeff and Colin had been arrested for attempted murder outside a nightclub in Southend-on-Sea, and it had all been caught on CCTV; and it was shortly after that he joined the police.

'All units please respond.' The radio sprung into life as Tom's car pulled out of Hellen's car park and onto the main road, and his thoughts returned to his duties. 'Disturbance at Cosham railway station; anyone able to attend?'

Tom replied, 'Unit 756 responding. On the old A3 heading towards Widley, e.t.a. under four minutes.' He put the lights on and accelerated up the hill towards the station. When he arrived, he found two men fighting, and PC Sally Carter trying to keep them apart. She had her Asp drawn, but as he pulled up, the smaller man shoved her from behind into the larger, dirty-looking man with tattoos, and ran for the footbridge over the tracks. Sally seemed to have the man under control and was now in the process of cuffing him, so Tom ran after the other one. He may be scrawny, but he was damn fast. 'Hawthorne in pursuit of a white male, brown hair, dark tracksuit bottoms and a red top. Heading down the High Street and turning left... left into Windsor Road,' he shouted into his radio as he raced after the suspect. Tom prided himself on his fitness as he worked out every day, no matter how long his shift had been, but as he turned the corner his suspect had gone. He was nowhere to be seen. Slowly picking up his radio, he said, 'I have lost the suspect; repeat, suspect is out of sight. I will check the gardens'; and he made his way along the road slowly, looking into the small front gardens, and checking side gates were locked.

About halfway down the dark road he came to a bigger, detached house with ivy covering its entire front, only allowing glimpses of the windows to show. No lights were on, and the 'Sold' sign screwed to the wall was hanging crooked, but the wooden street door was ajar. Perhaps he was hiding inside. Turning on his torch, Tom pushed open the door with his Asp. 'Hello,' he called out. 'Police, anyone there?' There was no reply except a large rat which came running out, stopped to look at him with disdain, and then scurried off down the road. Tom stepped inside carefully, shining the light around the room: everything seemed empty. Perhaps no one had moved in yet; there certainly wasn't anywhere to hide. He made his way through the house but found nothing, until he got to the kitchen. The units had all been torn out by vandals, leaving huge scars in the wall, and there was a large pile of earth on the floor with a spade in it. *'Why on earth would anyone put that inside for?'* he thought, as he tried the handle to what he guessed was the door to the basement. It was locked, but he did notice that muddy footprints came out from that door, or at least he hoped it was mud — could be shit if any pipes had burst. Not finding anything else, he left, clicking the door shut behind him. Strange, he thought to himself, very strange.

'Did you get him?' Sally asked as he walked back to the train station.

'No, he just disappeared.'

'You're getting old, Tom,' she quipped as she rubbed the bruise on her cheek. 'This one's far too drunk to make sense tonight,' she said, pointing to the large man being taken off in the police van, who seemed to be doing his best to head-butt his way through the van's back door. 'I turned up, but it was as if I wasn't there. The smaller man seemed terrified of the bigger one, but I swear he had a crowbar or something like it. Anyway, we'll question him in the morning. See you later, Slow Joe', with which she headed back to her patrol car and pulled out of the station.

'Odd,' Tom said to no one in particular, and went to go, but noticed the small man standing by his car. He was visibly twitchy and shuffling from foot to foot — he was either frightened or high on something, probably crystal meths.

'I'm sorry,' he said, 'I didn't mean to. It was just a job like you know. You know, a bit of money, lift and carry like.' This man wasn't drunk like the other one, or high; he was definitely worried, which was perhaps why he had returned. He had begun wringing his hands.

'What job was that, then?' Tom tried to ask in a calm voice whilst edging forward.

'We just had to do a delivery from London to Portsmouth last week, and take it just around the corner from here, man. It was easy money, just ask no questions.'

'You mean that house with the ivy on it, don't you?'

'Yes, yes, but quiet, man, he has ways of hearing things, like,' he said in an ever more hushed voice. 'Damn cargo turned out to be fucking coffins, man, coffins and earth — stunk to high hell. Heavy they were, too. I wish I hadn't done it. I didn't want to see that.' He was looking all around him, his twitching becoming painful to watch. 'It's here... in Portsmouth. I saw it. God, I wish I hadn't seen it. I looked inside, and it moved.'

'Seen what?'

'If you got any sense, pig, leave! It's looking for something, searching. It talked to me in my mind.' His eyes were over-wide, and Tom felt that the man was losing it, as increasing madness crossed his face.

'Why do we need to leave?' he said carefully, beginning to feel worried.

'It will destroy everything... everything.' A crow called out from where it was perched on the lamp post, and the man let out a squeak of fear and he took off, running like he was being chased by the devil himself, and the bird flew after him, flying low, and it strangely looked like it was following him. But for some reason Tom did not follow.

'*Looking for something,*' he thought, '*or someone?*' A sense of worry stabbed through his stomach. London, looking for someone, shadows. The fear in that man's eyes. Gary's death. '*Oh my God, Hellen!*' he thought, and jumped into his car.

Tom pulled into the car park to make one last check on Hellen. After his encounter with the man, he was very worried. He felt drawn to her like no other woman he had met, and the evidence pointed in this direction for some reason, but why? All seemed quiet as he approached, and he stopped the car. Maybe he was wrong, but the last time he had that feeling his partner had been shot on a drugs raid. Then the open door of the block caught his attention, and his fear rose. He quickly reached for his torch, which had fallen into the footwell, so that he could get out and investigate, when his windscreen exploded inwards, showering him with glass. Something then reached in with talon-like fingers and grabbed his stab vest, pulling him out through the gap in the glass, its jagged edges tearing at his flesh. The hazy man-shaped mass of darkness was incredibly strong, and Tom couldn't break its grip no matter how he struggled; its blazing red eyes pierced into him, and there was a crackle of static as his hairs began to stand on end. Then the shape said in a dry voice that Tom felt sure was just in his head, 'She is mine'. He went to draw his baton, but the black shape struck him and everything went black.

Chapter 7
Only Death Awaits

'Thou shalt also consider in thine heart,
That as a man chasteneth his son,
So the Lord thy God chasteneth thee'
Deuteronomy 8:5
(King James version)

Four thirty a.m.

'Shit!' Aaron said as he finished running, finding himself back on Cosham's station platform at half four in the morning. 'Shit, shit, shit!' And he punched the wall in frustration, leaving two bloody knuckle marks behind, but the pain that ran up his arm seemed to calm him a little.

'He'll fucking know, man, me and my big fucking mouth. Why couldn't I keep it shut?' He reached into his tracksuit trousers and tried to steady his hand enough to light a cigarette. All he had wanted was some quick money; he'd run out of weed and needed it so bad, and when Paul had asked him to help out shifting a load, it had seemed like a good idea and easy money — it was two grand each, just to deliver a box. God, he wished he hadn't done it! Paul was now in the fucking nick, probably getting charged for assaulting a cop, and he'd gone one step worse: he had blabbed. 'I fucking snitched, man,' he said to himself, pacing up and down the platform, breaking into a violent cough, projecting brown crap out of his lungs. It had been inside his fucking mind the whole way back from London, working its way in, talking to him, and it had emphasised that silence was essential, his life depended on it. Paul had not heard it, it had not spoken to him, but invaded his mind. The things that it knew and had shown him as his partner-in-crime had driven back to Portsmouth were horrific; the monster was old, three hundred years old, and that wasn't right, nothing got that old. He inhaled deeply, tasting the smoke in his lungs and knowing that he had to get out of the area, maybe go and visit his aunt in Wales. She lived in a very remote area; maybe it couldn't find him there! They had to move him after all, it might just work! Maybe it wouldn't bother following or finding him. He was, after all, only a little fucking fish in a big fucking pond; surely, he wouldn't be worth bothering with?

* * *

Four thirty-five a.m.

Paul sat in the cell with his head over the stainless-steel toilet, vomiting the drink out of his system. His head was beginning to feel clearer and he couldn't remember why he had been fighting with Aaron now; something he had just kept prattling on about — he must have been back on the drugs again. He had sounded really paranoid, like a man on the edge of sanity. Why couldn't he just have a drink like him? Worked far better than anything else, or at least he thought so. He sat on the bed and wiped his mouth with his hand, which in turn got wiped on his jeans, leaving a snail-like trail across the fabric. Not long until morning now and he would be released. There was no way Aaron would press charges, and the pigs would probably drop the assault on a police officer shit to save on the paperwork. As he lay out on the bed, attempting to get some sleep, he failed to notice a gathering of mist in the corner of his cell. Even if he had, he would probably have put it down to the drink… but it swirled around and began to take shape.

* * *

Four thirty-six a.m.

The light on the front of the freight train approached the station at speed. Aaron was sure that it stopped to pick up goods there, and he could sneak on and ride down to Southampton so that he could catch a train north. Out of the corner of his eye he saw a curl of mist gathering into a human shape, and for the first time in his life since he was a kid, he shat himself.

'Shit, man,' he stammered, stepping backwards. 'Fuck, no!'

He was too late: it was coming to get him. He could feel its pull on his mind, and it seemed furious. The tall man began to approach him, and he couldn't help but notice the apparition's mouth was burnt, his lips twisted into a snarl, and blood already ran down his face and shirt.

'No, no!' Aaron screamed at it. 'You won't take me. I don't want it. I don't want to be like you!'

* * *

Four thirty-seven a.m.

The mist in the cell took the shape of a lady in her sixties, and it walked towards the snoring shape on the bed. Her hands reached out towards his throat.

* * *

Four thirty-eight a.m.

Aaron shook in fear as the man approached nearer and nearer, and he could hear the voice in his head. It was like an army of rats trying to scratch their way out of his skull, and the building static added to his pain.

'You gave my location away, Aaron. I am very, very disappointed in you. I thought we understood each other? It was such a simple job, but you couldn't even do that. Perhaps I won't kill you; you don't deserve a

quick release. Perhaps I will keep you alive to serve me forever.'

Aaron put his hands up to his head and screamed, as if his mind was being torn apart from the inside. Several blood vessels in his eyes burst, and two drops of blood made their way down his cheeks as his eyes turned red.

On the tracks, the train was not slowing down. The safety barriers descended in preparation for the train to pass through, as it sped towards the platform.

'Come, Aaron, give me your hand... Preparations must be made for your service...'

'No!' he screamed, and as the train shot through, he stepped in front of it, and its brakes went on far too late to make any possible difference.

On the platform, Adam looked away in distaste at what remained of the weak-minded Aaron, smeared across the tracks and train. The driver never saw Adam's shape fade and slowly disappear.

* * *

Four forty a.m.

The old woman had found it easy to be invited into the station: an old pro in her thirties had said the words for a twenty-pound note, and that was all she needed to go anywhere in the building. She looked with disdain at

117

the crumpled form drowned in the toilet. What a waste of good hot blood, but Adam had been specific: he was to die and not turn, and you couldn't refuse Adam, it was impossible. She had tried when she had first woken after death, but the hunger was too much for her to resist, and his commands echoed through her mind. The alarm in the station sounded and her shape quickly faded.

Chapter 8
Death, Blood, Awakening

'Now the works of the flesh are manifest,
Which are these; adultery, fornication,
Uncleanness lasciviousness,
Idolatry, witchcraft, hatred, variance,
Emulations, wrath, strife, seditions, heresies,
Envyings, murders, drunkenness, revellings, and
Such like: of the which I tell you before, as I have
Also told you in time past, that they which do such
Things shall not inherit the kingdom of god'
Galatians 5:19-21
(King James Version)

'This is your fault, Hellen...'
    'You should have been a good girl and come to me when I asked...'
    'You will come... everyone does...'
    'When I command it... you will come...'
    'You will obey me...'
    'You will be mine...'

Hellen's eyes opened slowly and she felt that she was suffering from the worst hangover she had ever had in her life. She found herself lying on the fallen leaves outside, curled up in a foetal position and once again naked. 'Shit!' It had happened again. Taking a moment to get her bearings, she discovered her nightdress crumpled up in the mud, and, like her, it was wet and muddy; but given the alternative of walking home naked, she stretched out a trembling and dirty arm and put it back on to cover herself up. Shivering as it touched her skin, she unsteadily got to her feet, which were also bare and covered in scratches. The trees spun around her, and she had to reach out for a lower branch for support to prevent herself from falling on her face. After a minute, the world stopped spinning and she started making her way slowly and nervously back to her flat. On coming out of the woods, the hairs stood up on her neck and she began to experience a feeling of foreboding. She noticed the police car and headed towards it. 'Tom,' she called out, and stopped suddenly as something sharp cut into her foot. 'Shit, damn it.' She looked down to find broken glass all over the tarmac, and on looking around saw that it all seemed to come from the car, along with a path of blood, which was streaked over the bonnet, along the path and, as her eyes followed it, she saw that it led to a tree. Bracing herself, she looked up and had to bend over and vomit, her small frame heaving. She retched again, emptying the remaining contents of her stomach onto the floor, which left an unexpectedly large puddle, happily steaming by her feet in the cold of the early morning. She forced herself to look up again and her eyes met Tom, or what was left of him. A tear ran down her face, and she murmured, 'No... no!' He was hanging upside down by his feet, which were tied to the tree branch above, with his arms spread out in an occult southern cross crucified position, like they sometimes did to witches many years ago. She had seen enough of its imagery at metal concerts. He was completely white, and his neck had been almost completely cut through, his head hanging on with just a few fibres and sinews. As she looked closer, a crow flew off his face to reveal that his eyes had been pecked out. Below him lay an unextended Asp and his radio lying in a pool of gradually congealing blood. She staggered backwards towards the police car, leaving a trail of bloody footprints in her wake from all the cuts on her feet, and fell over in a dead faint.

Hellen was woken by the paramedics as they began to lift her into the ambulance. She shrugged them off, and with tears in her eyes began to unsteadily walk back towards her flat.

'Miss,' one of them called after her, 'your feet need to be treated; we'll sort them out for you. Come back.'

'I'll be fine,' she said without turning back, partly limping due to the pain.

'But the police also want to speak to you!'

Turning around, flushed with pain and anger, she shouted, 'Well, they goddamn know where to find me!' And she slammed the door behind her. 'Why the fuck is this happening to me?' she mumbled to herself. 'It's like a fucking film.' She collapsed on the sofa and inspected her damaged feet. Damn, they really weren't good, and she felt a bit ashamed that she had been rude to the ambulance crew; but this whole situation was unreal. Apparitions following her around, wandering the forest naked, two fucking murders right where she lived, and now she had two feet full of glass to add to her problems. God, she wished she had locked the door, but that voice was so hard to resist. It commanded, and you just did it, you had to do it. How could she resist on some occasions and not on another, though? She felt humiliated and degraded; at no point in her life had she ever been so submissive. True, she didn't like conflict, but that had never stopped her from following her own path; but here she couldn't. She damn well tried, but here she was, going along with what was asked of her. Christ, had she had sex with him? And her hands protectively cupped her sex as if guarding it from further attack, but she didn't think so. Had he bitten her? Actually, bitten her? Everything was hazy, but she felt sure he had bitten her, and then he had left almost immediately. Why? She reached up and found the bite marks bleeding — so she had been bitten! She knew now for certain who was in the woods; she had seen his face clearly as it had moved towards her. It was Adam from the club, but apparently, according to the police, he didn't exist. 'Maybe I'm going mad?' she questioned herself repeatedly as she hobbled over to her dressing table and shuffled through its drawers, looking for where she had last put her eyebrow tweezers.

Once she had found them, which for some reason had been hiding in her underwear drawer, she set about pulling out the pieces of glass embedded deep within her feet. She had never been a squeamish girl, learning this in Year 9, when one of the girls in her PE class had got her leg broken in a rather competitive hockey match, and she had been the one who had managed to calm her down. She couldn't remember her name now, but had actually managed to stem the bleeding with her pull-over bib until the ambulance had arrived.

She made quick work of the job, systematically digging the tweezers, that she had cleaned by heating over the hob, into the wounds and working out the few bits of glass that remained. Most were thankfully just cuts, only deep. Once she had finished removing the offending shards, Hellen found herself just staring at the blood as it covered her feet, and the way it swelled from the cuts and trickled down her foot towards the heel and dripped onto the floor. As she savoured its warm smell and deep redness, her eyes glinted, and a ring of red began to form around the iris of her eyes as she watched. A trickle of saliva ran down from the side of her mouth and dripped onto the floor. She tried to look up as the doorbell rang, but couldn't pull herself away, and to her shock she bent forward, unable to stop herself, and licked her foot slowly from the heel to the toes. '*Eew, shit!*' she thought as her tongue did it again. She could taste the salt and iron of her blood and began to feel the static build up as it had before. Suddenly, there was a call from the door, and she managed to break the invisible pull and her foot dropped to the floor. There were some occasions when being flexible just turned out to be gross. Hellen took a deep breath and called out, 'Just coming', and tenderly walked over to the sink and washed her mouth out before opening the door, pulling the wet fabric of her muddy nightdress tighter around her as she shivered self-consciously.

* * *

After a painful conversation with the police that was taking far too long, two men that were way too young to be detectives seemed convinced that she was thoroughly mad, thankfully not the suspect, but still crazy middle-age-woman mad, and would do well to seek help. Despite her repeated claims that Tom had been killed by a man named Adam from London, and that she had also been assaulted, she could see the disbelief on their faces and their lack of writing anything down. Although she hated herself for doing it, she just wanted them gone; they were not going to provide any help, so she did what she knew would work quickly. She began flirting with them. There was no surer way to get rid of unwanted male attention than to be confident, self-assured and demanding, and it did its job well. Most men were frightened of women if they were in positions of power, or well educated, and she was both. The two young men looked absolutely terrified, and hurriedly finished their questioning and excused themselves as fast as they could and stumbled out of the door, colliding with each other as they went. She allowed herself a sigh of relief as she heard the outer door click shut, when the phone rang. 'Shit.' When would she get a chance to get out of these wet clothes?

'Hello, is that Dr Hellen Oswold?' an older voice asked politely.

'Yes,' she said hesitantly, 'who is that?'

'I believe that your GP told you I would be ringing. I'm Professor Harker from the London Tropical Disease Centre. I was asked to investigate your bite marks. I would have called sooner but have only just arrived back today from South America, trying to sort out a potential outbreak of an unknown disease there, but had to leave in a hurry as an anti-government group moved into the area and we got caught up in some, well, trouble. All very nasty really, but you don't want to hear about me. I've had a look at the photos that your doctor sent me, and I have to say they are quite intriguing.'

'I'm glad they are... well... interesting, but they keep bleeding, and bloody hurt. What are they?'

'If I didn't know better, I would say they were from a vampire bat, but I was led to believe that you got these in London, and unless the bat was over twenty times larger than that of the species we know, it can't be that option, so I am afraid to say that it's got me baffled. Sorry to have to say that, but no point talking bollocks for nothing. I just don't know. Would you be able to come up to London to let me look at them more closely, and maybe run some tests?' His voice sounded eager, and slightly excited.

'Well, I suppose,' Hellen said, somewhat taken aback. 'I wasn't keen after my last experience up there, but...'

'Oh, it would only be quick, and not until the week after next as I'm away again until then, so I will book you in and my secretary will be in touch with a day and time.'

And with that he was gone. '*I can't take much more of this,*' she thought, and headed to the shower to get the mud off her skin and from the crevices that it had no right being in, and finally got into something clean, although she still felt that she couldn't really get clean — she felt violated and had her intimacy intruded upon. Without thinking about it, her hand moved up and protectively cradled her neck. Was she really dreaming it, or had Adam really turned up and bitten her? She had heard somewhere about cults that drank blood, but she couldn't remember where now, other than it did exist. Her neck hurt again, and she rubbed it, and cried as she felt vulnerable and abused. Looking at the clock, she noted that it was still only early in the day. Bollocks.

That night, Hellen went to bed early, making a start on *Dracula*, and from the outset her mind began to swim. This just couldn't be right; some things were so similar to what she was experiencing. 'Shit!' she said out loud. 'This just can't be fucking happening to me!'

She didn't sleep that night, and just kept reading instead, despite her eyes getting sore. Since the release of the *Harry Potter* series, she had never stayed up all night reading, but tonight she did. By the time the morning light was beginning to come through the window, she had finished the book — she had always been a fast reader — and was more terrified than she had ever been in her life. '*I really must be going mad,*' she thought, clutching her head in her hands. '*I'm actually believing a work of fiction; but the symptoms are so close. I don't want to end up like Lucy.*' Her mind started to rush. 'That's why it left me so quickly,' she mouthed, thinking about the previous night. 'The shape disappeared when it saw my cross. It hypnotises me, the bite marks, my lack of control, the feelings of desire?' She took in a deep breath as she considered what she was saying. 'Fuck me, I'm turning into a vampire! How long have I got?' She stopped, breathed deeply again and smacked herself hard across the face, leaving an angry red mark across her pretty features and a trickle of blood running down her lip. 'Get a grip, Hellen,' she told herself. 'You're a scientist, for God's sake, and are talking complete fucking shit. It's fantasy, just a novel written by a journalist' — or she thought that was what Bram Stoker had been. 'It's completely unreal.' Her heart was now beating fast, and she could hear it echo through her ears. But her mind kept being drawn back to the thought and wouldn't let it go. She phoned work and made an excuse about not being able to come in and sat down with her computer and did what she knew very well to do — she started researching. Although this time, instead of science, it was folklore, and vampirism throughout history, including references in popular culture.

An internet search first of all brought up the 1920s work *Vampires and Vampirism* by Montague Summers, which led to his other book, *Vampires in Lore and Legend.* There were hundreds of works available and she scanned as many of them as she could, including Nick Groom's *Vampire: A New History* and P. Barber's *Vampires, Burial and Death.* The list was endless and all suggested the same: she had been bitten by a vampire, and probably had a certain amount of time left before she would eventually die and be turned, by which it meant changing into a vampire. The trouble with all of this was that there was no proof, there were no proven cases and no evidence. All her life she had relied on evidence, it was necessary, but by God was life pushing her in this direction.

For the first time since she was sixteen and had lost her virginity to a young teen called Hugh in the school's sixth form art room after a party, she looked out the small rosewood box at the bottom of her wardrobe, and ran her finger gently over its surface, and the inscription her parents had engraved on it when they gave her the present on her eleventh birthday.

'Hellen dearest, we all live in the eyes of God, let him in and you shall never be alone. With all the love in the world, Mum and Dad.'

She drew out the band of rosary beads from its navy felt padding and having not been a believer for over twenty years, she kissed the cross, feeling the slight burn it created on her lips, and tears slowly crept down her face. If all this wasn't real, it was making a bloody good pretence. As she stood up, she ran her fingers along the beads again, this time beginning to recite her prayers, the ones that she had said so many times during her childhood, but now she kept stumbling through the words, and felt a growing pain in her chest as she recited them. She just managed to make the sign of the cross, but it felt difficult, and her hand moved clumsily. She took a deep breath and started with the Apostles' Creed.

'I believe in... in... God,' she stammered, 'the Father Almighty... Creator of... of... Heaven and... and... and... Earth; and in J... Jesus... Christ... His...' She choked back another sob. 'Only... Son... Our Lord... I believe... I believe...' Her eyes reddened and she was now crying. She tried another. 'Our... Our Father, who... who... art in... in... Heaven, Hall... Hallow be... Be... Be... Thy name.'

She closed her eyes, teeth clenched in pain. 'No!' she mouthed to herself. 'No!' and she sank to her knees, clutching the rosary tightly in her hand. She focused hard, beads of sweat forming on her forehead with the effort, and she forced the words out slowly. 'Thy

Kingdom... come. Thy... will be done... on... Earth as it... is... in... Heaven.' She pushed harder, her face turning red. 'Give us the day... The day our daily bread: and forgive us our... our trespasses as... we... forgive those who... who... trespass against us; and... lead... lead us not... not... not... into temptation, but deliver us... from... evil... A... Amen...' She sucked in air as if drowning, shaking with the effort, but she had managed to recite one of them. My God, it felt like she had run a marathon, and she panted with a mixture of exhaustion and fear.

Hellen knelt on the floor trembling for ten minutes before standing. Damn, was this more fictional proof of her curse? That, or she was a witch! Either way, still a curse. Stifling another sob, she decided that she needed to do something, anything that would set about proving her fears wrong. She disliked not being in control, the feeling of being powerless; she had to find a way to start controlling the situation. She decided that she would do this by carrying out some of the easier protective precautions listed within the pages of the books, no matter how silly they sounded. Ones that might stop Adam getting to her again, hastening her demise. Was she really thinking like this? She had hoped on her search that she would find some type of definitive ancient text with all the answers, but there wasn't. Only vagueness and probably incorrectly recorded legends and exaggerations, but she had to grasp onto something. She needed hope. She had the cross already, which was helping, but she needed to stop wandering out whenever he commanded her to; break that control he had exerted over her. She wasn't a staunch or active feminist, but she didn't like being commanded — it really pissed her off. So, she created a list; she liked lists, something about them always made her feel better and calmed her down. With a list, you knew where you stood. Perhaps it was the sense of moving forward.

(1) Fresh garlic and garlic tablets. Get the bastard both inside and out. Maybe that was what he choked on when she was in the woods, and in annoyance killed Tom? Which would make it her fault.

(2) A mirror for the door. She could hang this on her street door; as they supposedly couldn't bear their own reflection, it would make them leave, and it might work, as so far, he had not appeared on camera.

(3) She could put up one of those camera doorbells and maybe some wireless CCTV cameras in her house and looking out the windows, she could then see what was happening, what the bastard was up to.

(4) Hawthorn branches. These could be placed across the windows and doors.

(5) Salt lines. Yes, she would definitely put a circle around the bed, although she could swear that they were used in witchcraft as well for protective circles. Maybe that's why they were used?

(6) Iron was easy: she had a hefty iron hammer from her father. If he didn't like the iron, she could always try and hit him with it.

'*How did he get across the River Thames?*' she thought absent-mindedly to herself as she wrote her list — they can't cross running water. She was sure that she had read that somewhere last night, so someone must have moved him across in a coffin, she supposed. Shit, that would mean he could be nearby; now that was really scary. 'Fuck!' What was she doing? She really must be going mad — she was letting events screw with her head. With that thought, she headed out whilst it was light to get the equipment that she needed, and again felt the lump that formed in her throat and tried not to cry as she had to return quickly for her sunglasses and a baseball cap, as the sun was hurting her eyes. '*Goddamn it,*' she thought, '*how long do I have left?*' If I'm right, I will end up dead and haunting the streets at night for blood for ever, and if I'm making this up, I'll end up like Renfield in *Dracula*, or Randle Patrick McMurphy in *One Flew Over the Cuckoo's Nest* — except, unlike him faking insanity, I won't be faking it.

After a hard day of work, Hellen finally felt prepared for the evening. She had crudely nailed branches of Hawthorn across the door and windows and thought how much like a prison it made her nice flat look. She must have appeared completely crazy stopping in a layby and pulling the branches out of the nearest hedge, but the garden centres hadn't had any, and she definitely considered this an emergency. The mirror was on the outside of her front door, and cameras were in place, although getting her computer to detect them had taken several hours. Finally, the salt ring she would put in place before she went to bed. Not a bad job, she thought, as she swallowed a handful of garlic tablets. They burnt as they went down and made her feel hot and ill, but she consoled herself with the thought that she wasn't a full vampire yet, not by a long shot, and if that bastard did manage to get her to come out, or get in, she sure as hell wasn't going to taste nice; with a bit of luck, it might kill him. She couldn't help but wonder if that would be enough to free her from the curse, or if a stake would still be necessary.

* * *

'*Hellen...*'

There was a scraping at the window.

'*Come, Hellen. Don't fight it. You belong to me...*' [*Fuck you*]

'*Come... rise... come to me...*' [*No*]

There was a hum as the cameras started recording. The scratching at the window continued, the latch rose and unclicked.

'*Let me in, Hellen... Invite me in, be mine...*' [*Fuck, no*]

Then there was a hiss of pain from the window and the scraping stopped as the hawthorn rustled.

'*Hellen... You must obey me...*' [*No*]

'*You cannot resist me...*' [*I... I... No*]

133

'Come…' [*Please don't… No*]

In her bed, Hellen sat bolt upright, the cross around her neck seeming to pulsate and her veins bulging as the blood raced through them from her quickening heartbeat, as if in answer to Adam's call.

'You will come to me…' [*I… I… No*]
'Come…' [*… No*]
'Now…' [*Please… I beg… No…*]

Hellen's eyes opened. 'No!' she shouted aloud again, but she was not truly awake, for her eyes were still rolled back in her head, showing the whites. The static feel washed over her as before, and it began to resonate through the deepest parts of her body as she gasped with fear at the evil, and shock of unrelenting pleasure that seemed to come with his words.

'You will come to me now…' Hellen sobbed… [*No*]

The desire became stronger, and her fist involuntarily gripped tight the rosary in her hand, her knuckles turning white. Then her arm jerked up out of her control and she used the edge of the cross on it to cut across her left wrist, wincing in pain. Guided by a force she could not hold back or fight, she cut again, leaving a dark angry red welt on her pale skin. She then did it again, and again and again, harder and harder until it cut into

134

her flesh and the blood began to flow from the wounds to a whooshing that hammered in her head. Hellen lifted the cross again and drew it down from her left shoulder, across her breast until it reached the nipple, ripping across it, cutting through the thin cotton and skin alike until blood dripped from its erect peak onto the bed sheets, forming a scarlet pool. She cut again, and again, across her ribs, across her stomach — she could no longer stop herself, despite her attempts to stop her arms' involuntary movement, as pleasure and pain flowed through her, her face contorted as she attempted to stop herself.

'*Give in to your desire, Hellen...*' [*I... don't... I... Please leave me alone*]
'*No, Hellen... You're mine... Drink... Drink...*' [*No... I don't want to... Please don't*]
'*Stop the pain, stop your deep hunger and drink...*' [*No... please... Don't make me*]
'*Drink...*' [*Daddy... Help me...*]

Hellen slowly bent forward and licked her cut wrists, greedily lapping up the hot, rushing warmth of her own blood as her body shook, wracked with pleasure as she shuddered and orgasmed uncontrollably. Her mind was still weakly fighting him, but her body was not listening. Then she tasted the garlic at the back of her throat. Saved by such a common and simple cooking ingredient. It burnt her tongue, and that burning awoke her as it seared through her veins, rushing through her body like an uncontrollable fire, sending her nerves into spasm. But now, she found herself suddenly awake in her own bed. It had not managed to lure her out or get in, but had still managed to influence her, and she reminded herself that if she died that was it, or wasn't it as the case might actually be. She would join the undead forever; but she didn't know how to stop its influence further, and a feeling of helplessness came upon her. With time, all sources pointed towards the fact that she would eventually die and become a vampire. She had been bitten after all, so that was it — lore said that she must kill it to cure herself, but that seemed an impossible task on her own; but if others were involved, she would put them in danger from Adam and herself. How wrong the modern tales were of romantic vampires, their love for mortals and companionship, she thought bitterly, clutching herself in pain and anguish. All they wanted was to feed and pleasure for themselves. Was she just meat to them? Food to be taken and consumed when required? A pleasuring food source, a blood prostitute to fulfil their desires? It was nothing less than assault, vampiric rape of her veins and possibly her body — there was nothing erotic or desirable about that. The thought made her shudder. Did vampires even have cocks? She found herself wondering, as she pictured a film she had seen years ago with a young teen girl passionately making love to a hunky teen vampire boy with a six-pack. She shuddered again at the thought and felt sure that she had seen another series where after being bitten, all the victims' bits dropped off. *Yuck.*

Well, she didn't want to find out. Having them suck her blood was bad enough, and she made an effort to tuck the thoughts to a dark box in her mind and lock them in. She just couldn't bear to think about those possibilities.

With an immense effort, she dragged her aching body up from the bed and its blood- and mucus-stained sheets and looked at herself in the mirror, finding that she had to force herself to maintain her gaze; but she still had a reflection for now. Although she might be imagining it as she was tired and hurting, but it seemed a little blurry around the edges, and a rather sorry sight she was. The cuts were all over her, red and bleeding. Her white nightdress was torn and bloody, revealing more than it concealed, so she stripped it off and did the best she could at cleaning all her wounds with a towel and a bottle of TCP, which stung like hell, and then she sat on the dressing table chair, crying until the morning. Never before had she felt so alone!

Chapter 9
Confession, Hope, Pain

'Yea, though I walk through the
valley of the shadow of death,
I will fear no evil, for thou art
with me; thy rod and thy staff,
they comfort me'
Psalm 23:4
(King James version)

Hellen once again stood in front of her mirror and
inspected the previous night's damage on her body
whilst the washing machine fought to remove the blood
from her sheets. She had binned the nightdress, which
was beyond saving. All her wounds had for now stopped
bleeding, but horrible red welts now covered her
previously delicate and pale skin, criss-crossing her in
lines with a certain randomness like a Picasso painting.
She also noted that her weight had dropped again,
despite eating well: her ribs were becoming more
prominent along with her hip bones, but the problem
came in that what she was eating was not blood. She
paused, remembering the books that she had read, where
after feeding, vampires often looked less gaunt and
younger, like when Dracula's moustache had turned

from grey to black. Hellen felt that this probably meant that if she was to drink enough blood that horrific scarring on her body would heal over, and she wouldn't be left permanently marked — but there was no way that she would allow herself to consider that option; it was disgusting, and she would rather keep the marks. She put on a long-sleeved jumper to hide the cuts on her wrists and decided to go without a bra in case the rubbing opened up her cuts again. Besides, her torn nipple really hurt. She also thought that if they did open up again, there would be a good chance that the blood would soak through thinner clothes. The hospital really would commit her if she suddenly whipped her top off in public and started licking up her own blood, as the temptation was getting bigger. That would have her in a straitjacket quicker than a pig into a pile of shit. Damn, this was fucked-up.

Hesitantly, Hellen opened her computer and began reviewing the night's video footage; she didn't want to, but she had to know what had happened, as she only remembered parts and they were hazy, like trying to remember a dream upon waking. Camera 1 looked out of her bedroom window, and revealed a large and ugly bat fly up and land on the windowsill, where it walked along for a bit before stopping and then appeared to be struggling to open the window. It had just succeeded and was reaching in, when its claws touched the hawthorn, and it withdrew quickly as if it had been burnt. She shivered, but it had worked. The doorbell camera showed nothing, but it probably couldn't get to that as she remembered that they had to be invited in, or at least she hoped so. Camera 2 focused on her bed, and she hesitated again before she put it on, her fingers hovering above the button, steeling herself for the footage that she knew was to come, and she forced her fingers to click play. She seemed to be spending too much time watching events that she couldn't remember properly via CCTV; it felt like voyeurism and made her feel cheap and dirty, a sexual plaything for a dead man, although food was probably his main thought. It was intrusive. She played the events of the night, and her head slowly sank, and her eyes reddened, tears forming in their corners, as she watched herself writhing on the bed, and then sitting up and cutting herself. She winced as she watched herself make each cut, and unintentionally found herself tracing the cuts on her body with her fingers, and the pain that her torn nipple emitted at her touch. Once again tears began to run from her emerald eyes and zigzag down her freckled cheeks, and she hung her head lower, watching the footage again and again.

[Rewind]… Cut… One red wound ran across her skin.

[Rewind]… Wrists cut… Blood oozed from the next track across her skin.

[Rewind]… Ribs cut… Another deep wound was made across her torso.

[Rewind]… Breast cut… Nipple cut… More blood, torn flesh.

[Rewind]… Cut…

[Rewind]… Cut…

Hellen's vision became blurred with so many tears she could no longer see the screen, and she screamed; not a scream of anger alone, but of deep and personal pain. She clenched her fists tightly and closed the computer, gasping back a sob, and threw the vase standing next to her on the desk across the room, where it collided with the bathroom door and shattered with a large crash. She was beginning to fear the night now, and what might happen without her being able to control herself, and she determined to stay awake that night instead, and tried to pick up as much sleep during the day as possible. Maybe if she stayed awake, she would be able to resist the calling? She hadn't been bothered when she had stayed up reading, had she? Maybe it wouldn't happen at all? But she guessed that this was probably just wishful thinking.

Hellen remembered back to when she had been thirteen and had a horrendous nightmare. She couldn't recall every detail of it now, other than she had been kidnapped and was being held captive in a basement and was trying to escape, but she still remembered the fear as clear as anything; even all these years later, it still made her skin prickle. She could still recall her captors' faces in every minute detail and how she had tried desperately to squeeze herself through a tiny window to escape, and they had grabbed her feet, pulling her back towards them, towards the inevitable rape, and just as they started to tear her t-shirt off, she had woken screaming, and dashed to her parents' room and climbed into bed with them and clung onto her father for dear life, and refused to return to her room that night.

'Don't worry, Emerald,' her father had said in his ever-calm voice. 'It's all going to be all right.' And he held her protectively as her Mum had stroked her hair. For as long as she could remember, her dad had nicknamed her Emerald because of her bright green eyes, which neither of them had, and she missed him so much, now more than ever. He would have known what to do, he would have protected her from this mess.

'Your Mother and I will never let anything happen to you as long as we're alive,' he had said to her in the warmth of their bed on that night, and a tear rolled down her cheek at this, for neither of them were alive now, and she really didn't have anyone to help her. Both her parents had been only children as well, and she had no brothers or sisters. Her grandparents were mostly dead, except Grandma Jo, who was in a nursing home with advanced dementia.

She had not shared a bed with her parents since she had been six, but that night she had been unable to sleep at all and shook for hours. It just kept repeating in her head, over and over again.

'Your mind is a fascinating thing, Emerald,' her dad had said to try and calm her down. 'It's just trying to make sense of the events from the day, and these things are seldom easy to understand. You have a wonderful mind and will do great things in the future. You have every opportunity open to you, and all you need do is just take them when they arise. Don't hesitate, don't regret the choices you make, learn from them and move on. Always have faith in yourself, don't doubt and live life to the full.' And she had spent the rest of the night hugging him as he nodded off to sleep, starting to plan in her mind what she might do with her life until the nightmare drifted out of her conscious.

Her father had not been a well-educated man and always had to work extremely hard manually throughout his life to provide enough money to look after her, as had her mother. His rough and cracked hands were a testament to this. He seldom chatted to outsiders, and only ever seemed to open up and talk for hours with her. It had always made her feel so special, and she felt that her time with him was irreplaceable. She loved her mother just as much, but it was always her father that she had chosen to confide in, even in the most unexpected areas where most girls would speak to their mother or older sister, from when she had started menstruating, to her first kiss, and even her first sexual encounter. He was always so understanding and never angered, and most of all he just unconditionally loved her. 'Daddy,' she mouthed to herself, and closed her eyes, picturing his face, 'what on earth do I do?' She felt so lonely and cold sitting there on her bed alone, and she couldn't stop herself shivering, despite having turned the radiator up to full.

She lay there thinking, and decided that she needed to remain positive, and think of the better things in life, and what she could do to actually affect her future — she worked better to a plan. She remembered back to when she had graduated, and how proud she had been to collect her first-class certificate — she felt a giant, or at least as tall as her five-foot-four would allow — and how she had jumped up to kiss Ben when he had received his. He had always been tall, about six one, she estimated, and to reach his face she had always had to hop or jump up and cling onto him with her legs. Then there was her Masters, although that had been a little overshadowed by that event she never spoke of, and her temporary withdrawal into herself; but seeing how proud her parents were had actually helped her recover. Then there was her PhD and the publication of her first paper: for that she had cried and didn't care who saw. It really meant something, along with her appointment at Portsmouth University. She smiled and relaxed a little. Her father was right, there was hope; she had to cling onto the small things and make happen what she could.

She would storm the interview this time, she would prepare better, but what to do about Ben? The more she thought about him, and their past, the more convinced she became that he had loved her a lot, and most likely as more than a friend, and had just been too frightened to ask her out. He had always been sensitive and perhaps she should have realised, but should she make herself vulnerable and ask him out when they met again? She felt so fragile at the moment, and she had effectively ghosted him for no reason other than a bad experience that he knew nothing of, what must he think of her? Why couldn't love be like science, a strict right and wrong answer, and a sequence of steps to be followed? Shit, why did thinking about him make her feel so excited? She pulled her knees up to her chest and hugged them. Perhaps she should ask him out? But then how far should she go on the first date? She didn't want to seem easy, but she was potentially dying here, and it could be her last chance for love, to feel someone else, someone close to her, loving her. There was something about Ben that made her think it was the right decision, but the risk — damn, why couldn't these things be planned? She decided that she would have to see how things went; maybe she was jumping the gun. He could, of course, be married and have kids! That would fuck up her plans, and she realised at that thought that she did feel a desire for him, a strong deep desire and an unquenchable aching. Or it could, of course, be fear of her current predicament, panic at growing older alone and possibly sexual lust, but she didn't think so, despite the growing throb in her groin that would not go away whilst she was thinking about him. And for the first time in twenty-two years, she thought back to how they had embraced in that cold tent as students! Her parents had been right, the signs had been there, and she shuddered, involuntarily stroking her inner thighs and running her hand up over her panties and clutching her sex. How could she not have seen it? She reprimanded herself for her stupidity, and went to the bathroom and washed her face in cold water as she had flushed up a deep red and despite no one being present, she felt ashamed and embarrassed at what she considered her foolishness at not asking him out back then. 'Damn stupid girl,' she said aloud and fetched her tablet, before getting back into bed.

By the time it got to midnight, Hellen was having trouble staying up. She lay on her bed watching heavy metal videos on her tablet in the hope that the fast tempo and hammering drumbeat would keep her going, but her chin slowly kept drifting down towards her chest, and something seemed to keep whispering [*Sleep now, my child... Sleep...*], until her eyes eventually closed, and the device fell to the floor.

'*Come, Hellen...*'

 '*You crave blood... Why do you resist...?*' [*No...*]

 '*You need it... It's healing properties...*' [*Daddy, help me...*]

 '*It tempers the hunger... Supresses the madness...*' [*Please, Daddy...*]

 '*Drink... now...*'

146

Her stomach rumbled, screaming at her for food, and in her sleep, she rubbed it.

'*Hunt! Hellen... hunt...*' [*No... please, no...*]

'*You desire it... Take it...*' [*No... No...*]

'*You desire me...*' [*No... I want Ben... Help me, Ben... Help me...*]

Hellen awoke in her bed with a start, feeling wet and sticky, and her nose picked up a horrible acrid smell. It was still dark outside, and morning was a while off yet! Outside, she could hear someone calling out a name, and then calling from further away. She was naked again, but this time covered in blood, and she was terrified. What had she done to herself this time? She looked around the room frantically like a caged wild animal, seeing that all her sheets were also soaked in blood as well. She rapidly felt over the scars that covered her body to find where it had come from, but she couldn't find any open wounds, only the rough peaks and edges of the scabs she had carved into herself previously. She wasn't due yet, but finally ran her fingers down and checked between her legs in case she had menstruated, but the blood definitely wasn't hers, and at that thought her stomach turned over and tied itself in a knot, causing her to double over. As she gingerly got out of bed one shaking leg at a time, her eyes were drawn to a smear of blood from the bed which ran across the floor, and she then noticed it — the small body on the floor — and she stiffened a cry as she went

147

over to the pile of flesh and cooling meat, and finally the red leather collar, and she realised that it was the shredded remains of the neighbour's dog.

'My God, what have I done!' she cried, bending over the remains. 'No… no…' Tears formed in her eyes and she collapsed backwards, hitting the wall with a thud, sliding down towards the floor leaving a smear of blood as she went. 'What on Earth have I done, what have you made me do?' Hellen remembered the CCTV cameras she had set up, and she moved to her laptop without bothering to dress to see what terrible thing had happened. The effort of moving made her tremble. Her fingers shook as she moved them over the trace pad to select the camera's play icon, smearing blood on the pad as she moved her fingers.

Camera 2 (Bedroom): She watched her body writhe on the bed, shouting and fighting an unseen presence. Throwing herself up and down whilst roughly pleasuring herself, tearing her clothes off in the process. Her body suddenly stopped still like a statue, and stiffly got out of bed as if possessed, and headed out of the door. Hellen shivered as she noticed the size of her teeth, which seemed to glint in the night vision of the camera, and she unconsciously felt them as she watched.

Camera 3 (Front Door): Her naked form walked along the landing in the slow fashion that she was becoming accustomed to watching, and down the stairs. Just as she vanished from the screen, the neighbour's door opened and its owner appeared carrying his dog, and he seemed to be telling it off. After a minute, he headed off in the same direction that she had taken. '*Oh, my God, not him, too,*' she thought, panicking, and she looked back at the dog's remains as if expecting to see a body there as well.

Camera 4 (Block's main door): Hellen appeared, and walked down the steps, her scars shining white as they caught the moonlight. She then turned right and moved along the side of the building.

Camera 1 (Bedroom Window): She appeared into shot, and froze there, unmoving; she just stood there in the cold, looking into the woods, moving as if to take a step towards it, and then stepping back in indecision, her hair blowing in the breeze and steam coming from her mouth.

Camera 4 (Block main door): The main front door opened for a second time and showed the man appear. He dropped the dog on the floor, where it ran off, presumably to do its business in the bushes; but the man, on the other hand, went off in the other direction towards the bins, opened the door of the area that concealed them from view and went inside and closed it again. A small light sparked for a second and a drifting trail of smoke rose into the air. He was using the dog as an excuse for a crafty cigarette, as his wife hated him smoking and he had supposed to have given up.

Camera 1 (Bedroom Window): Her head suddenly swung to the right as she must have heard something, and then the dog ran into sight, growling and barking at her. Hellen watched in horror as it backed away from her, growling, and then her image on the screen pounced on it. She grabbed it tightly around the throat as it tried to bite her and she smashed it against the wall until it went limp, and she then ripped its throat out, with her teeth, and like a hare, she sprang up the stairs towards her flat.

Steeling herself for what she was going to see, Hellen turned her attention to the internal cameras once again.

Camera 2 (Bedroom): She reappeared and jumped onto the bed, ripping and tearing at the body in her hands, lapping up the blood, whilst smearing it across her body, before discarding the remains on the floor and collapsing on the bed from the exertion.

Camera 4 (Block main door): The man was looking around, calling for a dog that was not going to return.

Hellen noticed that the timer on the camera was only minutes earlier; she still had time before she started absorbing any of the blood and she ran to the bathroom and bent over the toilet, sticking her first two fingers deep down into her throat, forcing herself to vomit. Her body shuddered as she repeated the process again and again, until nothing else would come up and she was just retching, and she collapsed into a heap on the floor, sobbing hysterically, the toilet filled with blood and small lumps of flesh and gristle. This was a new low — how could she come back from this? She felt defiled, dirty and out of control, and she was disgusted with herself. She managed to stand and started scraping up the remains of the dog into a bag, along with all the bed coverings. She had to get rid of it, as the eyes seemed to be continually watching her. She wiped down the floor and wall, before cleaning the toilet, removing all traces of blood. Still crying, she climbed into the shower to clean herself up, hoping the hot water would wash away her sin, but it didn't — she still felt terrible. Her doorbell rang, but she didn't answer — it would be the man going around asking if anyone had seen his pet, and she couldn't face talking to him, not after what she had done to it. She just sat curled up in a foetal ball in her bed with the sheets covering her head as she rocked forwards and backwards, quietly crying herself to sleep.

Sleep did not come, and whilst still in her dressing gown, she drove out a couple of miles into the country, placed the bag of sheets and meat on the floor, poured lighter fuel onto it and set it on fire, watching the items curl up and blacken as they turned to cinders, before heading home. There was nothing that she could do. She couldn't tell anyone; this was too bad to disclose she felt, and shivered. She had killed it. Killed a dog and eaten it, and she spent the next two hours forcing herself to recite her prayers as she cried onto her rosary. It was getting harder, but she could still just force herself to say the words, just.

Hellen's mind was in turmoil, and she just found herself walking around Waterlooville town centre like a zombie at seven in the morning, trying to avoid being alone. After two hours, she found herself stood outside the Catholic church that she had attended as a child. A place that she had not visited in years, and it now looked rundown and deserted, with graffiti covering the side wall and weeds sprouting up between the cracks in the paving slabs. She slowly ascended the steps leading towards the large wooden doors. Her hesitancy was not purely caused by her long absence, and she knew it; it was deeper than that. But she forced herself forward, and with an effort, pushed herself through the door, and although she could still make herself enter the building at the moment, she knew that the curse was tightening its grip on her. The inside had been done up since she had last been there and made the outside look deceptive. She made her way to the front but could not see anyone around, and hesitantly drew an empty water bottle from her bag and approached the statue which held a basin of holy water, and she guiltily filled up the container, murmuring her apologies, and returned it to her bag, noticing that where it had splashed on her fingers it had left behind light red marks.

'Are you all right, my child?' came a quiet voice from behind her. She jumped and turned around to see Father Thomas approaching from a small side room. He seemed a lot older than she remembered, but it was over twenty years ago now and he had not been young then. He must be over seventy now, she thought, seeing his wispy receding hair and heavily lined face.

'Is that you, Hellen?' he said, looking at her carefully, and he put his glasses on to take a better look. 'My dear Hellen, I haven't seen you for so long!'

She smiled, and finally had to sit down on the front pew, as past memories she'd locked up for years and the effort she was having to exert in resisting the curse hit her. It all washed over her and she gripped the oak of the pew in a tight grip.

'Father,' she said, 'I'm so glad it's you. I have not confessed for so long, and I have sinned so badly. I always meant to come back, I really did, but my pride and youth stopped me.' Unintentionally, she started rubbing her left hand with the right, which was holding her rosary, and it started leaving more cuts across the top of her hand.

'You are shaking, my child,' he said, and sat down beside her, noticing from the corner of his eye the blood beginning to form at the light cuts she was creating. 'Tell me what is wrong, Hellen. Forget the past and the embarrassment it must have caused, God will forgive all sins, no matter how bad; it is us as humans that have trouble forgiving. It is not for you to judge; allow yourself peace, child.' He tenderly took her hand, pretending not to notice the marks the water and rosary had caused, and to stop her continuing with the cutting, as her actions were getting more aggressive. 'Tell me what is wrong. I'm told that I am a good listener, and only slightly deaf, so you won't have to speak too

loudly. This new hearing aid is excellent, you know.'
He smiled, trying to encourage her.

'I really don't know where to start, Father,' she said, fighting not to pull her hand away but failing. 'I thought I had a good understanding of the world, that everything had its place and fitted in, it was ordered. But now I just don't know. In the past few weeks, the things I have seen, experienced, I don't know if there is a God.' Tears began to flow down her cheeks, and she began to sob, her head bent forward, red hair falling over her face.

'My dear. Things in our lives have a way of testing us and our resolve; these are opportunities for us to shine. The Lord would never make us face challenges that we could not overcome; it is a test of our faith,' and he took her hands in his again, and she flinched as if electrocuted and pulled her hands away.

'I'm sorry, Father,' she sobbed again. 'But with respect, you have no idea how bad my problems are. Look!' She pulled her jumper down enough to show the burn mark her cross had made on her skin. 'How do you explain that? I've never done anything badly wrong, yet the cross burns me. I'm having to fight myself to just sit in this building and look what the holy water did to my hands! Is it that I am forsaken, claimed by the devil and therefore shunned by God?' And with a great effort she held his hand, fighting the urge to pull them away.

'It could simply be an allergic reaction, Hellen. What do you think, that you are possessed? I have never seen a true case of demonic possession myself, although it is not unheard of at the Vatican, and is extremely rare.'

'What do you call this, then?' she asked, pulling up her jumper's sleeve, showing Father Thomas the cuts all over her arm 'It's not an exorcism that I need — I'm turning into the undead.'

He winced at the network of deep cuts across her arm, and then sighed.

'Hellen, I have known many young girls that tragically self-harm; you wouldn't be the first.'

'This isn't fucking self-harming, Father. I think a vampire has set its sights on me; he has bitten me several times... He makes me do things... I don't want to do them, but... he insists. He made me cut myself because I resisted him and wouldn't invite him in. I don't know how long I have left until I turn. I don't know what to do. I can't keep fighting him. I'm losing the fight, Father. I ate a fucking dog last night!' She revealed the bite marks on her neck, which were bleeding again. 'I got these in London, a month ago, now I'm losing control of my life.'

Father Thomas for the first time looked really concerned. 'I have seen this once before, many years ago, when I was studying Latin in Italy. In a case that was never resolved, and the church refused to get involved, but many people died. I remember looking it up. May I try something, Hellen? It will most probably hurt slightly, but please humour an old man.'

'That's fine, nothing could hurt more than I do myself at the moment,' she said. With this, he dipped his fingers into the holy water and pressed them against the wounds on her neck, one finger on each bump. She stifled a scream as the water burnt her, but she managed to stay seated as he went on to mark the shape of the cross over her wound. Through gritted teeth she said, 'This pain to holy water is not normal now, is it?'

He frowned, his eyebrows like two out-of-control bushes fighting for dominance on his face. 'It could be many things,' he muttered in a matter-of-fact voice. 'You could be faking it, disturbed, or just attention-seeking.'

Hellen's heart began to sink, and she couldn't help but think that he might be right: maybe she was having a breakdown. He then looked her straight in the eyes and said, 'But I believe you. I made your mother a promise before she died, that if you ever came back to me seeking help, I would always be there for you, and help you find your faith again. And I will not break my promise to her.'

No longer able to contain her emotions, she started crying again and he hugged her, saying, 'I need to speak to my superiors, maybe even the Vatican itself, but I will, and see what I can do. Remember that this church is a sacred place and no evil can pass through those doors. If you ever need sanction, come here. Secondly, I would not normally advise anyone to get a tattoo, but I have seen protective inking before, and you would be wise to go and get one of the holy cross, done on your neck, where the bite mark is. I saw you take the holy water, and you are most welcome to it. Place a little in the ink that that is to be used and it will aid in protecting you. Do it now, and I will seek help. I only hope that it is not true, but if it is we have a battle on our hands with a true evil, that will be very hard to win.'

Hellen thanked Father Thomas and left to find a tattoo shop that was open. As she left the church, she felt better, and the swelling of the bite marks even seemed to be a little less. She spent the next half an hour looking for a suitable tattoo studio, and eventually found one in Southsea. It was a disreputable-looking dive from the outside, and even worse inside.

'All right, love, what you looking for?' said Lou as he came out from the back. 'Know what you're looking for, love?' The cloth he was cleaning his hands with looked like it would fail any health and safety examinations it might be given, but she couldn't be choosey.

'I'm looking for a custom job,' she said, and she outlined her request, much to the surprise of Lou.

'Well, if that's what you want, hop up. I'll do it, but you'll have to pay for the whole container of ink. Once I've contaminated it with something you've brought with you, I can't use it again on someone else.'

'That's fair enough'

'I also won't take responsibility if it gives you an allergic reaction either,' he added as an afterthought.

'Look, I really do understand. I will probably scream, I'll warn you in advance. I've never had a tattoo before, but just carry on, I have to get this done.'

'It's usually not the girls, Miss, they got quite a good threshold for pain — babies and all that, I guess. The problem is usually the big tough guys. I've had so many of them break into tears before; couple have even passed out. But if you're fine, I'll get going.' Lou turned out to be very good, and very gentle, despite the holy water burning into her flesh painfully, although it didn't seem as bad as it had been in the church. She winced and gritted her teeth together, clutching the padded chair tightly but managed not to scream like she had when having her belly pierced, but Ben had been there then. Once Lou had taped a cover over the newly inked work to keep it clean, she thanked and paid him, and headed out into the street. Realising that it was beginning to get dark, she hurried back home, hoping that she wouldn't get caught in traffic. The last thing she wanted was to get caught outside after sundown. Unseen from within the shadows, a black shape watched her go.

York 1820
First Interlude of the Nosferatu

'Be sober, be vigilant; Because
your adversary the devil, as a
roaring lion, walketh about, seeking
whom he may devour:'
Peter 5:8
(King James version)

Over the years money never seemed to be a problem for the Decker estate, and its lands were continually increased over the next fifty years. Whenever noble and wealthy locals died, they always left their money to the Decker family, and in some cases were buried within their personal crypts. James and Rebecca never appeared to visibly work, although they did make many considerable profitable investments, freely altering their political allegiances as required, not that they were visible members of the area. The locals that were lucky enough to spot them after dusk attributed their lack of work to their unnaturally youthful appearance in their seventies, which they kept right until their deaths were announced in 1760. The estate was taken over by a George and Anne Decker, who moved in by night and bore a remarkable resemblance to the late Lord James and Lady Rebecca. By the time it got to 1820, there was no one old enough that was still alive to have seen James and Rebecca themselves and the similarity between them was not noticed, along with the apparent lack of ageing within the family, let alone the estate being handed over that year to a Lord Robert and Lady Isabelle Decker, another couple in their forties that looked almost exactly like James and Rebecca, despite there never having been any whispers of children.

Most of the older locals now kept away from the Decker estate, citing a sense of dread or fear when close to its borders, and very few dared to attempt poaching on their land, as anyone who tried was never found — they simply disappeared. Typically, Lord and Lady Decker donated substantial amounts of money to the town over the next few years, especially into graveyards and children's health, for York was beginning to gain a reputation for its youth dying early through blood conditions which could not be cured. A large number of staff were required to run an estate of that size, and mainly consisted of teenage girls and boys. No one was permitted to lodge there or remain overnight, and to address this request, staff houses were built by the Lord just outside the walls, unusual for the time when most staff lived in, but the young workers were pleased along with their parents, and nobody seemed to notice the numerous visits both the Lord and Lady made to the teenage staff's quarters late at night. As the required hours were only ever during daylight hours, they were considered highly desirable posts due to the high pay, provided lodgings and short working hours.

However, the townsfolk had become very superstitious, and most of the households, hung crosses on their doors for protection. There was a spreading belief amongst the locals that the manor was cursed, and even entering its grounds brought ill on the hapless visitor. Talk was also spreading, regarding the packs of wild dogs that now seemed to haunt the surrounding woodland, and the sightings of bats and crows were on the increase; but the people feared even talking about such things, for those that spoke of it too often tended to vanish and never be seen again.

Chapter 10
Ben

'Charity suffereth long, and is.
Kind: charity envieth not; charity,
vaunteh not itself, is not puffed up
Doth not behave itself unseemly
Seeketh not her own, is not easily
Provoked, thinketh no evil;'
Corinthians 13:4-5
(King James version)

Ben was sitting in a lecture theatre within Southampton University. It was the first day after fresher's week, and he was worried about the amount of work that lie ahead. He knew that he was good at studying, but if he was being honest with himself, perhaps the anxiety came more about the possibility of making friends. He was naturally shy and had left school and college without any real friends, after being teased for years about his weight. The only reason that he had not been picked on more was because his size worked well for the rugby team, and that status had put him above the category of physical bullying, but only just. His trail of thought was broken when an extremely pretty girl with bright ginger wavy hair down to her waist sat next to him, her body brushing against him, and she introduced herself as Hellen Osborne. He could still remember that moment as if it was yesterday, her shapely summer dress revealing her body's curves to their best, the way she played with her hair and the sweet smell of her intoxicating perfume. Hellen, he thought, what a pretty name; and from then on, they were completely inseparable, like soulmates but without a lovers' relationship. At times they had even shared the same dreams and teased each other that they were telepathic. Ben had never wanted to push it further; his insecurities meant that he was worried about losing her as a friend if things didn't work out, and he didn't want that, even when he had to suffer silently as she dated other guys and he had to console her when they broke up. He was always there for her and could never forget the kiss that she had given him when drunk, and it had taken all his resolve not to take the opportunity when he had the chance, but he didn't. Over time he had convinced himself that it was because he had too much love for her to take advantage, but the real reason was most probably that he was too scared. Although his respect for her was indeed deep, and he always regretted not telling her his feelings before the end of the course, they drifted apart when she remained at Southampton for her Masters studies, and he was only offered a place in Dundee. Damn crazy, given his excellent results, but when you had a face and a mind like hers, no panel would refuse her to study wherever she wanted.

Ben awoke from the dream that had continually returned to him since he had come across Helen's job application in his university e-mail inbox. He had seen the name and had actually frozen for a couple of minutes; his mouth went dry and a single tear escaped from his eye and ran down his cheek. From that moment on he had experienced the recurring dream where Hellen would lean over to him, her lips brushing against his ear, her body so close to his, and she would go to whisper something to him while running her hand up his thigh, and that was always the point he would wake up. Damn, if it only went further!

He slid out of bed and started getting ready for work. He needed to speak to his friends on the interview panel to ensure Hellen had the best possibility of getting the job, although he would never mention it to her; he didn't want to upset her pride, which was why he would not sit in on the interview and would meet up with her afterwards instead. It had been so long since he had last seen her and it was now only three days until she would turn up, wow! The very thought of being near her again made his legs tremble. Ben had never been able to marry; sure, he had dated and had short-term relationships, but the problem was always the same: they just weren't Hellen. He knew he was fantasising, of course; if she only viewed him as a friend back then, why would there be any difference now? Except, of course, it might not even reignite their friendship. But he reprimanded himself that he had never actually asked her out. He had missed her badly over that time, her humour, her apparent lack of fear, her dedication. He sighed. Never mind, don't get your hopes up, she could be a completely different person now, she might even be married — women didn't have to change their last name. Damn, there was a depressing thought.

Ben distractedly shaved, which not surprisingly led to three cuts that wouldn't stop bleeding, washed and got dressed for work, taking a moment to decide which cufflinks would go best with his tie, and then cursing when he noticed that he had blood on his collar and had to change the shirt. His hand was hurting him this morning, as it did most mornings, a tightness and stabs of pain that shot through his fingers when he tried to do his tie up. His fingers on his right hand had never been the same since breaking them just before his final undergraduate exams in a rugby match, where the other team had been losing and one of their players had 'accidentally' stepped on his hand, and he had never forgotten Hellen's touch when she had held his left hand so gently while he waited for the ambulance, and delicately traced her fingers over his. He unlocked his garage door and absent-mindedly reversed his 1970s Pontiac Firebird out onto the drive, relaxing at the sound of the engine's throb of potential power. Although he would never have used it to accelerate that much as its 6.6l engine ate fuel like a thirsty camel does water at an oasis. He could only realistically have the classic car as he lived less than a mile from work, and that was expensive enough, and he swore that every time he pushed the accelerator pedal the fuel gauge went down. As soon as he had taken out the mortgage for his house, he had indulged himself by buying the car in an attempt to fill his loneliness and sadness at Hellen suddenly vanishing from his life, and his inability to find love. It hadn't worked, but it did cheer him up. If only she had said why she stopped talking to him it might have helped him move on? But perhaps it was best not to know.

The day had gone well and Ben was pleased with himself. All the relevant technology had worked for his lectures, his PhD student had passed his final viva, and it turned out that the panel were already strongly leaning in Hellen's favour — no real surprise there: she was a gifted scientist, and his support only helped what he thought would be a foregone conclusion. It was now getting late, so he had his dinner in his local pub with a cider and went home to relax for what was left of the evening. He quietly sat on the sofa on his own and watched a couple of episodes of *Bad Blood*, and the end of a foreign language zombie film that was really weird, but for some reason he couldn't stop watching. He put it down to the hero's last stand against the horde with only a tennis racket and a can of beer. How that fight had lasted the last thirty minutes of the film was ridiculous, but amusing.

His mind kept returning to Hellen. Sure, there was the physical attraction as she was an exceedingly

166

beautiful woman, but it was far more than that. It was all the little things about her that endeared her to him even more: the way her lips curled up when she smiled, the way her hips swayed when she ran, and by God, that twinkle in her eye. But it was her personality that did it for him. She always seemed so confident and in control of what she wanted to do, the way she would stand up when presenting work and own the room, yet when you knew her like he had, there was an incredible vulnerability deep inside her, and he felt that they had been complete together. He sighed. Maybe he was dreaming, but he wished that things had turned out differently, and that he had asked her out.

Ben rolled over and started to dream of the past, as he so often did; this time it was about one of their most precious moments. He opened his eyes and tried to blink away the beginnings of what would probably be an impressive hangover. Yesterday had been the first day of metal fest weekend and Hellen and himself had not got back to their tent until gone two in the morning. He had been nervous sharing a tent with her, as she was female and he fancied her, and would never have dreamed of asking her to do such a thing, but she had been nervous about going to the festival on her own and wanted him nearby, and she seemed one hundred percent happy with it, although it only helped to convince her parents that they were an item. '*If only*,' he thought to himself. He tried harder to focus on his watch and as the hands gradually stopped moving in front of his eyes and showed the time to be ten in the morning, and the gates would be opening again in just over an hour.

'Come on, Ben, we'll be late,' Hellen said, prodding him in the back with her foot. She sounded as bright as a daisy despite having drunk far more than him, and he was the member of the rugby team! He looked over to her, and had to stop his jaw from dropping, and quickly averted his gaze as she was standing almost right in front of him and was completely naked except for a skimpy red lace knickers, and was waving her gothic-style corset at him.

'Come on, you'll have to help me get this on, I can't lace it up myself,' she said, and prodded him with her foot again, her pert and delicately freckled breasts bouncing slightly as she did so.

'Coming,' he murmured, trying to hide his embarrassment, and his rock-hard arousal. She knelt down close to him and tucked herself into the garment, whilst he struggled to lace it up as his hands shook uncontrollably as he worried about touching something he shouldn't and upset her, like her small, firm breasts. 'Don't think about it,' he said to himself, looking down again, only to be met with her shapely hips and underwear. Sometimes he wondered if she was deliberately enticing him to persuade him to make a move on her, or whether he was just so far in the 'friend zone' that she had no concept of him as a sexual male. Now that was a depressing premise, but by God she was beautiful, he thought, as he moved her long wavy hair to one side to hook up the top of the corset. She leant forward, unaware or uncaring about his stare, searching through her pile of clothes for her short black 'vampire' skirt, as she called it, due to its hem's style of cut — again oblivious to how close her practically see-through panties were to his face, giving him a clear outline of her sex, and he had to steel himself and pull his jeans on before she noticed the size of his cock. Ben had known her now for over two years and they really were completely inseparable, but he just couldn't bring himself to ask her out: the risk of losing her as a friend was too high. The opening was potentially there as she hadn't really dated for a while, and there was even the chance that she was trying to get him to make the first move... but, no! Too much risk. He didn't even want to contemplate the possibility of losing her due to a clumsy proposition on his part. And it would be clumsy.

Hellen ducked out of the tent, smiling, waiting for Ben to get ready. Despite being top of her class in Organic and Inorganic Chemistry and that she was predicted a first-class honours degree, when it came to relationships she actually was painfully naïve, and had not given her seductive behaviour any thought consciously. She had needed help and he was her friend, and that was as far as it went, although she sometimes wished that he would ask her out; she dearly liked him, but maybe he wasn't interested in her that way, or perhaps he was gay, but he was so sensitive and she didn't like to ask, as it might break up their amazing friendship, but maybe she did test him a little unconsciously just in case, as they were so good together. Her parents had made a lot of less-than-subtle suggestions about her making the first move, but that wasn't proper. That was the boy's job to ask her out, and many did, but so far, she had only made love once at college, and that had been an awkward experience and somewhat of a disappointment for her, standing out for its strange mixture of her not wanting to be a virgin, mixed with the simple desire to just find out what it was like, with a dab of clumsiness and guilt. She had never been able to bring herself to confess to Father Thomas, the embarrassment would have been too much. She had spoken with Sophie the next day as she had always been more confident around men and had lost her virginity at just fourteen, or so she said, but she had not really been very helpful by suggesting that Hellen just needed more practice and had to get out there and shag more boys, which she found deeply embarrassing. Hellen felt deep inside that what she really needed was love for the act of sex to mean something, and on her first time it had just not been there.

Ben finished tying up his shoelaces and quickly rushed out to Hellen, and they both jogged off hand in hand to get a good place at the front of the stage. He really hated the front of stage with the moshing and joshing, but Hellen wanted to be up front, and as she was so petite, he worried that she would get hurt, squashed or groped, perhaps all three, so he always tried to position her by the rail, and he would stand behind her with his hands around her, holding onto the rail for dear life, trying to prevent others from knocking into her. Normally, he would have enjoyed the close contact of her jumping up and down so close to him, but this was harder work than scrums on the rugby field, and she always seemed to like the bands with the most mental fans. By lunchtime, they had moved back to a less rowdy part of the field, and Hellen was enjoying sitting on Ben's shoulders, waving her Devil's Rejects flag around even though they didn't come on until the evening. He also had to admit that she was so light it wasn't too much of a problem holding her there for prolonged periods; he had muscular shoulders, but there was also the fact, that he kind of liked the way her thighs clamped around his head and her panties rubbed against his neck as she bounced around, once again thinking 'one could dream'.

After getting lunch from one of the dubious-looking food stalls, they both laid out on the grass, chatting about their dreams and future aspirations. He loved just talking to her, and they would often picnic and talk for hours on end. She had an amazing laugh that could penetrate to his very heart.

'We both need to do our Masters at the same place, Ben' she said, fixing him with her piercing green eyes with the look that said she had already planned everything, which she probably had. 'Let's both apply to Southampton, and we can stay together for longer.'

'Sure, it would seem wrong somehow not to,' he said. 'I don't ever want us to be apart, you know, Hellen. I…' and he cut short. Damn, he'd been so close to telling her. Shit! Why did he have to bottle out?

'Ben, will you do something with me?' she asked, and his heart almost skipped a beat.

'*Maybe she's going to ask me out,*' he thought as he began to drown in her eyes; but with as much control as he could manage, he replied, 'Of… course, Hellen, you know I'll… always do anything with you.'

'I want to get a piercing, Ben, but I'm… well… scared of the pain… and don't want to go on my own. They have a place in the festival tent for that; will you come with me? Please?'

'Er, of course, what are you… erm… planning on getting pierced… then?' He couldn't help but stumble the words out, as certain images formed in his mind.

'Yeugh,' she said, involuntarily crossing her legs and clutching her crutch in assumed pain, 'not that! That would really hurt! No' — she playfully slapped his arm — 'I want my nipples done… You can kiss them better for me, they might be sore afterwards,' and then she laughed almost hysterically as his eyes widened and a look of fear crossed his face. 'I meant my belly button, silly! Geesh, I almost peed myself then — you should have seen your face,' and she got up, pulling him to his feet, and they both laughed.

'*Thank God,*' he thought to himself. 'You sure they will be hygienic and everything?' Ben asked her, as she led the way towards the tent. 'I don't know if they even have running water here.'

'They will be fine,' she said. 'Everyone has their belly pierced these days,' she said in a matter-of-fact way, as if trying to convince herself as well as him.

An hour later the pain had gone off in Ben's hand and he let Hellen lead him back to the music stages. She had been perfectly fine until the needle had gone in, at which point she had gripped his hand so hard he had been the one to scream out. For such a small girl, she had a massive grip, and had managed to bruise his fingers. She had been very apologetic about it, and even kissed them better, which had brought him around a bit, and she had been able to show him the small gold bar with pink stones in it, which he dutifully said was lovely, which it was, but his hand still hurt, and he had to have a large Scotch to recover fully.

That night was very cold on the field as a wind blew in from the East, and they skipped the last band to return to the tent for food and whatever heat they could get. By the time it got to two in the morning, Ben could actually hear Hellen shivering, and was not surprised when he got prodded in the back.

'Ben, are you fucking cold as well, or is it just me?' she said, leaning over him, so close, the mist from her breath blurring his vision.

'No, it's not just you, it's damn cold tonight. Do you want to put my coat on?' he suggested helpfully.

'No, can I get in your sleeping bag with you?' she asked nervously. 'It's so cold, and body heat is supposed to be best, isn't it? That's what the explorers say on the television, right?' If it had been lighter, she might have seen the sheer look of panic that passed across his face, but she didn't give him time to answer; her mind had really already been made up as it so often was, and she just climbed into his sleeping bag, hugging him tightly, whilst he shivered, realising that she wasn't wearing anything apart from her thin nightdress, and he could feel her rock-hard nipples brushing his back through it. Trying not to think about their abrasive action as she rubbed against him, he turned around and held her tight, lightly rubbing her arms, and at her request her legs as well to help warm her up, and her skin really was icy cold and she was shivering.

'You're so cold, Hellen, why haven't you put more, well, er, more layers on?'

'I tried, but it was too uncomfortable,' she whispered. 'I don't like much on at night — it stops me sleeping. I just sort of turn up the fire at home. Last night was warmer and I was able to just wear a t-shirt and my knickers, but tonight is savage.' Then her teeth gave a chatter as if to prove a point.

'Don't worry, I'll warm you up,' he said, hugging her more tightly until she eventually stopped shivering.

He was just beginning to drift off when he found her face right in front of his again, and her eyes swallowed him up whole and he was sure his heart stopped beating for those few minutes.

'Thank you so much, Ben,' she said, and kissed him lightly on the cheek. 'What would I do without you?' And she rolled over, pulling his arms around her stomach, where he could make out the light bulge of the piercing's gemstone and the slight wetness of the blood trickling from the side of it. As he did his best to control certain parts of his anatomy, he couldn't help but think to himself, '*If only this night would never end.*'

In the morning they collapsed the tent and waited for Hellen's Dad to collect them from the 'pick-up' zone, sitting on their bags, holding hands.

'I'm going to do a PhD as well, Ben. I assume you are as well? We both scored the best in our year; it would be a waste not to.' It was a statement more than a question. She probably did have a list for life goals.

'You've got this all planned, haven't you?' he said, looking lovingly at her. God, he loved her so much it hurt sometimes, but she always had a life plan. Until now he had never thought of anything past his exams. 'I expect I'll do one as well if you are; maybe we could carry out research on the same project together,' he mused, getting lost in her eyes again.

'That would be excellent,' she said, mentally ticking a secret off on her list, and she changed her position to sitting on his knee, arms around his neck, complaining that the bags were hard. 'That's another four years together then,' she quipped. 'People will be thinking we're married by then!' And she giggled, posing in a silent movies-style swoon, whilst he was struck dumb with shock. If only he could ask her! Hellen suddenly hopped up as her father's car, a battered blue Volvo estate, pulled up and she ran over to it.

'Mum, you came as well,' she said excitedly, and hopped in as Ben put their bags in the boot.

'All right, Mr, Mrs Oswold,' he said politely as he got in next to Hellen.

'Ben, you're almost family we see so much of you, you really must call us Ann and Jim,' her mother said kindly.

'Yes,' said her father jokingly, 'I want to hear everything you've been up to with my daughter.' He knew his daughter well, and that she was very sensible, but felt it his duty to give Ben a few jibes, even though it be jokingly, as he felt sure that he was his Hellen's boyfriend. He liked the lad, and in a way, hoped that he might end up as his son-in-law.

'Erm, well…' Ben stuttered, not quite knowing what to say.

'Dad, stop!' Hellen said. 'Ben, don't you tell my nosy father anything — what goes on in the tent, stays in the tent. He doesn't need to know how we made hot passionate love throughout the night,' she giggled, putting a finger up to her plump lips and making a shush sound, leaving Ben turning red and stuttering further.

'But… Nothing…'

'Oh, she's teasing you both!' Ann cut in. 'Hellen, stop, you're embarrassing him. We know you've had a good time, and Ben here has behaved himself like a true gentleman, haven't you?' He nodded his head in agreement.

Hellen smiled and kissed her dad on the head, and then Ben on the lips. 'Sorry, Ben, I know you don't mind,' she said, and she lay out on the back seat with her head on his lap as he ran his fingers through her hair and proceeded to snooze for the rest of the journey home, whilst Jim talked to Ben about the rugby. For memories, this weekend had to be one of the best in Ben's life, and for someone that didn't like planning, he certainly had created a lot of plans for his and Hellen's potential future, deciding that after the exams, he would ask her out, even if he had to get drunk to work up the courage or write it down and give it to her.

It was around one in the morning that Ben's dreams shifted in their mood to a somewhat darker tone.

Tonight, his dream about Hellen was different. She was now lying naked on her bed, and the dark was gradually obscuring her from his view. He tried to walk towards her but was fixed to the spot. He could make out that deep cuts were being slashed into her body by an unseen force, and her mouth was open, seductively moving her

177

tongue over large and pointed teeth. The dark had now almost completely veiled her from view when she opened her eyes!

'Aggggh!' He woke with a start, covered in sweat. '*Fucking hell,*' he thought, '*where the hell did that come from?*' Then he remembered that he had been watching *Bad Blood*, and he relaxed a little, still uncomfortable about it featuring Hellen. He got up and washed his face in cold water and sat in the chair beside his bed. He read for a while, but couldn't focus on the words: his mind kept drifting back to Hellen's eyes in the dream. He always clearly remembered her eyes — large emerald-green orbs that had the ability to melt and arouse you at the same time, a doorway into a truly fantastic mind — but in his dream, they had burnt uncontrollably and red, their intensity filled with hate and desire.

Before work, Ben started cleaning his house up, as he had been a bit slack for over a week due to his workload and considered that if he could pluck up the courage, he might ask Hellen over for dinner. But he worried that it might offend her and give the wrong impression, but he only had one shot at rekindling their friendship, and if he could be really brave, ask her out, and try to take it further; but no, that was jumping the gun. He knew that he stood just as big a chance of avoiding her and running off. She certainly looked the same sexy girl that he had known at university. He had felt bad, but he'd frequently looked her up on the

Portsmouth University site, and in her profile picture she looked as damn beautiful as ever, if not more so. He knew that she liked things ordered and tidy and he was going to make sure that everything was perfect. The Hoover shook as his hand trembled; it did that kind of thing when he was anxious, it was the damage from that accident, and most of the time he could control it, but since awaiting Hellen, it had become far more frequent.

He continued his clean-up that evening once back from work. He had even spent an hour cleaning the car, inside and out, which was a hard job, given the amount of metalwork in it. Despite the fact that there was still another day to go until the interview, he had already laid out his clothes for the event and bought a new suit as well. He changed all the bedding in all three bedrooms in case she wanted to stay the night like he had spent most holidays over at her parents' during university, and he even cleaned the toilet, which was typically a monthly chore. By the time he got to bed he was exhausted and fell asleep fully dressed.

Hellen lay naked on her bed, half obscured by shadow. She was incredibly pale, and her red hair stood out as if it was on fire by comparison. She was writhing around as if being flayed, arching up and down as cut lines formed in long tracks across her skin. The previous ones were still visible, and these cut across them, opening up the old wounds as well. He was fighting to get to her, but his movement was so slow, taking all his effort to move the smallest distance. A fuzzy, roughly human shape drifted in front of him, and seemed to put a finger up to where its lips should be and went 'shushhhhh'. It then moved over her, pulling her head to one side with one shadow-like arm, and cupped her left breast with the other. Ben fought even harder to get to her, but the shadow was spreading, eclipsing her from his view, and all he could see was her eyes, not burning this time, but their usual piercing green, and they were filled with tears, and then the shadow completely obscured his view and she screamed, a terrified sound made in desperation and fear that cut to his very bones...

Ben awoke screaming. His shirt was soaked with sweat, and his hands were clenched into fists, his right hand shaking uncontrollably, so much so that he had to hold it with his left hand and rub really hard to loosen up the rock-tight muscles. He panted with the exertion, trying to re-oxygenate his lungs and shake off the terror his nightmare had caused. He was still shaking. 'Bloody hell,' he said aloud to the room — he had a tendency of talking to himself as he lived on his own. The images had been so realistic, so horrible. Could Hellen actually be in need of help? Although they had joked about it as teens, he had never taken their discussions of sharing each other's thoughts that seriously — that was sci-fi stuff — but still it made him very uncomfortable, and it took him a long time before he managed to get back to sleep. The look in her eyes, and that scream, he could just not shake it off.

The next morning, he almost phoned Hellen using her details from the application form, but decided that might be breaking the professional line as he was involved in her interview, so held back. That day seemed to take forever to pass, and his thoughts were solely focused on seeing Hellen tomorrow. He needed to know that she was all right, and he was getting an uncomfortable feeling in his stomach that she might need help. That or his brain had been turned to shit and his cock was now in control, but it hadn't been a dream of lust, had it? If it was, he needed therapy. He had never dreamt of her naked before, and felt ashamed about that, as she seemed helpless and directly asking him for help. He sighed. Maybe it was white knight syndrome; he knew she was a very capable woman, one of the reasons he loved her, but that scream, and those eyes?

He ate out at the pub again that night, as he didn't want to create a mess after all the time he had spent cleaning, and got some shopping at the local all-nighter so that he could cook her a dinner if she did accept his invitation. When he turned in for the night, he had trouble getting off to sleep, as he was anxious about seeing Hellen again, and worried he might have another nightmare. But eventually he drifted off to the sound of the neighbours having an argument that managed to come clearly through the wall despite being detached.

Hellen was crying, curled up on her bed and crying. The shadow was circling around her and once again he was rooted to the spot and unable to move. All he could do was watch, but the scene was far darker this time, as if time was running out. The mist descended on her despite his shouting, and enveloped her, moving all over her body, as if caressing it. She started struggling again, as if trying to free herself from unseen chains, arching up, only to be pushed back down by the shadowy presence. Deep cuts started to appear across her body now, cutting through her naked skin, muscle and right down to the bone, revealing glints of their whiteness amongst the blood that flowed out of the wounds. Again, the shadow roughly formed a human-like shape and ran a claw-filled hand up from her thighs, over her pubic hair, up her stomach and chest until it reached her head and pulled it to one side, and he could see the green of her tear-filled eyes begin to turn red and burn with a fire, and she seemed now to be arching towards the shape in pleasure, and it moved in, tearing at her thin and pale neck with its teeth...

Chapter 11
Death of a Friend, Flight

'For I will forgive their iniquity
and I will remember their sins no more'
Jeremiah 31:34
(King James version)

Since her visit to the church, Hellen had a night of undisturbed sleep and was now feeling a bit more positive, but this morning she had woken to find herself bumping into the locked bedroom door, trying to get through it whilst closed. Still better than previously, but it had started the day off badly. She had, with an effort, looked at the surveillance footage, and painfully watched as she had thrown the sheets off, arched in pleasure as she tore off her clothes and then suddenly sat up and walked slowly to the door, tried to open it and failed, and then just kept stepping into it, and it seemed to last for over an hour before the handle had caught her belly ring and the pain had woken her up. She turned the images off and braved a look in the mirror and noticed that her canine teeth seemed to be getting larger, and her reflection was more blurred, and when she went out, she had to cover up more as her skin was becoming really sensitive to the light. She was also craving blood.

After returning from the church, she had eaten dinner, but the food had no taste, and her stomach had continually growled at her. Much to her disgust, she had gone out, bought a beef steak and drunk the loose blood that was contained in its wrapper, which seemed to taper the desire for a bit, but made her feel really sick and revolted with herself — but it was better than the dog incident. After drinking it and realising what she had done in a partial haze, she had dashed to the bathroom and forced herself to vomit again; she was not going to go down the blood-drinking route — her own was one thing, but not anything else. Tomorrow was her interview and she had booked a train and a hotel in advance, along with an overnight bag containing the flask of holy water, garlic cloves and a few spare crosses purchased at a market stall. She didn't like the idea of staying out given her current problems, but Father Thomas hadn't contacted her yet, and she needed work in case she managed to sort this out; and besides, how much worse could it bloody well get? When death was the endgame, why fucking worry?

She looked out the window after making a coffee and noticed that there was a crowd gathering outside the block next door, and an ambulance was pulling up, followed by two police cars, all of which were bustling around and taping an area off. She slid a coat on and quickly made her way downstairs, sliding her way through the crowd to see what was happening.

Oh my God, it was Jasmine's flat they were in, and they were wheeling a trolley out with a blanket over it. She frantically caught one of the police officers at the scene, WPC Sally Carter, a pretty girl with a large bruise on her cheek, and she confirmed that it was indeed her — a heart attack, they reckoned.

'May I see her?' Hellen asked. 'We were good friends. I can't believe it's her.'

'All right, but she has been dead for a few days' said Sally, leading her over to the ambulance and drawing back the sheet. Jasmine laid there with a calm expression on her face, but she was almost completely white, which looked grotesque. All the blood had gone from her face, but Hellen felt that she needed to check; no, not just check, she had to know. She turned her head to the side and checked the neck for marks, but there were none. She breathed a sigh of relief and turned it to the other side, and there they were, two angry red marks. She ran from the body — it didn't matter where, she just couldn't bear being anywhere near it.

'*Goddamn you, why her?*' she thought as she ran. After an hour, she found herself standing outside the church again, but the hairs on her neck were standing up again, and she had the feeling that she was being watched. She spun around, looking into every corner, then…

'*Hello, Hellen.*'

My God, it was him. She could hear the blood rushing through her ears.

'*Why don't you come to me, my lady? We belong together. I'll forgive your attempts to poison me. Come...*'

'Fuck you! I hope it burnt fucking badly!' she spat at Adam. 'You don't own me, nobody fucking owns me!'

'*Oh, but, Hellen, are you that naïve child? I do own you. I claimed you back in London; you were not just sustenance, you were for me. Now come.*'

She started forcing herself to back away, step by step, ascending the stairs towards the church. At the last moment, she turned to face the door, but he was standing there, and he pulled her towards him. One hand around her neck, and the other lifting her leg up, and she began to tremble and ache deep within herself.

'No!' she screamed at him, trying to push him away, when suddenly the door opened, surprising him, and Father Thomas appeared. He was wielding a large gold cross which he brought down on the centre of the vampire's face. The scream was terrible and he threw Hellen to one side, her head smashing into the stone wall, where she crumpled onto the floor. Flashing lights danced in front of her eyes as she saw Father Thomas continue his attack by chucking a jug of holy water after the retreating Adam, who then turned into a dark blur and vanished, just as she lost consciousness.

Hellen awoke with Father Thomas leaning over her, attending to a large cut on her scalp. She reached up and her hand felt the sticky blood running down her temple. She tried not to, but her hand just seemed to move towards her mouth, but he gently reached forward and restrained the hand, wiping the blood from it quickly, before bandaging her head.

'Don't forget, my child, that you have been ingesting garlic. I don't know how that would affect you; it is already in your body, but I don't know the effect it would have on you if you ingested the blood as food.' The flare in her eyes reduced.

'At the moment, not that much, Father,' she said, sitting up. 'It is like a mild allergy and for now just creates a tingling sensation. I've drunk it a few times and I haven't had a major reaction. Thank you, but you have put yourself in massive danger. He has killed my friend. Drank her dry. He will come after you I fear.'

'I am eighty years old, my dear, and not very well. I do not have long left. If I can protect you with my life, so be it; you have years left ahead of you, it is my pleasure to help.'

She noticed that he was still panting from the confrontation. 'Father, have you had any luck with getting help?'

'I am awaiting their answer, but this meeting will force the issue in our favour now that I have seen it. They will act, but they will take their time, meaning we must hold out for now.'

'I am going to Nottingham tonight for an interview in the morning. What if he follows me?'

'He will not follow. His place of rest will be around here, and he can't leave it for long, so you should be safe. It might be for the best. I will stay in the church; I feel his attention will be on me sooner rather than later. Get off while he's returned to his coffin. Go now — it will be safer. I will do what I can whilst you are away.'

She thanked him and headed off, quickly returning home to collect her bag and driving straight to Petersfield Station, terrified of being followed.

It seemed a very long journey to Nottingham, as she was continually looking over her shoulder and at every shadow, but as she got further from Portsmouth, she seemed to feel better, and began to relax more. She even allowed herself to have a coffee and a flapjack from the hostess trolley. It was bland, but rail food was, and therefore wasn't an indicator of her condition. She got a taxi to the hotel and locked the door as soon as she was inside, curling into a ball on the bed to await morning. Her thoughts kept drifting to the interview, and in particular Ben. What would she say to him? What could she say to him? She had not contacted him for years, and in effect had cut off their friendship, and she felt her stomach turn at the thought. Hellen wished that she had kept in touch, and now more than ever she missed him so much it hurt, and she kept running through ways to apologise, but couldn't come up with anything that sounded right. She really would have to improvise when she met him, but she hated doing that as she liked to plan things. She decided at that point she would not lose her opportunity this time; she loved him and felt sure of it, and at the very least she would have to open her heart to him, even though the very thought of exposing her feelings terrified her. Science had defined answers, and typically things behaved as expected — people didn't, they were complicated. Maybe he hadn't made a move on her because she was guessing his feelings wrongly, or he liked her but not in that way? Shit, why was life so difficult? But no, she must take the chance. She felt deep in her heart that he would not pluck up the courage to ask her, and she had to know. She felt the ache grow in her heart, and the intense loneliness she felt.

That night, Hellen remained fully dressed and surrounded herself with a ring of salt and garlic bulbs, clutching one of her crosses as she drifted off to sleep.

Chapter 12
Interview, Old Friends, Passion

'Owe no man any thing, but to love one another:
for he that loveth another hath fulfilled the law.'
Romans 13:8
(King James version)

Hellen awoke suddenly, looking around quickly to see where she was, and breathed a sigh of relief to find that she was still in her hotel bed in the early hours of the morning. '*Phew,*' she thought, '*the relief of small mercies.*' Sleeping away from home had seemed to refresh her no end, and she took her time getting ready for her interview, wearing her new leather skirt, white blouse with a fancy lace decoration around the neck and a smart black velvet jacket, finished off with black high-heels and a thigh-length black wool coat. She enjoyed the breakfast buffet and had a coffee to fully wake her up, and realised that she could taste it. Being away from Portsmouth, from him, did make a difference.

She arrived for the meeting early, probably for the first time in her life, and was able to calm her nerves by running through her presentation; and by the time they called her in, she actually felt prepared. The interview panel were really positive, and genuinely seemed to be aware of her research and valued her opinions, which did digress from the accepted norms on occasions, and had caused her problems with traditional thinkers in the past. To her disappointment, Ben was not there, and she felt an emptiness in her chest. She had felt sure that he would be on the panel, but she was offered the post at the end, and she accepted it quickly, starting after Easter, if she was still alive then, she thought.

After the pleasantries, and a lunch in the University canteen, she started to make her way off campus, when she bumped into someone whilst searching through her bag and not looking where she was going.

'Sorry,' she said, and bent down to help pick up the papers that the man had dropped; and then, as she looked up, she realised that she knew his face — older and a few more lines, but it was him, it was Ben, and he looked good, and she felt needles piercing her heart.

'Hi,' he said hesitantly as he desperately fought to keep his bad hand from shaking, which it had a habit of doing when he was stressed. But to his surprise, Hellen grabbed him in a massive bear hug, linking her arms around his neck, and hopping up, she locked her legs around his hips so she could reach up to him and kiss him full on the lips, making him turn the colour of her hair. Of everything that had run through his mind on how this moment could play out, he had not expected that.

'Ben, I was just coming to look for you. Where were you? I expected to see you on the panel as you replied to me; it said you were managing staffing.' She dropped down off him and straightened her dress out, back to a more decent level from where it had rucked up, surprised that her legs were shaking.

'I know, but I didn't want to throw you, and it seemed, I don't know, inappropriate as we sort of have a history, and I hadn't seen you for so long! I just... Well, I wasn't sure that... well... If you...'

'I'm so sorry, Ben. I lost your phone number when my mobile was stolen, and time just moved on,' she blurted out, talking way too fast, and realising that it sounded a poor excuse. 'I focused on my work and that seemed to become the only thing that I saw. I never had time. I wish I had made more of an effort; I could have found you but, I don't know. I was in a bad place, and just needed space, I suppose. You didn't worry, did you? Oh, I'm so sorry,' she said, seeing the pain in his face. He had never been able to hide his emotions very well: it was one of the things that she found so endearing about him, and he had averted his eyes to hide the forming tears. 'Surely you didn't think it was in any way your fault?'

Ben reached forward and pulled Hellen closer to him, crying, 'I thought you didn't want to speak to me.' His voice was beginning to crack up. 'I thought... I... don't know what I thought. I suppose I tried not to.' He sobbed, in turn making her cry. They separated still holding hands, and looked each other over, their gaze lasting for what seemed like hours, taking in the most minute details. Both were much the same, except older, although Ben noticed the weariness and hidden pain in Hellen's eyes, like in the last dream he had seen her in that night, and she was so painfully thin. 'Why don't we catch up? We could go to a nice little Italian place I know, or I don't want to be presumptuous, but you could come to my house and I'll cook.'

She smiled, and thought to herself, '*I've got a second chance, he still loves me. I have been alone all this time, and he's always been there waiting, you damn fool, Hellen! Why didn't you find him earlier?*' She took a deep breath and whispered, 'Yes, let's go to yours. I always loved your cooking.' So, they headed to his car and without thinking about it, they had found each other's hands again and interlocked their fingers.

'My God, really!' she said on seeing his car. 'That is retro!' A playful smile lifted the corner of her mouth. 'Midlife crisis retro. It must cost a fortune to run.'

'You don't know the half of it,' he said with the bright smile that had endeared her to talk to him all those years ago in Lecture Theatre A, and they got into the car. He went to start the engine, but she stopped him.

'Ben, I owe you a real explanation about why I didn't contact you. I feel so bad and now it seems silly that I didn't, but at the time I shrank into myself when I should have looked for support. I haven't told this to anyone, but I need to.'

'You're worrying me a bit, Hellen. You don't owe me anything.'

'No, I need to tell someone, it's been buried in me for too long. Shortly after you went to Dundee, I decided to try and reconnect with my faith, and I met what seemed to be a decent bloke there, at the church, I mean, and we started going out, but he was very pushy when it came to… well… you know, demanding things that I wasn't ready for, and he didn't like it; it seemed all he wanted was, well… and it accumulated and came to a head when it was late after a movie and he had just walked me back to mine, but he changed, and sort of pushed his way in and started to get really aggressive, and I couldn't understand why, it was so sudden, but he wasn't listening. He kept calling me a whore and a slut, and I was frightened. He kept hitting me… hard, I mean really hard. He split my lip and knocked one of my lower teeth out, so I had to have an implant. I, well… I managed to push him off me after he had torn my blouse and I didn't think, I just kicked him straight in the balls,' and she stopped for a moment, licking her dry lips.

'Good for you; that bastard deserved it.'

'Yeah, he did, but I don't know, he went down all right, but didn't get up; I thought that he would just give up and go away, but he just kept screaming. It was horrible. His jeans turned red, Ben. I wanted to get rid of him, but… It turned out I had managed to split him open and literally rip his balls open. The police were very understanding, and he was arrested for ABH, but… I suppose I retreated into myself. I jumped at everything for a while, especially if they were male. So, I just

194

focused on my work, and relinquished my faith completely… I mean, he was meant to be a religious man, but… how could he do that? I… It wasn't what he said. We had only been going out for a couple of weeks; it's not even as if we had slept together or something, we had barely even kissed. I'm sorry, Ben… I… well…' She looked pleadingly at him, her eyes desperate for him to say something.

'Hellen, you can't blame yourself, it's not your fault. The world is full of maniacs, and I guess if you're female you'll meet more of them, but… please don't feel bad about not contacting me; I just wish I could have been there to talk to you. If I hadn't been so damn shy. I… should have come back to see you… I felt something was wrong… But I was… I suppose I still am too afraid of rejection.' He hung his head and they both looked away from each other, but their fingers re-locked together and they looked back, probing each other's eyes. 'I'm pleased you told me,' he said, and they both remained quiet for the rest of the journey.

Ben led Hellen into his house and took her coat, involuntarily gasping when he saw the blood lines on her blouse. She followed his eyes and blushed, looking away ashamed, as he bustled to hang up her coat. '*Shit, they have re-opened,*' she thought, and without realising, she nervously attempted to smooth out her blouse, which started her nipple bleeding again, leaving another red stain. '*He's lost weight since I saw him last,*' she thought as they sat down, '*he's so fit now.*' Hellen noticed his hand shaking again and slipping back into old habits from over twenty years ago, took it in hers, gently stroking the fingers, rubbing each joint in turn. 'Your hand never fixed up, did it?' she said in a low voice filled with concern.

'No, the nerves were permanently damaged. It never will, but I get by; it's worse some days than others, but you always knew how to ease the pain.' She smiled, and kicked off her heels, kissing his fingers. He looked embarrassed, but knew he had to ask, and said, 'Hellen, I don't want to offend you. I've never had any doubts that you could look after yourself, but what's with the cuts? Are you OK now? No one's still hurting you, are they? I'm not as strong as I used to be, but I'll sort out anyone if they are hurting you. It breaks my heart to think about it. Not again.'

'No, Ben, it's not like that. It's a long story, complicated, but…' She leant forward and took his other hand in hers. 'I have to ask this first. It's been so long and we both deserve the truth and I need to know' — she felt like she was going to faint as all her blood seemed to rush to her cheeks — 'you used to love me, didn't you, Ben? Don't answer that, I know you did, but do you still love me?' This was it, she thought, the moment of truth, but she needed to know, and her heart was aching, throbbing loudly in her chest.

Ben was startled by her bluntness, and he started stuttering, 'I'm sorry… I didn't… Was it really that obvious? I'm sorry to make you uncomfortable. I didn't realise it was that obvious. I've always tried to hide…'

She interrupted him. 'I felt that you did. You shouldn't have to hide it. You were always there for me and I missed the signs and I let you slip through my hands like a bloody fool, and we have lost so many years that we might have had together. I was unfair to you and myself, because… I love you. I just never saw what was right in front of my face.' A tear ran down her cheek and they gazed at each other for a minute before hugging, and Ben felt more relaxed, the pain of rejection gone; he felt better, he felt free.

'I am in trouble, Ben,' she said quietly, kissing him. It felt good to be so near to someone, to feel their heat, their chest rise and fall as they breathed. 'It's difficult to explain… I, well, that is to say… I've been having these dreams… And they… Well, look.' She stood up, hesitated for a moment, and then slowly undid the buttons and let her blouse slide off onto the floor. She had undressed many times in front of him and never worried about it, but this time was somehow different. Now she knew he loved her, she felt like a teenager again, and trembled nervously with anticipation. As the blouse fell to the floor it revealed the network of cuts and welts that ran across her body and arms, along with her visible bones showing on her overly thin body. Ben welled up and cried to see her hurt, all the wounds. It was unbearable, and so like his dreams. 'I… had problems in London, and well… it got worse from there on.' She took a deep breath and outlined the events to him while he sat open-mouthed in shock from her story, and also from the freckles that were speckled across her cleavage and the way that they seemed to hide seductively behind the lace of her black bra.

'I know it's unbelievable,' she pleaded, her eyes begging him to believe her. 'I've thought that I was going mad... maybe I am. I'm a scientist and this should be insane, but I have no other explanation.'

'Well, I don't know what to say,' he said, closing his mouth and taking a breath, forcing his gaze away from her breasts and back to her sparkling eyes.

Hellen looked crestfallen: he wasn't going to believe her. Pain filled her now intensely gleaming green eyes, and she quickly in a last-ditch attempt for validation took out her rosary. 'Look... Look... I can show you, watch this!' she said, and laid it in her open palm, and to Ben's horror there was the faint smell of burning flesh as Hellen winced. She then offered her hand to him, opening her fingers to reveal the burn mark that the cross had left on her palm.

'Oh, Hellen,' he said, hugging her again. 'Stop... stop... I believe you.' He started tracing the shape of the burn on her hand and kissed it. 'Don't hurt yourself further. I believed you before you did that. I have never seen you lie — I'm just getting my head around it, that's all. It's a lot to take in. I love you, Hellen, and always have.' It felt good to finally admit it. 'I never stopped loving you for all these years; it's burnt an indelible mark into my heart. Of course I'll help you, look after you, whatever you need from me.' Their eyes met again and they were suddenly kissing passionately, falling back onto the sofa and its soft cushions. She pulled off his tie and accidentally ripped his shirt buttons off in her rush to be near to his warm body and press herself against his bare chest, she could hear his heartbeat and it aroused her. He fumbled with her bra clasp, fighting a battle to undo it. They both laughed, kissed and she managed to unfasten it, and he cupped her small, pert breasts in his hands, playfully teasing her nipples with his thumbs, taking care of the one that was torn and freshly bleeding, as she arched into him. He delicately kissed her all the way from her now erect nipples to her skirt's waistband, and slid it down, along with her tights and panties, and she stroked his hairy chest. He looked back up to her face and kissed her lips again and started kissing her neck. Hellen gasped in pleasure, and caressing his manhood into life, she looked down at his neck, kissing it in return. The veins showed prominently, pulsating with blood and passion. That hot warm blood, flowing with such life and warmth. Her eyes began to glow, and she tried to pull her gaze away. '*Oh God, not now, not now!*' But a familiar tingling ran through her, stimulating every nerve in her body, and as he went down again towards her moist yawning sex, she leant forward, her mouth opened and her teeth gleamed as her lips pulled back, uncovering their new true size. She leant in closer and closer towards him… the smell of blood and sweat was intoxicating. She could hear the rush of his life blood... each fresh pulse as it was sent from his heart.

Ben had reached Hellen's midriff again, tracing the contours of her muscles with his tongue, when there was a sudden scream of 'No...' from above him. He looked up and Hellen threw herself away from him, pushing him in the other direction with such amazing strength and force that he flew six feet before crashing into the side table, and she crawled into the corner of the room, curling up into a ball, repeating 'No... no...' whilst sobbing. He rapidly drew breath and quickly ran to her.

'I'm so sorry, I didn't mean to do anything wrong. What did I do? I...'

Her eyes were burning red and were filled with terror, and tears dropped onto her knees, where they were pulled up to her chest. She looked up at him with red, tear-filled eyes that were beginning to dim from the previous burning glow, the eyes from his dreams.

'It's not you... You've done nothing wrong, Ben. It was me, I lost control, I could have hurt you... I nearly... I nearly bit you. I... I shouldn't have dragged you into this. I love you too much, and knowing that I could kill you, I... I should go.'

Ben took her in his arms and cradled her small frame close to him.

'Hellen, if it meant being with you I would do it gratefully. I have always loved you, and I will help you. I've had dreams about you the last few nights, Hellen.'

She couldn't help but smile. 'Oh, did you now, you dirty boy.' And she ran her hand down the side of his face.

'No, not like that… It must have been more of a premonition, because I saw the cuts… I saw you cutting yourself, and a dark shape slowly obscuring you from my vision, taking you away from me… That's not going to happen, Hellen. Now I've found you again I'm not going to lose you to anyone, least of all a guy with no pulse.'

She laughed. He was so cute when he tried to be tough, and she shifted around so that she was straddled across him. She smiled a fiendishly naughty smile, and reached into her bag, producing a large cross and hanging it around his neck. 'If you're willing to chance it,' she said seductively, whilst stroking his neck. 'It's not much, but it should work; my willpower is stronger away from Portsmouth, and I can control it more if I'm aware its coming, and I need you. And…' She caught a whiff of her breath which burnt her nose. 'And if you can stand my breath…' — he coughed and her eyes motioned upstairs — 'we could see how it goes. I'll try not to bite!' And with that, Ben picked her up and carried her upstairs.

Ben gently pushed her onto the bed, taking a moment to admire her slender body again, taking in every detail, her long ginger hair curling delicately across her firm breasts, the smooth swell of her stomach, the fiery hair covering her pubic mound down to the soft pink lips below, which now slowly opened and closed with anticipation. Despite the network of cuts across her body, she was more beautiful than he could ever have dreamt, and he climbed slowly up the bed, kissing her as he went, trying to value every single one of her delicate freckles until he reached her pouting lips, and probed deeper with his tongue, tracing her teeth, feeling the shape of her enlarged canines and then deeper. Her hands caressed his back, leaving faint nail marks across it, as she forced back her vampiritic desire to let his blood flow from the bulging veins in his neck, tracing the cross she had given him to drive the thoughts further back in her mind, feeling the light burns the chain's links caused on her fingers. She could and would control her unnatural vampiric desires. He again took one of her breasts in each hand, teasing the nipples erect with his mouth as her moaning aroused him to full size. Hellen loved the sensation that his slightly trembling hand sent through her as he stroked her inner thigh; the simple human desire of touch filled her heart with hope, dispelling her fears of the future. She had the now, she had this moment, and she was in control now for the first time in days; this was her own decision, and she wanted it so badly. She rolled him over and went down on him, her firm lips sending spikes of pleasure searing through him, burning like nothing he had experienced before, her teeth delicately nibbling the tip of his manhood, until he pulled her up for another kiss on the lips. Ben leant back, cupping her face, and she spread her legs wide in invitation, her vagina opening like a summer flower, exposing its centre, which pulsated rhythmically, gaping open and demanding more from him. His fingers sought out her strip of red pubic hairs and he slid his first two fingers gently inside her, making her gasp in pleasure, arching her back and grabbing him tighter, moving her hand down to make him explore deeper inside her, whilst rubbing her clitoris with the other. His cock began to jerk up and down with anticipation, waiting for its chance in the warmth and moisture that it craved, and when her nipples brushed against his chest, it made him think that he would explode immediately. He quickly withdrew his fingers and tightened his grip on her ass as she guided him inside her, wrapping her legs around his waist tightly to help maximise the hardness and depth of his thrusts. It was as if she was trying to pull him so close that they became one, arching and rolling in unison, both sweating with desire, with no thought of anything other than each other. The warmth of ecstasy rushed through them, and she shuddered in an uncontrollable orgasm just as he came, and they both moaned, before collapsing in a tangle of limbs, fingers locked, and embroiled in a kiss that they both hoped would never end.

Hellen woke at seven, just as the sun peeked through the curtains and stung her exposed skin. A painful reminder of reality. She rolled over and put her arms and legs around Ben, pulling him close to her just to make sure that he was still there and she wasn't just dreaming, clinging on to the few fragile moments of the dream before reality fully caught up with her again, and she had to face her problems. He kissed her gently and traced his fingers over the tattoo on her neck.

'Where do we go from here?' he asked, hugging her, squeezing as if to prevent her from running away.

'Staying alive would be a good start,' she joked.

'I'm serious, Hellen. I have no intention of losing you this time.' He sat up and looked at her as if she might suddenly disappear in a puff of smoke. 'Tell me everything again, all the details; we need to plan our next move, outsmart him, do something.'

'I think he knows what I'm thinking, Ben, or at least it feels that way. I don't know where to go from here. I doubt tropical diseases will be of any use. I see them soon, and Father Thomas is speaking to his superiors, but I put him in massive danger, Ben. Adam knows of him, and he's vengeful. I have to get back to check on him…'

'Well, I could act independently from you, I suppose, but I don't want to leave you.' He playfully squeezed her. 'Tell me everything, so I have a full and clear background of events. We must be able to do something. I'll take time off work, I'll come back with you right now, I'll…'

She looked up at him with her big green eyes and he melted, but knew he wasn't going to like what she said.

'I must return to check on Father Thomas, I must, and then go to London to see this so-called specialist. You could meet me in London for that. I'd really like you to.' Her eyes pleaded for him to say yes.

'Of course, that's my research day at home, I'll skive it and come down, then it's the weekend and I could... you know, stay with you.'

Hellen beamed a scheming grin; she was plotting, he could see that clearly, he'd seen it before. 'I might have something else for you to do for me, something special. Meet me for the appointment and I'll fill you in then. But promise me that you won't take that cross off, it's really important — and take these.' She handed him a tub of garlic pills. 'These will help, but when he commands, it's very hard to resist... Or maybe not for you as you haven't been bitten.' A distant look came across her and he kissed her on the cheek.

'I will, I promise.'

'I have a while until my train,' she giggled, stroking his leg with her foot. 'We could always... you know, take advantage of it,' and she disappeared under the sheets.

Ben just managed to get Hellen on the train in time, although no matter how hard they looked her earring remained missing in action — he would have to search the living room floor more carefully later. They just had time to kiss, before the train pulled out, and he felt the tug on his heart as she gradually got further away. He went home and packed a travel bag. There was no way that he was going to leave her on her own with that thing; for some reason he did not doubt her, maybe it was his love for her, maybe the dreams he had experienced which now made far more sense, but he couldn't just sit and do nothing, so he went out to his shed and started shaping some crude wooden stakes, which he wrapped in a cloth and placed in his sports bag along with a hefty hammer. He took the garlic pills, stopped at the nearby church to pick up some holy water. There never seemed to be anyone there, and today was no different. He just walked in, filled up an old Pepsi bottle, and walked out. He then gritted his teeth and paid for a full tank of petrol — 'Ouch!' — and headed off down the M1 towards London. He had a few things to do before meeting up with Hellen, and at that thought he gunned the gas pedal and was gone with a smoky cloud and a whiff of incomplete combustion as the Firebird shot down the road.

Chapter 13
Where is She? The Call, Intervention

'For if they fall, the one will
Will lift up his fellow:
But woe to him that is alone
When he falleth: for he hath not
Another to help him up'
Ecclesiastes 4:10
(King James version)

Sophie was beginning to get worried about Hellen. For a short time after they had parted following that strange night, she had kept regular contact as promised, ringing her every other day, but now nothing, and it had been almost a week without a call. She waited, fidgeting with the fabric of her leggings, whilst she tried Hellen's number for the sixth time that morning. As before, no answer. Something was wrong; it was early, but she should have been at home. It was a typical approach for her friend to withdraw into herself when serious problems arose, and she would sometimes not talk to anyone for days. It had happened before, years ago, and Sophie had never found out why, and had to assume that she would talk when she was ready; but on that occasion she never had, and it even went as far as her leaving the church she had been so fond of when they were both little. She had loved Father Thomas's sermons, and he had really been a family friend due to his long friendship with her parents.

Sophie had never really enjoyed the church herself and found it too preachy. As soon as she had reached sixteen, and after a series of furious arguments with her mother, she chose not to attend church. The situation had finally reached a head when Sophie had been having her eighteenth birthday party, which had got off to such a good start. Her parents had bought her a lovely pale blue dress for the event, which, given its short length, amazed her as her parents were very Churchy. She had received a call from the judo association confirming her place on the national under-twenty-one team, and best of all, her parents had gone out for a while as the music was giving them a headache, and she could relax more. Hellen, who was already twenty-one, seemed to be enjoying arranging the music playlist and deciding on what to play next — that girl definitely liked her lists — which gave Sophie time to sneak off with Dave, an eighteen-year-old college drop-out who had spent the last half an hour giving her the eye, and catching a feel under the table, which she found quite to her satisfaction, and prompted her to slip her panties off and hand them to him, before winking and dashing off towards the garage, and he had quickly followed.

'In here,' Sophie said, and pushed him into the back seat of her father's BMW, with its plush cream leather seats. Sophie had roughly kissed Dave, before unzipping his jeans. She was fairly sure she would never keep in contact with him after this, it was just sex, but she needed it now, and she was never afraid to take what she wanted. She straddled him quickly, allowing him to enter her, and started to hop up and down on him vigorously.

'Sophie?' a voice called her.

'*Damn, not now!*' she thought, quickening her pace. '*Maybe she won't notice.*'

'Sophie!' it called again, and a face appeared at the steamed-up back window. 'What the hell are you doing?'

Shit, it was her mother. '*Well, I can't stop now,*' she thought as her muscles began to shudder and she quickened her rhythm.

'Sophie, you stop that right now, you sinful child. I'm getting your father!'

'Fuck off, Mum!' she screamed as she came with a shudder. Somewhere behind her there was a crash in the background as a door slammed shut, but she was past noticing at that moment.

'Right, Dave, you'd better head off before Mum tells Dad,' Sophie said, climbing off him. 'Dad can get in a bad temper once Mum's worked him up.' Dave didn't need asking twice and shot out of the garage like grease lightning, not even remembering to zip up his flies. She sighed and headed indoors to face the inevitable argument that awaited. The music had been turned off and her friends were looking worried, getting the impression that there was going to be fireworks, as most of them had experienced both Sophie and her mum's arguments before, and they had stopped being amusing to watch and become an uncomfortable and sometimes violent affair. As she entered the room, she saw everyone's eyes on her, and it annoyed her; no, more than that, it made her angry.

'What?' Sophie demanded loudly, her cheeks still flushed from her encounter with Dave, and annoyance at being caught. 'What's fucking wrong this time?'

'Your behaviour is terrible, young lady,' her mother practically screamed at her, whilst her dad's face had turned red, and looked a mixture of terrible embarrassment and red-mist anger. More than once she had been at the receiving end of his belt when she was younger, but it was usually her mother who disciplined her, and she was far less controlled when it came to a physical beating. Her dad's punishment was usually symbolic and there to appease his wife, and he had never struck her hard, if at all — it was just a show to prevent a harder beating from her mum, who was very Old Testament, and had come from a large family, where their father had regularly beaten them hard with a belt. Her dad was not good at words, but she knew that he loved her, and was touched by his poorly articulated but incredibly heartfelt apologies after the punishment when her mother had left the room. They often brought her to tears.

'What have I done wrong?' she asked, deliberately making the situation worse, shrugging her shoulders defiantly.

'I don't think now's the right time, Soph,' Hellen whispered to her friend quickly.

Unfortunately, the advice was that bit too late, and Sophie was caught with a hard slap around the face from her mother, and as she was unprepared, she staggered backwards and would have fallen over if it hadn't been for Hellen stopping her.

'You wicked child, having... sex in your father's car. How could you? You gave in to the Devil and must repent, ask the Lord for forgiveness.'

Sophie felt the trickle of blood run down her lip and the sting from the blow, and tears started forming in her eyes and she turned red with anger, her fists gripped tightly together, which Hellen knew could mean trouble.

'Wicked, mum, really? Since when was fucking someone ever wicked? It's an expression of love' The level of her voice was trembling but shouting nonetheless. Her party guests quickly took the chance to drift off and Hellen shrank into the background, for this was going to explode, and she had never liked head-on confrontation if it could be avoided. She had never had these sorts of problems with her parents.

'It is a sin, girl, lust is what it is, filthy dirty lust! Sex before marriage is a sin as well, or had you forgotten? You have spoiled yourself, given away your virtue.' Her mother was now screaming at her, spit shooting from her mouth, and she was clutching her leather-bound bible in shaking hands as if it was a shield to protect her from her evil daughter; in her eyes all she could see was Sophie in the car embroiled in sin.

'Mother, this is not my first fucking time. I lost my virginity when I was fourteen. Mum. But you know what, OK, have your way. It's filthy fucking dirty lust, and the best thing is that I loved it. I fucked him witless and I enjoyed having him inside me. I fucked him as hard as I could and I fucking loved it. I'm fed up with your religious bullshit, Mum. Yes, that's right it's bullshit, the whole fucking lot of it. I believe in God, but I do not believe that he would have made sex so enjoyable if he meant it to be wrong.'

'Blasphemy!' her mother screamed. 'Blasphemy! Renounce the devil, girl, renounce him.' At this point, her mum looked like she was about to have a stroke, and began to tremble. She then smacked her daughter again, this time accidentally catching her with her engagement ring, leaving an angry and bloody cut across her cheek, just missing her eye. It was one that never did fully fade with time and remained a constant reminder of that fateful birthday party that she could never forget. She went to strike her daughter again and this time Sophie caught her by the wrist, stopping the blow from connecting, and held it there. She would never have hit her parents, but knew that she could defend herself, and just pushed her mother away. She staggered back and raised her hands, expecting a blow, but instead Sophie grabbed her crotch.

'You might as well know I fucking got this pierced as well bitch and it feels so fucking amazing, see what your God says to that' she shouted, giving her parents the fingers up, and then she ran off crying, quickly followed by Hellen, leaving her mum and dad screaming after her.

Sophie did not return home for a week and spent her time at her Aunt Kim's. She was an old ex-hippy and had no real problems with her behaviour and just wanted to keep her safe. She did her best to encourage Sophie to return home and make peace with her mother. This she had done reluctantly, after her father had come to see her at Kim's, and for the first time in her life she had seen him cry. He had sat in Aunt Kim's large flowery armchair and cried. She hadn't really known what to do, as it had never happened before, and he begged, yes, begged her to come home as he didn't want to lose his little girl, and she gave way and returned home the next day. Her parents were both very apologetic, and never hit her again, but her mum still wished her to confess to Father Thomas and kept asking her to purify her soul and confess, which was the point when she refused to go back to church ever, but they didn't push the issue and let her leave. The rift was deep and her mother never really recovered from her daughter not going to church, but had accepted it and they had both continually tried to make it up to her, hence the car given to her on her nineteenth.

As soon as she reached twenty, she had taken a job as an assistant in the local library, which she found that she really liked, and moved into her own place. She sighed. She didn't blame her parents, they were from an older generation, and she knew she could be a difficult teen, a real bitch sometimes, but she was not going to be hit; she was used to blows in her martial arts, but she knew that it was wrong. It had taken years for her to speak directly to her mother about their fight and had been amazed to realise that her mum had carried a massive guilt about hitting her daughter on that day, and still repeatedly confessed about causing the scar on her face even now. It was then that Sophie had truly forgiven her, and they had both been able to really talk again, although she was more discrete with her relationships and would never bring any boys to see her parents, not that she really had any long-term boyfriends. The only thing that would never leave her was the look of disappointment on her father's face when she had argued with them. No father liked to think of their daughter as having sex, no boy would ever be good enough, and there she was telling him that a strange man had given her intimate piercings. She felt bad about that, and it had been wrong of her, and she would never forget his face. Despite leaving the church herself, she had always respected Hellen's dedication and had always been confused and felt it was strange that she had left in the first place.

Sophie sighed, and put her phone down, unknowingly stroking the faint scar line under her eye, a nervous trait she had developed since the incident. This was getting silly; maybe she had hurt herself? She had, after all, found Hellen naked in the woods, which was odd for anyone, particularly at that time of year, let alone for her; she had always been so prim and proper, and really ignored anything that wasn't involved in her work. She was similar to Hellen in some ways, like her determination to succeed and focus, but when it came to relationships, they were a mile apart. Hellen always had a lot of male attention, and could flirt like a pro, but the thing was that she didn't know that she was doing it; there was a certain naiveness to her, and she worried about her, fearing that she would get hurt. Sophie was far more confident around men and was good at manipulating them to get what she wanted, although a long-term relationship had as yet evaded her. She got up from the sofa and changed for work.

She liked her job in the University library and had been sad when Hellen had left to care for her ailing mother. They had always met up every lunchtime and had dinner together and talked about their dreams and plans. It had been a depressing time for Hellen looking after her mother, but at least it had been expected, and in a way, Sophie felt that she had had time to prepare and say goodbye. But her father's death had been worse, and Sophie had at the time feared her friend would drown in her grief and commit suicide, although she had hoped that her religion might taper those thoughts, given that it was viewed as a sin, and therefore you couldn't get into Heaven. But her father's death had been so sudden and unexpected, a massive freak accident, really. He had been nearing retirement at the time and had worked at the dockyards in Portsmouth since he was a teen, but on that fateful day he had been assisting with the unloading of containers from a ship as usual, and the chains had broken, letting one of the large crates fall, and it crushed him. She shivered; it was horrible, and Hellen had always been a Daddy's girl, and she actually collapsed when the police had broken the news to her and her mother. It had taken months to get Hellen to talk about it, and open up to her, but it did give a real cause for concern now.

Sophie quickly brushed her short dark hair, spending time with a can of hairspray to ensure its spikes stayed in place. She quickly checked her appearance in the mirror, smoothing down the creases in her clothes, proudly running her hands over her athletic physique. She was still pleased with her muscle structure and trained at the gym almost every day. Tonight, she would focus on her legs, as her knees were starting to feel stiff, especially the one that had been injured, and she needed the structures around it to remain strong. The injury had been quite impressive really, looking back at it, and had happened at the under-twenty-five's kickboxing finals, where her opponent had brought her elbow down to block her kick and it had hit her knee instead, breaking the patella and detaching some of the surrounding ligaments. The pain had been so bad that for the first time at a sports event she had screamed in pain and cried, and that was only the start of her problems with it. It had taken several operations and months and months of physio to get her walking again, which was the point that she gave up. Despite her track record with relationships, she desperately wanted children, and to be able to play and run around with them, and the risk of further damage if she continued professionally was so large that she quit.

She put a bowl of food down for Alfie, her dog, who was still curled up in his basket by the fire and was refusing to move and headed out to her car. If she didn't get off soon, she would not get parked, and the old Beetle needed a while to warm up in this weather before it would consider moving anywhere. It was a good little runner that she had driven from her youth, after many weeks pestering her dad to get her a car rather than a large party, which, given the past, he had agreed with and convinced her mum, and in the end she had enjoyed more good fun in it than a camper van had seen during the summer of love, but it was getting temperamental these days, and was getting near the point of needing a proper restoration, but she didn't have the money for that at the moment and hoped it would hold out.

She kept ringing Hellen throughout the day, to no avail, and by the time Jim took over from her at six in the evening, she had made her mind up to go and see her. She had a spare key for her flat and would be able to check that she hadn't collapsed or something if she didn't answer the door. Sophie sped down the A3, wincing at the farting noise that came from the exhaust, making a mental note to herself that she would have to pop into the garage and get that fixed. She always got a good deal there — Dave, who worked in the garage, fancied her, and as long as she wore a short skirt, about the only time that she did, as she preferred trousers, they hid the scars all around her knee. She would play silly and flirt and giggle with him, and he would always give her a good price. 'Men are so easily manipulated,' she chuckled to herself, and besides, she enjoyed the banter as well, a bit of harmless fun; but she was beginning to feel that she and Hellen were the only two women in Portsmouth that were still single at their age. But she wanted a man that was sophisticated and a charmer, who was loyal and would not cheat on her, and be able to keep up with her in the bedroom. She sighed. A rare breed these days; most of the men she had been out with lately were complete dicks, and she had decided to give up on her attempts at internet dating after spending an evening with a handsome forty-something who couldn't stop talking about himself and his ex-wife. She had been too polite to walk out, but by God what a jerk; she was fairly sure that he hadn't even asked her name.

It was seven by the time she pulled into Hellen's car park and noticed a police car pulling away from the block opposite, having boarded up the doors and windows, and placed a 'crime scene' notice up. Frowning, she made her way up to her friend's flat, and to her surprise found a door-length mirror hung up facing her. *'Why would Hellen put that up there?'* she thought, ringing the doorbell. After another two attempts, she let herself in, and gasped in shock at the changes to the room. The windows had what looked like branches nailed over them, and crosses were everywhere. Her heart started beating more quickly when she noticed what looked like bloody footprints all over the floor, and on closer inspection she found a pile of Hellen's sheets in the basket by the washing machine, along with the torn remains of her nightdress, blood all down the front. *'What the fuck happened here?'* she thought and jumped slightly when the phone went off. Not quite sure whether or not to answer it, she eventually did.

'Hi,' said the cheery voice on the other end.

'Er, hello,' she said, 'Hellen's place. Can I help?'

'Oh, this is Tim. Becky and myself were getting a bit worried about Hellen, as she hasn't been in for work, and we wanted to check that she was all right.'

Sophie thought quickly, as she knew that Hellen needed the money from the job and had to think of something to cover for her with, before finding out what was really going on.

'Oh, Sophie here, Tim; she's not well, I'm afraid, so I've come over for a couple of days to look after her. She'll be back soon. I'll get her to call you tomorrow if she's feeling better.'

'That would be excellent if you could. Pass on our regards and I hope to speak to her tomorrow.'

'Will do, bye.' She put the phone down and sighed. Where had she gone?

Sophie spent the night at Hellen's in case she returned, but she didn't, and she ended up having a disturbed night. Some animals outside kept pecking at the window, really annoying her, and she started having horrible dreams, where she was lost, wandering in the dark, unable to find Hellen no matter how hard she tried, and something was following her. Were these the dreams that Hellen was talking about? If so, they were terribly oppressive. The door phone had rung at two in the morning, but there was no one on the other end, just the buzz of static, and she had put it down to a group of annoying teens with nothing better to do with their time. She decided that if it rang again, she would throw a bucket of water out the window at them.

After a very bad night's sleep, she woke at nine, and phoned into her work sick, telling them that she had the shits — no one ever wanted to question that excuse. There was that thing of too much detail, and she remembered to phone and ask her mum to look after Alfie. She had another look around the flat and kept coming back to the bloody sheets. 'What has she done to herself?' she kept asking. It was far too much blood for a period, and why was her nightdress so torn up? Sophie made up her mind to look around outside, on the off chance that Hellen was out naked in the woods again, lying helpless with hypothermia. After spending a couple of hours wandering around the forest, she was beginning to feel agitated. Better head back, she might phone the flat or she could return home, she thought. Sophie was pleased to get out from the trees, as it seemed that they were closing in on her, creaking and groaning as she made her way through them. She couldn't shake the feeling that she was being watched by the birds; their eyes seemed to follow her, tracking her every move, and their calls eerily sounded like 'go… go…' She knew that it sounded mad, but by the time she got back to the flat she was very jumpy and decided to take her mind off the experience by cleaning up her friend's floor. All she could do was wait, and the longer she waited, the more she felt the heavy atmosphere within the flat, and then become even more worried herself. If this was what Hellen was experiencing, no wonder she wasn't well. She didn't scare easily, but there was something odd about the atmosphere here that made her feel unsafe.

Chapter 14
The Holy Debate, Visitation

'For a just man falleth seven times,
And riseth up again: but the wicked shall
Fall into into mischief'
Proverbs 24:16
(King James version)

Father Thomas waited patiently on the telephone, as he had been for the past hour. No one had contacted him back after what he had considered to be a productive conservation a few days back with several of his superiors, and he had been convinced that the result was going to be positive, and when he hadn't heard anything, he had tried contacting them, and was now defiantly confident that he was being blocked. He twisted and untwisted the phone cord in annoyance; he had said that it was a matter of urgency and he was being ignored. Hellen had little time left and he felt sure that the unholy monster was going to come for him tonight. The tinny voice of the queueing machine repeated for the hundredth time, 'We value your custom, please hold and we will be with you as soon as possible. Your call is important to us. You are number ten in the queue.' He had damn well been number ten in the queue for the last half an hour and he was getting annoyed. Why did the Church need a holding machine anyway? The number was only for regional priests to contact them. He tried to calm himself by reciting his prayers, but it wasn't helping.

It was almost dark outside, and the wind was picking up. As long as he didn't leave the church, he felt that he would remain safe, but he wasn't worried about himself. He feared for Hellen. She had seemed in a bad way when he saw her and appeared almost defeated; she hadn't seemed like the bouncy and wilful girl that he had known, she seemed so alone. He had known her since the day she was born. He had conducted her christening and been very good friends with her parents. They had been so proud when she became a member of the church's choir. She had always been a beautiful girl, who was usually willing to please, but if she set her mind against doing something, she could be amazingly stubborn, and it was unlikely anyone would be able to get her to change her mind, except perhaps her father. He smiled as he remembered her confessing to having forgotten to get her mother a birthday card for the actual morning, and how she had cried uncontrollably. She had only been seven at the time, and he had been able to help her make a card and pick some flowers for her to give her mother from his own personal garden. In many ways, Hellen's mother had been like a surrogate daughter to him as she had lost her parents when she was very young, and had sort of adopted him as her surrogate father, which deeply touched him, and Hellen had been a substitute grand-daughter, for his wife had died giving birth to his daughter, who had also died a few days later despite the amazing efforts of the hospital, and being able to help them had made him feel needed. Having seen her in such pain had greatly upset him. She had grown into a highly successful and independent woman, and he knew all her achievements through regular conversations with her mother; but it had still pained him greatly when she had left the church and was determined to get help for her now.

The phone suddenly clicked into life, making him jump.

'Hello, Father Thomas, its Daulton here, how are you doing?'

'Oh, hello there, Father Daulton, I was expecting someone else. I haven't heard from you for a bit; what's happening here? I can't get through to anyone.'

'Well, my friend, unfortunately that's why I'm speaking to you. Putting it bluntly, they think you've gone mad! You must be aware of the Catholic Church's stance on these supernatural matters. It may have loosened its position on exorcisms, but vampires are a completely different issue.'

'But you saw it with me, James,' he implored, 'we were both there — the bites, the death, the chaos! What we had to do to end it, it's forever engraved in my mind. If only we had been given clearance to act sooner, those children would still be alive!'

'I know, I know, but we were young then and they managed to cover it up.'

'But we know the problem is real. There have been cases on and off for years. This is my friend we're talking about here. I fear this curse will kill her.'

'David, many women can be hysterical and self-harm. It doesn't mean that they are turning into the undead,' said Daulton. Father Thomas felt sure that he was making the sign of the cross on the very mention of the word.

'I've damn well seen the vampire, James, in person. It is most definitely real. I marked him with the cross to save Hellen, but I fear he will kill me tonight. I do not fear my own death, you understand — in a way it would be a relief. But not sweet Hellen.'

'My God!' James gasped. 'You've seen him? For real!'

'As real as I'm speaking to you now, as real as back then.' He was sure that he could hear his friend curse in the background. 'The cross damn well burnt its shape onto his face. I saw it.'

'I will speak up for you, David, and do what I can, but do not hold out for hope; they are unlikely to change their mind on my behalf.'

'I thank you, James, and it's been good to know you all these years. When I am gone, please look after Hellen for me. Keep an eye on her.'

'You talk as if it's over, David.'

'For me I fear that it is, James. I know he will come tonight. I will stay here in the church for protection, but I fear his power, James, I fear him. The look in those eyes when he stared at me… Goodbye, my friend.'

'Goodbye, David. I'll get back to you as soon as possible.'

Father Thomas shakily replaced the receiver and began to pray.

[*Bang*]… It came from the main door of the church.

[*Bang… bang…*] The noise was repeated, as something heavy pounded on the church door. Father Thomas rose to his feet and clutched a large gold crucifix to his chest.

'*Come now, Father, let me in. You must have known that I would come.*'

He chose not to reply but jumped as something started to knock on the back door as well.

[*Bang*]… It echoed as the sound spread out and dissipated through the church.

[*Bang… bang… bang…*]

'*Come and face your demise with courage, don't be a worm of the Church.*'

'O God, you are the preserver of men!' Father Thomas jumped as tapping began on the stained-glass windows. 'And the keeper of our lives. We commit ourselves [*Bang… bang…*] to your perfect care on the journey that awaits us.' The doors began to rattle on their hinges, and dark shapes shifted behind the windows. 'We pray for a safe and promising journey.'

[*Bang… bang… bang…*]

'Give… give your Angels charge over us to keep us in all our ways.' The light dimmed, but came up again.

'Let no evil befall us, nor any harm come to our dwelling that we leave behind.' His voice began to get louder as his confidence grew.

'Although we are uncertain of what the days may bring, may we be prepared for any event or delay, and greet such with patience and understanding.'

The whole church was alive with noises now, and Father Thomas began to worry that the glass in the windows would shatter.

'Bless us, O Lord, that we may complete our journey safely and successfully under your ever-watchful care.'

The noise reached an ear-shattering pinnacle, then the lights went out.

Chapter 15
Father Above, Sophie, A Long Night

'For all that is in the world, the lust of the flesh and
the lust of the eyes, and the pride of life,
is not of the Father, but is of the world'
John 2:16
(King James version)

Hellen sat on the train with her foot bouncing nervously
up and down, as many different themes circled her
mind, from her newfound love with Ben and where that
was going to go, how to stop Adam from turning her
completely and how to control her own growing
Vampiric addictions so that she could retain enough
self-control to save herself from damnation. The closer
she got to Portsmouth, the heavier the air seemed to get.
She had never expected their relationship to develop so
quickly, let alone instigating sex with him on their first
meeting — twice! That was so unlike her, but it had
been so good, and she had controlled the curse, and that
pleased her. She had managed to fight back the blood
lust and take control, and it felt so empowering. She had
never realised that she could be so forward with that
kind of thing, though, but it had just felt right, and for
once in her life she had no regrets over her decision. She

felt well, fulfilled, and needed — he had definitely needed and wanted her, as much as she had wanted him. '*My God, I love him,*' she thought to herself and subconsciously hugged herself, remembering Ben's embrace. '*Wow!*' she thought and allowed herself a small smile of pleasure.

During her journey, Hellen kept struggling to pull her thoughts away from Ben and their night of passion, as every time she thought of it, she had a warm tingle run through her body. If only she could just curl up with him forever; but there would be no future for them if she couldn't sort out her vampire problems. She tried again to focus and looked through the folklore guide she had downloaded onto her computer, and struggled to read the text as she had forgotten her reading glasses. The only permanent solution, of course, would be to kill Adam, but the police would be of no use; she felt sure that they didn't deal with dead criminals, meaning that she would have to do it, and would she be able to resist him for long enough to get close enough to him to do it, and what would be the legal repercussions if she did succeed? Scrolling down the page, she looked for any title referring to 'How to kill a vampire'. Of course, she knew the famous ones like exposure to direct sunlight and a stake through the heart were meant to work, but there must be more:

— Burning it 'alive', so to speak [Possible, she could get lighter fuel and a lighter]

— Decapitation with a gravedigger's spade [Perhaps she could nick one from the graveyard off Hulbert Road]

— Burial at a crossroad face down, so it would dig out the wrong way and become lost [Sounds silly, and difficult getting said undead bastard to the right place]

— Decapitation with garlic in the mouth [Might as well use a stake as well to make sure]

— Cut out the heart and cut it in two [Ditto]

— Drive a nail through its temple [Stick with hammer and stake]

The trouble was that they all involved you catching the vampire during daylight, and then actually being able to do the prescribed deed. They all seemed difficult and filled with danger, and she didn't think she would be able to wrestle a vampire into submission. Hellen mulled these ideas right until the train pulled into Petersfield Station. She took a few minutes to buy her ticket for tomorrow and made her way to the church to check on Father Thomas. When she pulled up and got out of the car, the deathly silence that surrounded the building was ominous, especially with the dark mist hanging in the air that tasted of earth, and her stomach tightened. Something was wrong. Looking around, all the trees, ledges and roofs were lined with what must have been hundreds of crows, all of which seemed to watch her approach as she walked towards the church door. For the first time it was locked, and she called out,

'Father... Father Thomas?' A fear was beginning to descend on her and she wanted to be inside, and away from the gaze of the birds. She could hear the sound of many locks being undone and bolts being drawn back. She was greeted by the haggard and unshaven face of the old man, and he quickly ushered her in, re-bolting the door behind her.

'You should not have come back here, my child, I am being watched. I do not feel I have long left, and it is not safe for you here. Now listen carefully. The Church will do nothing — they refuse to accept the facts and claim that I am apparently "just working too hard",' he snorted. 'I haven't ever worked hard, not for years now. The arrogance! Anyway, you must go, now. He was outside last night and will return again. You must not leave your house tonight, do you hear me. I had these specially made for you by the blacksmith.' He handed her a pair of what looked like silver handcuffs. 'These will make sure that you cannot leave the room. Do not come looking for me as I do not expect to survive the night. I will try and stop him if I can, but don't hold out too much hope there. I am an old man, but we will see what the Lord has in store for me. I will do his bidding. Now go... go!'

'But, Father, surely we stand a better chance together? I don't want to leave you here on your own.'

'No,' he interrupted, 'you are still young and have a chance. He's furious that I scarred him, and he will not let that go unanswered. I am never on my own, for God is always with me, and you if you let him. Now go.' He ushered her to the door and after checking she had reached her car, bolted the door again, gripping his chest to try and control the pain.

Hellen stopped at the local garage, worriedly watching the sunlight diminish as the mist got worse, and bought a couple of lighters and some lighter fuel, and hurried back to her flat. She got to the top of her stairs and her door, but heard noises from inside, and felt her gut twist. She drew a deodorant can from her bag along with her lighter and quickly pushed the door open, letting loose with a blast of flame.

'Jesus Christ!' a woman's voice cried out, and a shape dived to the floor. 'What the fuck was that about?'

'Oh my God, I'm so sorry, Sophie! I wasn't expecting anyone, I heard the noise and...'

'You were expecting someone, though; who the fuck were you expecting? Who possibly requires a flamethrower as a welcome?' Sophie said, grabbing a towel and frantically trying to smother the now growing flames on the arm of the chair. 'What the hell's going on, Hellen? You stopped phoning me, I come around and you've not been to work in days. Tim has phoned several times. Your windows have, I don't know, branches nailed to them, you have a goddamn mirror on the front of the door. What's that for, the postman to comb his hair in? Then you turn up and almost burn my fucking face off. Come on, get talking, lady!' Sophie had a stern but worried look on her face and her hands were now on her hips, and Hellen sighed: this was going to be difficult, and she didn't think that she would be able to lie to Sophie, she knew her too well. She shut and bolted the door and went over to her friend and hugged her.

'I'm sorry, Soph, I really am. I'll tell you, but please, you're going to need to sit down, but first you must wear this,' and she hung a cross around her neck.

'What's this for, Hellen? I'm not religious any more, I gave up that path a long time ago.'

'Doesn't matter, you just need it, it will protect you from me, and perhaps him.'

'Unless it folds out into a fire blanket, I doubt it's going to be of much use, protecting me from you' she said sarcastically, as she smothered the last of the flames. 'And who the fuck is him?'.

'All right, all right, not against that, but seriously it will protect you from something else.' Hellen sat down and told Sophie a shortened version of her story, realising how crazy it sounded.

'I've been your friend for years, Hellen, and someone has to tell you, you're losing it. These ideas are mad, can't you see that? This isn't *Twilight* or *Buffy the Vampire Slayer*! It's fantasy.'

'Fantasy, is it? Well, what are these then?' said Hellen, baring her pointed teeth, rather annoyed, and Sophie looked a bit shocked. 'And what about these? Allergic reactions, are they?' and she revealed the burns from the cross on her neck and hands. 'And this.' She pulled her sleeve up, showing the cuts on her arms. 'I could go on.'

'You're not well, Hellen,' Sophie pleaded. 'I found you naked in the street, remember? You need help! Let me call an ambulance, get your wounds dressed, you could talk to someone... A specialist?'

'I need help, but not in that way. I'm not mad, I know I'm not! Now you have to go, it's dangerous being around me at the moment. You need to go before it gets any darker. Go before the sun completely sets... Please, Soph, we've known each other for years; keep yourself safe and go now, while you still can. If you stay, there may be no going back once he's seen you.' Sophie looked at the fear and concern in her friend's face and softened to her plight.

'I can't leave you like this, Hellen, I can't. You're obviously terrified of something, that is clear. What sort of friend would I be if I didn't question it, though? You have to admit it's far-fetched! I'm going to stay whether you like it or not — we need to talk about this,' and she changed her approach a little, knowing her friend's stubbornness, and she gave her a sly smile, for she might as well catch up on the gossip as she was here. 'And you need to fill me in on this Ben. I want to hear everything, you understand, every dirty and sordid little detail. Is he the one from Uni that I never got to see? And your parents thought you were sleeping with?'

'Don't change the topic. You shouldn't stay, Soph, I don't know what will happen tonight. It's far worse than when you were here before, and it's getting more difficult for me to control and I don't want to hurt you. But if I can't change your mind, you must at least take precautions. You have to take these garlic pills, please, for me.'

'Oh, all right,' Sophie said, and she swallowed them down without water. 'Yeugh, horrible, no kissing for a while, then,' she added, pulling a face. After their initial argument, the heat had dissipated and the two women settled down to enjoy each other's company.

'I have to say that I am glad not to be alone,' Hellen said, 'but I do worry for you. As I told you, I almost bit Ben; I was only just able to resist — but thanks for staying.' A thought then occurred to Hellen: she could show her. It was all on camera, and she showed Sophie the footage from the CCTV, and it seemed to bring her around a little, including making her cry, and Hellen gave her friend a hug.

Hellen pulled a chair into her bedroom for Sophie to sleep on and set about preparing the room for the night. 'Now, some of this will seem a little weird, Sophie, I understand that, but please humour me.' With the salt rings set up around both Sophie and herself, Hellen asked her friend a final request. 'Now I know this is going to seem really odd…'

'Odder than the rest of this crap?'

'Well, now you come to say it, probably not, but please handcuff my left wrist to the bedhead; it might serve to protect you from me if things go bad, and it might save my life. Remember the CCTV I showed you, the harm that I can do to myself and others, that poor dog...' and she swallowed hard, pushing the incident back in her mind.

'Hellen, please, this is ridiculous! Save that sort of thing for Ben. What if you need to get up?'

'I can ask you for the key, of course, and don't let anyone in, under any circumstances, you understand. Don't invite anyone in, and unless there is no choice, don't let me out either, no matter how much I beg.'

'OK, OK,' she said, "whatever you want,' and she shackled her friend to the bed. 'Is that burning you?' she said as Hellen flinched when it was tightened, and a red line started to form around her wrist where the metal made contact with her skin.

'Yep, but it will keep us safe and a little burn won't hurt me for now; it's nothing compared to the others. Good night.' And she turned the light down but not off.

'Hellen...'
'Hellen... did you think you could avoid me...?'
'Come out, Hellen... Come to me...' [*clink*]

'What?' Sophie sat up to several noises. Hellen was struggling to free herself from the cuff, and there was a scraping from the window. She looked out to see a large crow pecking the glass. On looking back to Hellen, she noticed that she was not awake, but seemed to be arching in pleasure on the bed, running her free hand over her thighs and crotch, and she seemed to be having a conversation with herself.

'Please, no, I will not come... do you hear me, I will not fucking come!' There was a pause and then, 'No... Leave me alone you bastard...'

'Hellen, are you all right?' Sophie quietly asked. 'Hellen?'

'No... I will not let you... you in here, I...'

The door phone then rang, which didn't seem to draw Hellen's attention, so Sophie crept over to it and slowly lifted the receiver to her ear, and had to swallow before she could croak, 'Hello?' Her hand was now shaking.

'*Let us in,*' a lady's voice said.

'*Let us in, Sophie, it's so cold out here, let us in.*'

Sophie dropped the receiver. No one here knew her name, or, in fact, knew that she was here. She forced herself to peek out the curtain, and there were two dark shapes at the door, and they looked up at her with terrible, hateful red eyes.

'Shit!' she thought. 'Shit!' And she quickly let the curtain fall back into place and there was a banging at the door. She looked back to Hellen, who still seemed to be arguing with herself and arousing herself at the same time. Her eyes suddenly sprang open, two burning pits of fire which focused on Sophie, and she hissed, making a rush at Sophie, causing her to flinch, but she was held fast by the silver chain of the handcuffs, and jerked to a stop. She emitted an animal howl and kept pulling at the restraints, and it slowly began to cut into her skin.

'Let me out, Sophie,' she said in an almost unrecognisable voice. 'Let me out, I must go to him.' It was deep and animalistic, but then she spoke again in her normal voice ['Don't, Sophie, don't free me, for God's sake help me.']

'No!' said Sophie, and she got up, but without thinking left her salt ring to move closer to her friend, and Hellen's free hand shot out at speed and gripped her arm in a vice-like grip.

'Hellen, you're hurting me, let go!' She struggled to free herself, but the grip was unnaturally strong. Instead, she went with the pull, reversed the force, swung around onto the bed and put her friend into a judo head lock, which seemed to make her madder, but she kept her grip.

'Let me go, bitch, you will be mine! I will feed on your blood tonight.' ['I... can't stop... Help me!']

'*Fuck, she was bloody right*,' Sophie thought, and she tightened her grip. 'I'm sorry, Hellen, but you will understand when you're yourself, I hope,' and she spun her around and smacked her round the face really hard, leaving a massive red mark, but it was enough to make her loosen her grip and fall back so that Sophie could pull free and throw herself out of the salt circle, where she was able to regain her breath and rub the bruise forming around her wrist. My God, she was strong. She had always been able to restrain her in training, but

238

now! Hellen, meanwhile, fell limp onto the bed groaning, and the window began to rattle violently.

'*Let me in, Sophie. You may go, but she is mine. Let me in,*' another voice sounded from nowhere.

Shit! She felt herself shifting towards the door, a strong pull — my God, no wonder Hellen couldn't resist — but she hadn't been bitten, and the pull was slightly less on her. 'Fuck you!' she shouted out to the air.

Hellen sat back up on the bed, looking dazed, but her eyes were more normal; she was awake this time. 'You can't get me here,' she whispered. 'You can never come in, you son of a bitch!'

'*Have it your way... But your friends will suffer... One by one... Give yourself to me now and perhaps they can live.*'

'Sod off!' said Sophie and Hellen together. There was a loud bang as a large crack split down the glass in the window and it was suddenly silent.

'Is that it?' Sophie asked Hellen warily.

'Not by a long shot; he's going after Father Thomas, and there is nothing I can do, not at night. We must stay here.' A tear ran down her swelling cheek, as her thoughts turned towards the church. 'It's worth a try, though,' and she rang the police and told them that there was an assault happening at the church. '*Well,*' she thought, '*they might get there in time, and scare him off. Maybe.*' And she sat down on the bed, breathing deeply from the exertion.

'I'm sorry, Hellen. I mean, you were right... I... I've never seen anything like it. Who was the woman?'

'There was a woman?' Hellen said, worried.

'Yes, on the door phone. I... saw her from the window, an older lady.'

'Fuck no... no... not her. Damn, I should have known.'

'Known what?'

'It's Jasmine,' she said sadly, remembering some of the texts that she had read. 'Gary and Tom didn't come back because they couldn't. They were mutilated — Gary was torn to pieces and Tom was decapitated — but Jasmine... I saw the bites but it didn't click, not then. I was so upset that I didn't see it, but damn that bastard! Sophie, he left her able to turn, to be able to join him... help him.'

Sophie sighed and sat down, clutching her head. 'I just gotta get my head around this,' she said. 'I... well... Fuck me, vampires are real, shit!'

'It takes a while to accept, I know,' Hellen said. 'Don't suppose you could get me some ice from the freezer? You really hit me hard there and I can feel it swelling up.'

'I am so sorry, Hellen,' she said, quickly fetching the ice cube tray and wrapping a towel around them before handing them to her friend.

'It's all right, there was nothing else that you could have done. Things would have got a lot worse if I had invited them in or gone outside, but I managed to resist that, but not all of it. You did what you had to. I attacked you after all! At least this will go down,' and she paused, looking really sad, and Sophie felt sure that she could see her lip tremble. 'I don't think the others will, though,' and she self-consciously rubbed the wounds on her chest. Sophie sat down next to her and hugged her, squeezing her hard, and stroking her hair.

'They might do, you never know, they are not that bad,' she said, trying not to look too hard at her friend's cuts in case her face exposed the lie she was now making. She knew that they were deep, and the chances of them vanishing completely were small, but she didn't need to hear that right now. Sophie hugged her again. 'Well, as we're up anyway, coffee?'

York 1920
Second Interlude of the Nosferatu

'For it is the life of all flesh; the blood of it is
For the life thereof: therefore I said unto the
Children of Israel, Ye shall eat the blood of no
Manner of flesh: for the life of all flesh is the
Blood thereof; whosoever eateth it shall be cut off.'
Leviticus 17:14
(King James version)

The Great War had brought hard times on the whole
country, as the effects of mass death sank into the
consciousness of a nation. The shortages had even had
an effect on the Decker estate, which was now heavily
overgrown and noticeably unkempt and in need of
repair, despite the manor being inherited by Charles and
Elizabeth Decker, and the eventual halt of their grand
social events in 1917. No staff now worked there at all
as the fear of the place had grown over the last few
years, along with an outbreak of deaths in the nearby
village. The Doctor's thirteen-year-old daughter, and
the Blacksmith's fifteen-year-old cousin had both died
of blood loss within a week, and now several other
young ladies were suffering the same symptoms. There
had been talk in the local tavern of the policeman

finding a tall, beautiful lady in his son's bedroom who had disappeared through the window when spotted, leaving him with bite marks on his throat. One of the local farmers had a similar story of finding a shadowy man in his seventeen-year-old daughter's bedroom when he had walked in, and she had been standing there naked to the waist as the stranger caressed her and sucked at her neck. He had chased him with his rifle, and swore that he went into the Deckers' estate, but he didn't have the courage to follow the man, despite his anger. The next week he was found dead with a broken neck in the woods, alongside his naked wife and daughter, who both had their throats ripped out.

It was not until 1921, when the mayor's daughter was found dead, that the town reacted in fear and anger, and a mob had set off in the direction of the Deckers' estate at dusk armed with forks and torches. They had torn the gates down and set the house on fire. Two coaches had attempted to leave, but only one got through, carrying wooden boxes. The other was stopped, and Lord Charles and Lady Elizabeth had been dragged from the carriage and set upon by the crowd. Both had fought with the strength of twenty men, and many of the villagers dropped injured, but one got lucky and managed to thrust an iron pitchfork into Lady Elizabeth's chest, where she collapsed with a howl, blood soaking her white blouse. Lord Charles had let loose with a howl of grief that left the villagers on their knees, clutching their heads, before he disappeared in a cloud of shadow. The mob had watched the house burn until midnight, before dispersing, and no one noticed the tall, dark shape that returned in the darkness and crouched over the body of Lady Decker, caressing her beautiful face and hair, before delicately carrying the body away. Although many people did hear the wolf-like howls as the moon rose in the sky. For the years to follow, no one went near the burnt remains of the manor, and no more children went missing or died.

No one returned to claim the estate until the 1960s, when a pale man with sad blue eyes called Adam Decker appeared with his wife Jill Cooper and their exceedingly beautiful and busty daughter Izzy Cooper. They had then spent many years restoring the property to its former glory and were seldom seen to start with due to their extensive European travel. It was reported in the press that Adam Decker and his family were not related to the manor's previous dynasty, and no one thought to check, as it was about forty years since the events that had burnt the building down. Towards the end of the 1960s Adam and Jill began to be seen around far more than any of the previous owners, although in dark garb with wide-brim hats, which many took to be a product of the time's odd fashion and his work as a musician, which was discovered when he chose to play several events a year in the city, typically for charity-based events.

Most eyes, though, lie on their daughter Izzy, who was a regular figure around the town's night-time scene, with her curvy figure and love of mini-skirts and cleavage-revealing tops. She was never short of male attention, and seemed to party all night, every night, the locals putting it down to the youth movement and their promiscuity. Several braver ladies on the town council had tactfully tried to mention her antics to Adam when he was chairing a committee meeting, but he seemed unconcerned at his daughter's flirting, claiming that she was fine, and more than able to look after herself. No one noticed that many young men began disappearing in the area — all those that had last been seen flirting with Izzy in the clubs.

Chapter 16
Confrontation and Desecrations

'Woe unto them that call evil good and good evil;
that put darkness for light and light for darkness;
that put bitter for sweet and sweet for bitter!'
Isaiah 5:20
(King James version)

Father Thomas hadn't slept well for years, and the creaks and bangs an old building like the church made at night didn't help him in this endeavour. He had given up on sleep at two in the morning and was instead searching the bible for anything that might help him if, or more likely when, the vampire turned up. He felt sure that it would visit Hellen first, and hoped she was all right. She was young, and had a lot more life left to live, whereas his body had slowly been packing up on him for years now. The only reason the Church hadn't made him retire was because attendance had always been low in the area, and those that attended did so because they had known him for years, plus the fact that no one wanted to cover this church, a reason that he could never understand as he had run the church for over fifty years and liked the area and the people.

His mind kept drifting back to the events in Italy, and the horrors that he had seen. The damage that one vampire could do to a village over a short time was unspeakable, and his discovery was burnt into his mind, and would remain so until he died. He had tried, he had done the right thing and told his superiors about the problem, but they wouldn't listen. Both James Daulton and himself had been made to wait and observe as the curse spread, because the Church didn't want to believe. It was right in front of them and they refused to see it. It was not until James and himself acted independently, without approval, that the foul disease had been ended; but it forever stained his soul. By the time they had acted, over ten adults and twenty children had been turned. Dealing with the adults was hard enough, but the children... He prayed every day for God to forgive him for the deaths his inaction had caused. The Church had finally intervened at the end, and had absolved James and himself of any sin, but that didn't clear his conscience, not by a long shot. He had had to end their torment of living undead, the people they had gone on to hurt...

'*Father, let me in, Father*,' a voice called from behind the church's main door. It sounded like Hellen, and he hurried over to the door. '*Why has she come out after dark, silly, silly, girl.*'

'*Father, help me, let me in, he is coming, help.*'

'I'm coming, my child,' he said as he fumbled with the keys and started unlocking the many bolts. Maybe she had been forced to flee, and he cursed the fact that he was so slow.

'*Help me!*'

He drew the bolts aside and opened the door.

'*Hello, Father,*' Adam said as he stood in the doorway.

'*You, stupid old fool,*' Father Thomas thought, as he felt his stomach sink through the floor. '*How could you have fallen for that?*' He went to lift his cross, but a long arm shot out and grabbed him by the throat, the long nails digging into his skin, and he was slowly lifted from the floor. All he could do was look down at the fiend holding him firm as he began to choke. Adam was tall, pale and many would have classed him as handsome, except for the burnt cross mark that was now seared across his face. It was fainter than when he had first burnt it on, but still there.

'*Did you think that because you have faith, I would not be able to get to you, Father?*' He spat the words out as if they hurt him to speak them, and Father Thomas could hear a faint hissing sound as the vampire's hand began to burn as it made contact with the cross around his neck, but Adam did not flinch — his grip remained like steel.

'*I have not survived for hundreds of years without learning to accept pain; it is a part of life and death. I live in continual hunger, one that can never be quenched, most certainly not by your pathetic watered-down old blood.*' His smile was evil. '*Hellen's sweet blood is far better,*' he taunted, '*the smell of her unpolluted skin; but you advised her poorly. She will be mine whatever she tries to do, and will come to an acceptance of it given time, and will learn to respect me and accept my love. Despite my abilities and hunger, it is the loneliness of time that cuts deepest, and in time she might come to love me.*' For a second a haunting pain flashed past his eyes, before the burning returned and he threw the priest down the stairs, causing a series of sickening cracks as he rolled down to the floor, and placed himself in front of the door.

'You will never win,' Father Thomas wheezed, pain surging through his body as he struggled to stand. 'Be gone, you cursed stain on God's Earth!' He again began to lift his cross, but a dog shot out from where it had been hiding in the shadows and closed its teeth around his wrist, tearing into his flesh and tendons, and it kept shaking until his fingers lost their strength and the cross fell from his hand. A crow then landed on his shoulder, screeching 'Death, death' into his ear and pecked the cross from his neck, flying off with it into the distance.

Adam descended the church stairs, making his way towards the old man, and the dog's shape seemed to shift, the edges blurring, and the haze shimmered to reveal a woman, potentially in her sixties, who then also started closing in on him. Both their eyes burnt like coals as they watched the blood run down from what remained of his hand and onto the floor. Father Thomas looked up towards the sky, knowing his end was near, and started muttering a prayer, and tried to make the sign of the cross, but he was interrupted as two more crows flew onto him, tearing at his eyes and the flesh on his face. In the distance, he could hear the sound of sirens, as the two figures wrapped in shadows descended down on him.

'Good luck, Hellen,' were the last words that he would ever say.

* * *

As WPC Sally Carter's patrol car pulled up, hundreds of birds lifted into the sky, blurring everything in sight. She got out of the car along with PC Lee Harper, and both lit up their torches. Blood and feathers covered the floor as they headed towards the church. On the cross outside, Father Thomas' head was rammed, its bloody eyeless sockets watching their approach. Lee shone his light up the stairs and onto the door, where the crucified body was nailed. Both officers gasped at the horrific sight, and as Sally bent over, reaching, Lee threw up over the wall. Across the front of the building scrawled in blood was written:

'In the Lord we trust,
Believe if you must,
For Death awaits,
For the fools that trust'

'WPC Carter, requesting an ambulance and back-up immediately,' she automatically shouted into her radio, before drawing her Taser to check out the rest of the building. They made their way around the inside of the building but found nothing. No one had been inside; the true horror, was outside.

'He must have gone out by his own choice,' Lee said as he looked at the undone locks lining the inside of the door. 'He must have been worried that something was coming for him.'

'Yeah, but why open up? No one could break through a door of that stature, it's nearly a foot of solid oak.' She frowned. 'Damn, it's going to be a long night.'

Chapter 17
A Grim Discovery, the Family, Reunion

'Fear thou not; for I am with thee: be not dismayed;
for I am thy God. I will strengthen thee; yea, I will
help thee, I will uphold thee with the right hand of
my righteousness'
Isaiah 41:10
(King James version)

Ben pulled his car into the only remaining space on
Soho Square with a parking meter and emptied all his
remaining change into it. '*That car got less than six
miles to the gallon,*' he thought, working out that it had
cost over a hundred pounds in petrol to get from
Nottingham to London. Thinking about trivialities
helped to divert his mind from the problematic issue of
what to do next and prevented his mind from dwelling
on the fearful dreams he had experienced about Hellen,
and their scary connection to reality. He kept seeing the
fear in her eyes from his dreams, and it was driving him
mad. He wanted to remember her as he had seen her just
the other night, when they had made love, eyes
sparkling emeralds of joy. He shook his head and took
a deep breath. The real question now was where to start
looking. He'd spent the whole journey thinking this

problem over, and the only answer that he could come up with was to see Detective James Dick, the one that Hellen had told him about, so he set off through the crowded streets to find the police station. After a frustrating push through what seemed like all of humanity squashed into a couple of rooms, he finally reached the station, and asked the bored-looking man at the front counter for the detective. As expected, he was asked to wait and spent half an hour in a room of very suspect-looking people, nursing a rather disgusting plastic cup of hot chocolate, which he eventually decided to feed to the unhealthy-looking cheese plant in the corner. Thinking about it, its health might have been caused by it being fed a diet of unwanted drinks, and he quickly disposed of the cup in case anyone saw.

'You wanted to see me,' said Detective Dick, appearing from a key code-locked side door.

'Er, yes, I wanted to have a talk to you about Dr Hellen Oswold.'

'Right, I need a bit more to go on than that, sir. I see a lot of people in my line of work.'

'Pretty, ginger hair, found in an alley, no signs of assault.'

'OK, and you are?'

'Oh, I'm her, er, her partner [*or at least I hope I am*], and she is still very worried about what happened, and I said I would talk to you and see what was happening about it.'

James sighed: another worried boyfriend. 'Look, I'm kind of busy at the moment. Come through and if you don't mind sitting around for a bit, I'll try to get to you when I can.'

'Yeah, thanks for that,' Ben said, and set off following the detective.

He was led through the corridors and stuck in the same room that Hellen had been taken to and left there. Most likely forgotten about, he thought. To his surprise, all the CCTV screens were showing images, and the computer had been left on without its previous owner having logged out. '*Now that is lucky*,' he thought, and looked around carefully; if he did this, he felt sure that it was probably illegal, and he could get arrested for it and lose his job, but he kept seeing Hellen's scarred body, and the fear in her eyes after she had almost bitten him, and he closed his eyes for a minute. His features hardened, and he sat down at the computer, and the flashing box with 'person search' on it. He typed in her name, and up came several reports from the incident, along with loads of CCTV footage, including the ones by, what was he called, PC Tom Hawthorne that had been added. But there was more footage than he had thought she had mentioned, and looking at the date, he felt that Detective Dick must have been looking for more evidence of what had happened, as it dated from the same night in London, but footage from a wider circumference of cameras was now present. Ben started viewing the footage that had been obtained and it all seemed to track the movement of the shadow, from after it disappeared from the shot after throwing Hellen into the trash bags, and down many side streets until it reached a boarded-up house under the train tracks at Waterloo Station, at which point it seemed to go inside. That was where he would start his search — better than walking the streets.

As he rose to get up, he saw the detective watching him from the doorway with what he assumed was a half-smile on his face and a look of amusement in his eyes.

'Shit!' It was the only thing he could think to say, as Dick released a loud cough, or it might have been a laugh: his face was difficult to read.

'Well, well, someone in here actually working, now that's a goddamn first.' He laughed at his own joke and sat down next to Ben. 'What do you think of it all, then?' he asked, rubbing his temples, and Ben noticed how tired the man looked.

'I'm, er, sorry, I just couldn't help looking. I'm very worried about her.'

'Yeah, yeah, I've heard it all before, awr... sit down, you're not in trouble. I was going to show it to you anyway; you saved me time. Damn strange, isn't it?'

'No mistaking that.'

'I see it happened to her again back in Portsmouth. Sorry, I saw the tapes on file. If she was my girl, I'd be worried, too. Unfortunately, it's still the same situation that I said to her: no faces, means we have nothing to go on, until I found this.' He moved to another file, and this was dated two days before Hellen was found naked outside for the first time. It showed the same house in London that Ben had seen on the other footage, but now the boards had been removed, and two men — one tall and fat, the other shorter and thinner — were loading a coffin into the back of an unlabelled van. The two men then seemed to have an argument, and the door was re-boarded, and they headed off.

'Now they are small-time crooks,' he said, pointing to the screen with a fat finger, 'typically handling stolen goods, common assault, things like that,' said the detective; 'and guess what, they both showed up in Portsmouth, along with the death of a good policeman. Both men are now dead themselves. One was found electrocuted on the rail tracks, and the other was found in his police cell, with grip marks round his throat and drowned in the toilet. Christ, what a way to go.'

'Have you checked out the house they go to in the footage?' Ben asked.

'They won't give me a warrant to do so yet. Not good enough cause, apparently, so I can't. But I promise you that I'll keep trying. You go home and keep that pretty little thing safe. I know it may be slow, but we'll get there.'

Ben thanked him for his help, whilst breathing a sigh of relief, and headed out of the station quickly. He wanted to check out the house before dark.

He pulled up on a double yellow line outside the house from the CCTV, just as the sun was starting to get lower in the sky. '*Shit, I haven't got that long,*' he thought as he took his bag from the boot, pulling out a large crowbar as well. Ben jogged up to the door and started prising off the boards that were blocking the door, trying to make as little noise as possible; every squeal released by the lever made him shiver. He turned on his torch and headed inside. Very little outside light penetrated the gloom of the interior, and he felt his heart pounding as he wandered from room to room, searching for anything that might tell him where the two crooks had delivered their load. He found various bits of paperwork and shoved them in his pocket to look at later, when a hatch in the floor caught his attention. He grabbed its metal handle and lifted it up, revealing a rickety set of stairs leading down into the darkness. Ben really didn't want to go down, but he took a few deep breaths to steady his racing pulse, and headed down, carefully testing each step before putting his weight on it.

At the bottom, he was surprised to find that it was an earth floor, with three wooden coffins laid out in a line in the middle of the room. He crept up to the first and found it empty. He breathed a sigh of relief, and then noticed that it had a name engraved on the front. It said *Adam Decker 1680–1720* on a decorative brass plaque. It was Adam's coffin, his resting place in London. Ben looked inside again and found several long ginger hairs stuck to the satin lining with blood. He felt his blood begin to boil. '*Bastard!*' he thought to himself. '*They're Hellen's.*' He poured some of the holy water into the coffin, and laid garlic at the head and footwell. 'Take that, you blood-sucking fucker, you will not be able to run back here to escape me!' Ben gritted his teeth and wiped a tear from his eyes, as his dream came back to memory, of the shape caressing Hellen, and the fear in her eyes as she was obscured from his vision.

He moved onto the next coffin, and silently removed the lid. 'Shit, shit!' he cursed to himself, and tried to calm himself by slowing his breathing. In it lay a young girl, who couldn't be more than eighteen, possibly younger, a schoolgirl even, dressed in what looked like a prom dress. She lay there as in death, but with no signs of decay. Her hands were clasped on her stomach, and her lips were an unnaturally bright red. A thin line of blood ran from them and trickled down her chin — she had been feeding. Ben looked for signs of life, but couldn't find any, which didn't surprise him, and he took a stake and the hammer from his bag and knelt there looking at her. Her age made it more difficult than he had thought it would. 'For God's sake, she was only a child!' Fuck, he was a lecturer, not an action hero. He remembered watching all the Hammer films as a teen, and how the Van Helsing character would always fearlessly drive a stake into the nubile vampire's heart. It always seemed so easy for them, but when faced with the innocent-looking face of a teenage girl young enough to be a fresher was really difficult. Christ, she was young enough to be his daughter, and he was going to mutilate her body. He slowly placed the tip of the stake between her ample breasts where her heart should be, the point just touching the fabric of her dress, and he looked at her face again. There was an eerie beauty in that cold white face, then her eyes sprung open and her hands grabbed his wrist, the one that was holding the stake. Her eyes were full of hate, burning into his brain, making him hold from bringing the hammer down, and he let out a cry of pain as the grip dug into his flesh. Beside him, the other coffin lid began to rise. He could see the red varnish on the nails of an emerging hand. Then events began to blur.

'Holy shit!' a voice called out from behind him, which broke Ben from his trance as everything seemed to happen at once. He brought the hammer down on the stake, driving it deep into the girl's breastbone with a loud crack, and the girl screamed a piercing, high-pitched howl as blood sprayed over him and soaked her dress. He brought the hammer down again and again until it went completely through her and he felt it hit the wood of the coffin below and it would go no further. She released his wrist, and the hate left her eyes, leaving a peaceful expression on her face, and her hands dropped back onto her stomach. At the same moment, the woman in the next coffin leapt at the other person in the room. There was a hum of electricity as a Taser discharged and did precisely nothing. The barbs stuck into the woman's face, but she kept going, pinning Detective Dick to the wall. Ben's hands searched around without taking his eyes off the scene and grabbed a shovel from the earth floor and ran towards them both. As the woman bent in to bite the policeman's neck, who she had fixed to the wall in a powerful grip, he swung the spade hard, smashing it deep into the vampire's neck. She howled and turned around, dropping the policeman onto the floor. Her head was leaning sideward, the neck half cut through and squirting blood in all directions. Ben took one more swing, but his bad hand was shaking badly now, and she moved at an astounding speed and knocked it out of his hands with ease, grabbing him by the lapels of his jacket and throwing him across the room, where he collided with a crash into the stairs, dropping to the floor winded. Eyes burning, she began to slowly make her approach. Ben clutched his chest in pain, struggled to get to his feet, but was grabbed again and lifted up into the air, her hand like a vice around his neck. Then suddenly he dropped to the floor, covered in blood. He desperately wiped his eyes and rolled to the side, but nothing came for him. He looked more carefully and found Detective Dick standing above the woman with the spade sunk into the ground, her body on one side of him and her head attached to the spade.

'You, OK?' Ben managed to croak at the detective.

'That is a poor choice of question,' he said, sinking to the ground. 'I think I just killed someone.'

'Don't worry yourself, they were both dead already, you know. Their names are on the coffins,' said Ben as he walked over and helped the detective to his feet. 'I must finish this,' he said, and dragged the woman's body back to the coffin, placed it inside along with the head and drove a stake through its heart, just to be sure. He also covered both with holy water, gently closing the women's eyes, before nailing the lids shut. Ben then took a moment to look at the name plates again more carefully. The young girl's stated *Izzy Cooper 1940–1957*, and the woman's read *Jill Cooper 1918– 1957*. Mother and daughter, by the look of it. He guessed Adam had bitten one of them, probably the mother, and she in turn had bitten her own daughter, or given her to him as commanded. He muttered a silent prayer for them and stood up.

'What now?' he said to the detective. 'Am I under arrest?'

'I… just don't know. I shouldn't even be here myself. I just had the feeling that it's where you were heading and I just followed my gut. Never been wrong yet, but usually gets me into a shit load of trouble. No, you're not arrested; hell, this never happened. I need my pension. I'll tidy it up and smooth it over with the boys on the beat, you get out of here. I don't want to remember this. I mean it, go, look after your girl. I'll report it and sort it out. Shit, that's going to be weeks of paperwork. Now go.'

'Thanks' was all Ben could think to say. 'I think you saved me there,' and before the detective changed his mind, he ran out into the moonlight and back to his car. He sat for a moment, hands trembling, as he changed his shirt. Then he turned the ignition and headed off into the night.

Ben parked up in a side road off Mortimer Market near the Hospital for Tropical Diseases. He wanted to be there for Hellen in the morning and adjusted his seat so that he could lay out more. Remembering the assortment of papers that he had picked up at the house, he started sorting through them to see if there was anything of any use, anything which might point him in the direction of Adam. Most of them were advertising, or trash, but one contained a hand-written address in Cosham, so he carefully placed it in his wallet and tried to get to sleep. A text from Hellen during the day had clearly stated that she was going to set off once the sun was up for safety, and should be there by ten thirty a.m., and he had a good view of the entrance from the car.

He slept badly that night; his thoughts kept returning to the women's faces, and how long they had been dead. Christ, one was just a little kid. He couldn't forget those eyes, and how Hellen's had shone the same when she had tried to bite him, and it kept him awake for a while, until he drifted off; but a short while later he dreamt about Hellen again, waking him up shaking. The shadow was almost completely hiding her from his sight now; it had to be symbolic. By the time it got to ten thirty, he was pacing the road waiting for her. To his relief he caught sight of her a few moments later hurrying up the road with another girl, and he rushed to meet them.

'Hellen!'

'Hi, lover boy,' she said with a smile, trying to sound cheerful, although her face showed the strain she was under, and the puffiness around her eyes when she removed her dark glasses showed that she had been crying, and there was a large bruise covering her cheek, which was showing a dark purple through the make-up she had tried to conceal it with. 'This is Sophie, she's been a friend of mine since... well, forever. She knows about the problem, and all about you.'

Sophie smiled and said, 'Hi, it's been a bad night, I'm afraid. Looks like you've had problems, too?'

'You're both all right, though?' he asked worriedly. 'He didn't get to you again?'

'Oh no, we survived, but he tried,' said Hellen.

'And she bloody attacked me,' said Sophie, smiling and pointing to Hellen.

'I just thought that was our special thing,' chipped in Ben, trying to lighten the mood.

'Father Thomas is dead, Ben. Adam got to him, and there's no help coming from the church,' said Hellen sadly.

'Well, I had a fun night as well. I think I met his family, or at least some of his friends. Detective Dick had found an address and we only just got out alive, but managed to lay them permanently to rest, and he won't ever be able to return there. I guess I sort of blessed his coffin.'

'My God, are you all right? I didn't know that you were tracking him down. You were just supposed to meet me here; my plan was to look for him afterwards, together,' and Hellen began to protectively check him over, running her fingers over the fresh scab on his forehead, the dark blue bruising around his throat, and they finally came to rest on the trembling of his bad hand, and she clutched it tight to her breasts.

'I'm fine,' he said. 'Detective Dick saved me. I killed one, and him the other. But what we do now know is that a stake through the heart definitely works, and so does decapitation.'

'Well, we're running late, so we had better get in there and we can talk more afterwards.'

Professor John Harker was waiting for them in his office, which was plushly decorated and looked like a throwback to a gentleman's club library in the Victorian era. He was a very tall man, approaching six foot three, very thin, with short grey hair and an insanely bushy moustache. His age was difficult to guess, but he must have been somewhere in his fifties. He walked over to them like an old war captain with his hands clasped behind his back.

'Well now, you must be Dr Oswold, and who are your friends?' His voice was deeper than when she had heard him on the phone.

'Well, this is my dear friend Sophie Jenner, and this is my, er, boyfriend, Professor Ben Harwood,' Hellen said, and they all shook hands in an awkward exchange, with Sophie remaining unusually quiet for her. She just seemed to be spending her time examining John closely, taking in every detail about him, trying to read his face, and in turn he kept nervously glancing at her.

'What a powerful grip you have, for such a petite little thing,' he said after shaking Hellen's hand. 'Yes, now, anyway, let us have a look at these strange bites then, shall we? No point wasting time.' He ushered her to sit down in a well-stuffed leather clubman chair, and once she had exposed her neck, he reached into his jacket pocket, removing a pair of gold-rimmed glasses and perched them on his thin nose, and bent over to have a look. 'I would assume that it's stopped bleeding by now, but it looks more irritated than it should do this long after the trauma.'

'Well, it still actually bleeds, and it hurts.'

'Well, most animals that bite secrete a saliva that contains anticoagulants, which inhibit the blood's clotting ability so that it can feed, but it would not be active now, and they rarely hurt.' As he spoke, a small trickle of blood made its way from the puncture and slowly trickled down her neck.

'Fascinating, fascinating,' he muttered, and dashed to his desk to collect a swab and container. 'We must take a sample; if there is still the species saliva present, it will make it easier to identify,' he said, and he bustled around getting enough blood into the tube.

'But what do you think caused it?' Ben asked, choosing his words carefully.

'Well, it does look like a vampire bat, as I said to the lady on the phone, but it's far too big. If it wasn't for the size, I would be almost certain we had our man, or bat, so to speak, ha, ha.'

'What would you say if I showed you these?' Hellen interrupted, drawing her lips back to reveal her pointed teeth, and Professor Harker nearly fell over, gripping the arm of the chair for support.

'I... well...' he said, trying to compose himself. 'That would be the sort of scale we would be looking at. But I am assuming that they weren't always like that?'

'Definitely not,' said Sophie. 'I've known her since she was little, and these beauties have developed over the last few weeks.'

'Few weeks! My God, the speed!' he stammered. 'May I?' — and he started examining them and got out a measure and began writing numbers into his notebook. 'I think we need a longer conversation here; please, all be seated.' They settled down. 'I would offer you a coffee, but I think that I need something stronger'; and without waiting for a response, he opened a side cabinet and brought over four glasses and a glass decanter of what looked like brandy. He poured them all out a glass and swallowed his in one gulp, before pouring another. 'Now, I think you had better tell me everything from the start. I need all the details and the symptoms. Everything is important, you understand, everything.' His eyes shone with interest and he leant back in his chair.

'I don't know if we should?' said Ben in a whisper; 'it's up to you, Hellen.'

'What choice do I have, Ben, after last night?' He put a reassuring hand on her knee, and she began to explain her situation to Harker, allowing spaces for Ben and Sophie to fill in where necessary. There was much crying on Hellen's part, particularly when she got to Father Thomas' death which hadn't fully sunk in yet. Professor Harker listened attentively, scribbling notes down as she went on with the story, until at last she had finished, and Ben gave her a hug.

The professor joined the tips of his fingers together and closed his eyes, leaving the trio to believe that it had all been too much for him, and he had fallen asleep. He then suddenly looked at them with an intense stare. 'Would you mind if I did a few quick tests?' he said, jumping up from his chair like a jack-in-the-box.

'If it will help,' said Hellen.

'It will, it will. I've never had the need to do this, but… I must get a few things. Have another drink and I will be back in a few minutes.' And he left the room like a rocket.

'What do you think?' Hellen asked her friends when the door closed.

'As you said, what options do we have left?' said Ben.

'I like him,' said Sophie slowly. 'I think he's trustworthy, and he's kind of sexy as well. Passionate about his work.'

'I didn't know you had a thing for older men?' Hellen teased in a whisper.

'Well, I don't normally,' said Sophie, turning red, 'but, well, I might reconsider my position on that stance. I've usually gone for younger men for their sex drive, but I have not had much luck with a more meaningful relationship, and that moustache. Grurr!'

'Sophie, I don't know if this is the right time,' Hellen whispered into her friend's ear, smiling.

'You really going to say that to me?' Sophie whispered back, raising her eyebrow and looking at Ben, who couldn't understand why his ears were burning.

It was closer to twenty minutes before Professor Harker returned with a box of odds and ends. 'I'm sorry, it all took a bit longer than I thought,' he said, and first produced a cross. 'Now, please bear with me, Hellen, but I need to test these things for myself. It's not that I disbelieve you, but... I need direct evidence.'

'It's OK, I understand,' said Hellen, and he proceeded to administer his tests, writing the results and his observations down by hand in clear and almost ornate handwriting.

(1) Reaction to cross — modest, no clear rejection, but mild skin irritation and feelings of discomfort and burning

(2) Reaction to holy water — burnt skin

(3) Exposure to UV light — moderate. Shies away, feels the need to cover up. Extended exposure causes reddening of the skin

(4) Observation of enlarged canine teeth — similar in appearance to a vampire bat.

(5) Obvious signs of self-harm — unclear if intentional or not. Would need to carry out sleep study tests, as the information would suggest it happens in the patient's sleep

(6) Recoils from iron metal objects, but able to manage with self-control

'Now,' he said, 'just one more test to do.' He sat down next to Hellen and drew an open-blade razor from his box. Ben and Sophie looked worried and shuffled around in their chairs. Professor Harker then drew the razor down the end of his finger, and blood started to come to the surface and run down towards his palm. Hellen's eyes burnt, and she gripped the sides of her chair; there were small cracking noises emitted from it due to the strength of her grip, as she tried to resist. He watched intently as her whole focus was absorbed by the blood and followed his finger as he moved it. She then suddenly grabbed his wrist with her left hand and his throat with her right, and started to pull his hand towards her.

'Erk!' he choked as her grip tightened.

'Quick, grab her!' Sophie said to Ben, and they both jumped from their seats and fought to pull her away, which proved very difficult; her strength was amazing, but together they managed to hold her in the chair, as Harker quickly covered his finger up with a bandage. At this removal of the blood from her vision, she suddenly relaxed into the seat, her muscles becoming less tense and her eyes filled with tears, and she looked away, ashamed.

'I'm so sorry,' she said.

'No, my dear, you did very well... Very well. I have never seen anything like it. Never. All the signs of Vampirism, as if it was a real infliction. Fascinating. This could be proof of the existence of a folklore legend; this could provide funded research for years.'

'That doesn't bloody help me,' Hellen said, raising her normally quiet voice. I won't be alive to be studied, even if I wanted to. He's getting too strong now, I don't have long left. I thought you would be able to help, but I think perhaps I was wrong.'

'Yes, yes. I get ahead of myself. I'm sorry, but you're a scientist yourself and you must understand why I got excited. I'm not sure what you really want me to do, though? This is no tropical disease that I know of and I'm sure you are now aware of that. But I will run the bloods and see what I can do. I will phone you tomorrow with the results and an update; maybe there might be a way of slowing the transformation process down, or something. Maybe an antibiotic or an anti-viral drug might slow it, if I can find out what it does to the blood to change you. If I can't find that out, it leaves us stuck.'

'Thank you, Professor,' Hellen said politely. She provided the larger blood sample that he requested and left quickly, just in case he tried to section her to aid his investigations. Sophie lingered by the door for a moment before pulling it closed behind them. It was as if she wanted to say something, but couldn't. Which was unlike her — Sophie was never usually tongue-tied, and she looked frustrated. Professor Harker was busying around his desk in excitement, but, feeling her eyes on him, he looked up. Their eyes locked for a brief second and then she closed the door, uttering a silent curse at herself.

Once outside, Hellen sat down on the bonnet of Ben's car and rubbed her temples, attempting to rid herself of a developing headache. 'Well, that was a waste of time,' she said to the air. 'I don't know what I really expected. I mean, I can still hardly believe this myself, let alone anyone else.' She seemed to visibly shrink with disappointment, and Ben put his arms around her and squeezed gently.

'We'll come up with something. I mean, we know that they will die — I killed two of them.' He smiled, and she hugged him back. 'I found a lead at the house,

271

though, and I just have to find the building in Portsmouth; maybe that will help us. But we had better start back to your place; it's midday now, and it will take us at least three hours to get to Portsmouth, only just before the sun starts setting at four.'

'Yeah, we'd better go,' said Sophie. She was frowning, and clearly had something on her mind.

Hellen looked up at the sun accusingly, and then back at Sophie and Ben, and she looked sad. 'You can't come with me, I love you both too much, and you've seen what I'm capable of on my own, let alone Adam. Go home and I'll sort it out.'

'There is no way we are leaving you on your own, lady,' said Sophie, pleased to be distracted from her thoughts.

'As I said before, I'm not losing you so quickly again,' said Ben. 'Besides, I've just killed what I think was Adam's family, or at the least his associated vamps, so I think for the moment I'll be in more danger than you. He's going to be really pissed.'

'OK,' she reluctantly gave in. She felt too tired to argue. 'You can come back, but not Sophie, you must stay safe, please.'

'I'm not being left out. Besides, they've seen me at yours, so in for a penny and all that.'

'Fine, I don't know what I've done to deserve you two!' And they all hugged, squeezed into the old car, and set off for the coast.

Sophie spent most of the journey sleeping on the back seat, and Ben steered with his left hand, whilst Hellen caressed his bad hand, which was still twitching, and she had laid it in the warmth of her lap and was holding it tightly. It was gradually beginning to feel better, if he was now not a little hot around the collar. Hellen looked at his hand and its slightly crooked fingers, whilst contemplating the severity of their situation. The church couldn't, or more likely wouldn't help, science was failing badly — the science that she had devoted her life to for so long could provide no answers — and she had trouble keeping herself under control, although she was pleased that she had proved it possible with Ben. He had a way of centring her in the moment, giving her a reason for hope, a desire to succeed.

'What are we actually going to do, Ben?' she asked, looking at him, and the slight stubble that was forming on his face. 'It's getting worse every night. I'm terrified that soon I will lose control completely and he will claim me.'

'You're stronger than you think, Hellen,' he said, glancing across at her. 'You can control it when it really matters; you controlled it for me, you prevented yourself biting me, and then continued, despite all the heat and rushing blood of the, er, moment, you managed it.'

'We were sort of preoccupied, though and a good distance away from him,' she said, lightly blushing. 'It's just that we are on our own here, there is no one coming! We are academics, Ben, not Buffy the fucking Vampire Slayer. Do you think that we can win this?'

'I would never lie to you, Hellen, I love you. I don't know if we can defeat him, but I managed to kill two of them, so there's a chance. And more than that, we have each other, and I promise you that I will do everything I can to help you fix this.' She smiled; she loved his simple view of things and felt somewhat better.

'I don't know how safe we will be at mine; he knows I'm there.'

'I know, but I feel that Sophie will help keep you safe.'

'I want you with me, Ben, please. It feels better when you're holding me. I find it easier to resist him.'

'I don't want to leave you, ever, but I must look for that house. Only the road name was written down, not a number. Besides, he can't be in two places at once, can he? Or at least I don't think he can. I have to find him and somehow finish this; then we can be together.' He smiled and turned his hand over and slid his fingers under the hem of her skirt, and walked them along the nylon of her tights.

'But what if he goes after you?'

'Then he does. Better me than you. Anyway, I'll think of something.'

She couldn't resist a giggle as he stroked her thigh, gradually creeping higher until his fingers were touching the elastic of her panties. '*My God*,' she thought, '*the simplest things mean so much to me now*.'

'Oh, damn!' he sighed.

'What is it?' she said, looking up.

'Going to have to stop for more fuel; this thing is thirstier than a drunk at opening time.' And he reluctantly pulled his hand back and signalled to pull in to the motorway service station that was approaching.

'When I get to Nottingham with you, it's going to have to go,' Helen said, crossing her legs and smoothing her skirt over, putting on her 'disappointed' face. 'It's spoiling my fun!' And she smiled as he got out to fill up the car, noticing the twinkle shining in her eyes from the mirror.

Chapter 18
Homecoming, Sleepwalking, Searching

'And they shall fight against thee; but they shall not
Prevail against thee; for I am with thee, saith the Lord,
to deliver thee'
Jeremiah 1:19
(King James version)

It was three thirty in the afternoon when Ben's Firebird pulled into the car park by Hellen's flat. A heavy fog was beginning to descend, spreading out its tendrils as if searching for them. He had insisted on stopping off at the DIY shop to buy some UV lights, and the sun was getting lower quicker than they had wanted. It wasn't that cold yet, but Hellen shivered as her gaze rose towards the trees, and she noticed that there were several large crows watching their approach, their expressionless eyes following them as they disembarked from the car.

'He's watching us, I know he is,' she said as calmly as she could. 'Something bad is going to happen tonight.'

Sophie calmly walked over to her car and pulled an air rifle out of her bag in its boot and shot two of them dead before the others scattered for cover. 'Bad fucking birdies,' she shouted between shots. The sound of gunfire filled the air, but the fog seemed to make the echo sound shallow, killing the sound prematurely. As the remaining birds scattered, one flew right at them as if to attack, making them crouch and put an arm in front of their faces to protect their eyes. But it didn't. The bird pulled up at the last moment with a grating, defiant scream, and flew towards the woods.

'Where the hell did you get that thing? Put it away before we get arrested!' Ben said, sounding rather shocked as he stood up.

'I used to shoot competitively,' Sophie said matter-of-factly; she was the only one of the trio who had not ducked and stood her ground without flinching. 'I started practising when my knee was buggered. Gave me something to do, and I got good at it. You don't have to have a licence or anything; probably should have to really, damn stupid kids can use these and end up hurting people's pets. I always keep it in the boot due to a lack of space indoors.'

'Good shot, though,' Hellen added. 'Now, we had better get inside, the night is coming in quickly.' She ushered them both inside; it was too open for her liking, and the birds were slowly returning, in greater numbers.

'Right, let's get these lights up,' said Ben, and he started setting up the UV lights by all the windows and the front door, so that they could be turned on and they would shine outwards. 'That should give him a shock if he comes by. But you should perhaps be a little careful with them, Hellen. I think they might burn you as well.'

'Er, them, I'm afraid,' added Sophie, emerging from the bedroom having nailed the old wooden window frames shut. 'Sorry, Ben, I forgot to mention it with everything going on, but he seems to have turned Helen's neighbour, you know, the gossip, and she turned up last night as well. She actually knew my name — so creepy.'

'Oh, great. Now they can split up. Never mind, give me your air gun pellets, will you?'

'OK, why? I am going to use them, you know? You can't stop me.'

'I know, and I wouldn't even try to stop you. I'm going to stick them in to soak in holy water — might add a bigger kick to your shots, or you might say let all your shots be blessed and all that.' He said this with an evil smile.

'Like it, Ben, I like it,' she said, and handed him the box of ammo. Not much, but at least twenty shots, and he bet that they would really hurt a vampire. Probably wouldn't kill it, though, perhaps if it penetrated enough to hit its heart, but he didn't think that it would be powerful enough to go through bone, but it might cause enough pain for the girls to escape if it came to that.

Ben kept one of the hand UV lights for himself and clipped it onto his belt for an emergency and went looking for Hellen. He found her coming out of the bathroom, wrapping a towel around herself. He steeled himself and followed her through to the bedroom. He didn't want to leave her, but they were running out of time and options, and he worried that if she asked him to stay again, he would not be able to resist her.

'I'm going to have to go, Hellen,' he said with a determination that he didn't feel. 'Everything is set, and please take care.' He trailed off, starting to trace the long cut that started on her shoulder and ran down her chest to beneath the towel. She placed a finger on his lips to stop him talking, and just gazed into his eyes, portraying a frailness that she never usually exposed, and it made him weak in the knees knowing that she trusted him enough to reveal it to him; but there was also a steeliness in her green eyes, and it frightened him a little.

'I know you must go, I do, but we could both end up dead tonight, you know that, don't you? And I... just don't know what to say; you're putting yourself in terrible danger for me, and I'm the one staying here.'

'It will be more dangerous for you, Hellen. You're the one he really wants; he will come for you over anything else, so please take care... I love you. You can resist him.' His voice shook as he said it, admitting to himself that this was probably a lie, and as time went on, she wouldn't be able to prevent doing as Adam asked; but what good would the truth do? She leant forward, wrapping her damp arms around him, and kissed him softly. It said everything. Before he changed his mind, he hurried out, and set off for Cosham. As he drove away, he noticed that the crows were still building up, and there were twice as many as when they had arrived. Hellen sighed, and went over to Sophie, who hugged her and finished drawing the curtains. 'He's coming,' she said. 'I can feel him, he's coming.'

'And we are ready. He won't know what hit him,' said Sophie, and she started loading her rifle.

Outside, the air carried a cold chill and a frost had started spreading across the grass. Ben didn't know the area very well, and it took him a while to find the road, where he drove to the end of the cul-de-sac and parked by the railway footbridge, turning off the engine and the lights and preparing to wait. On the drive down, he had spent time thinking carefully on how he could protect himself, and after leaving Hellen's, he had pulled over in a side road just around the corner and had hung a cross on the front mirror and used duct tape to stick one on the back window, and he had carefully spread holy water around and over each window, so he couldn't be trapped in his car. There wasn't much movement in the road yet, as people were still at work, so he leaned back in his seat and unwrapped a chocolate bar that he had got at the garage when paying for his fuel. Not a good dinner, but he wasn't really hungry. Hellen's kiss had provided him with enough energy to keep him going for days; a childish sentiment, but he felt true — he was a romantic at heart, after all. 'God, I'm so naïve,' he reprimanded himself. 'You've only just met up with her again.' One night of sex didn't mean that she would stay with him… But… they had known each other really well before, and… there was something about the way she was with him now that gave him hope, and he found his mind drifting to a life with her after all of this. 'No… I must pay attention,' he said to himself and sat up. 'I've got to keep her alive first, and I have to kill these things to have that chance.'

Hellen and Sophie had settled down in the bedroom and had already locked the door. Sophie cuffed Hellen to the bed, this time with both of her hands restrained. It was incredibly uncomfortable, but she was not going to risk her friend's safety, and she felt that last time she was so close to giving in to Adam that she had to take every precaution.

'What do you think of him then, Sophie?' Hellen asked her friend, desperately trying to keep positive and her mind off of the macabre. For some reason during her university days, Ben and Sophie had never met up, and she was keen to see what her childhood friend thought of him. It seemed strange, at least to her, but it was like there had never been a break in their friendship, and she was coming to terms with the fact that she had very strong feelings for him. Not just lust and passion, although she had never slept with anyone on a first date before, but with Ben it went beyond that: they had been really close and it was more like she felt complete again. She could be herself with him, trust him, and he loved her for it! Yes, he loved her.

'Seems nice; we haven't really had a chance to talk, though.'

'No, you slept all the way back.'

'Not all the way.' She gave a sly smile. 'You two seemed to be having fun; I didn't want to interrupt.'

'Oh God, Soph, you should have said. We were only talking, and...'

'I'm sorry. Didn't mean to embarrass you. You're good together and you deserve someone who loves you. You have put your work first for so long, I thought you'd never find anyone — somehow guessed you'd marry a test tube or something.'

'That's hardly fair... Is it? I... I don't know, but I do actually feel complete, for the first time in my life, a relationship that feels right. I know, I know that we only met again the other day after years apart, and most of that was sex, but I knew him before, when we weren't lovers, but true friends; I just didn't see it then. I think my Mum and Dad did, they just didn't want to interfere. They always thought that I was lying to them, and we were at it like rabbits the whole time. When he used to come and stay with us in the University holidays, they even asked if I wanted him in my room. I'm sure they saw it. They liked him, you know, he got on well with Mum and Dad.' She allowed herself a few tears, and then had to ask Sophie to wipe her eyes as her hands were cuffed up.

'I'm pleased for you, Hellen, I really am. You both just have to stay alive now, and hey... I can be bridesmaid, can't I? You can't say no, not after all this.'

Both women couldn't help but giggle at the absurdity of talking weddings when Hellen was handcuffed to the bed to prevent a vampire attacking them.

'No, I suppose I couldn't. And I'd love you to be, Sophie. Now we have a few moments, what's all this about with the Professor? You were mighty strange up in London.'

'I don't know, Hellen, I just don't know. You've known me for years and I've not had much luck in love really.'

'You've had massive attention from men, how can you say that?' Hellen said, rather surprised. 'You've always got a man on your arm!'

'Don't, Hellen, you make me sound like a black widow or something. I've dated a lot and have gained a lot of experience, if you know what I mean, but I don't think I have really loved any of them,' and for a moment Hellen thought that Sophie looked very sad. 'Did you know that I never had a relationship last longer than six months in my entire life?'

'Well, I hadn't been counting, but now that you mention it.'

'Sad, isn't it. I want them to last, but they never do. I think I scare them.'

'Surely not! Well, perhaps a little — you are very forthright about what you want.'

'I know, but when I saw John this morning, I don't know... But I sort of felt something I haven't felt before... I can't really explain it, but I couldn't say anything. I stayed back and was going to talk to him, but, well, I couldn't.'

Hellen couldn't help herself and laughed. 'Now there's a first!' she said, and Sophie smiled as well and hit her restrained friend with a pillow.

'If he phones again, I want to speak to him. Please put me on.'

'I will, I promise.'

The only thing they could really do was to keep cheery and wait for the inevitable, but Hellen knew that she had to ask her friend something first, something that she didn't want to have to ask her, but had no choice! She suddenly looked serious, and turned to face Sophie.

'Sophie, if I do turn, will you promise me something?' Hellen asked suddenly, her lip trembling and a lump forming in her throat.

'No, No, please don't ask me what I think you're going to, don't you dare,' and she fought to keep the tears from her eyes.

'I shouldn't ask you, I don't want to have to ask you, but I don't know if Ben would be able to do it. I think he would end up letting me kill him. He may not look it, but he's so sensitive. Will you please kill me, if it comes to that... please?' She looked imploringly at her friend. 'I don't want to harm anyone, especially you and Ben, and I don't want to live like that. You've always been stronger than me, Soph, you're the only one I know that could do it.'

She could hold them back no longer, and tears ran down Sophie's face.

'Shit, why did you have to ask me that? Why?' She looked heartbroken, as her face flushed and she fought back the tears. 'I don't want to lose you; there is always hope, but I will, Hellen, I will, if there's no other way and that's what you want, I will.'

Both sat silently for a while just holding hands. There was nothing else to say.

* * *

Ben was jolted awake by the noise of two cats fighting and looked out the side window to see a fat tabby squaring up to a shabby ginger cat that looked like an anorexic version of Garfield. Both circled each other slowly, sizing up the opposition, before both looked up at him, and decided to saunter off in different directions. 'Shit!' He looked at his watch to find that it was seven, and the road had filled up with cars and the smell of the residents cooking their evening meals drifted towards him. He sat up and cursed again — he couldn't afford to sleep. He didn't think that anything would happen this early, but just in case he must stay focused; it was dark, and that made anything possible. He had scanned the road earlier and most of the properties looked like well-used family houses, but one had stood out, and did so more now that people were home and their lights were on. One house had an estate agent's sold board up outside, and no lights could be seen coming from the windows. That had to be it. He pulled out his phone and texted Hellen just two things: 'Found' and 'The Ivy'. If he didn't manage to get away alive, it would give Hellen and Sophie one more chance to finish it, if they acted fast. There was always the possibility that Adam might try to move, or have another residence he didn't know about, and the girls would have to act quick to catch him if he didn't return alive.

As he sat in the car waiting, Ben began to wonder about the absurdity of the whole situation. A couple of days ago he had been at University, where his biggest worries had been students not handing work in by the deadline, and making sure that he got enough journal publications to appease management and keep his position. And now, here he was, united with the love of his life, fighting vampires. One might be forgiven for thinking that he was in the middle of a bad LSD trip. He, Professor Ben Harwood, had actually killed two people in as many days, one of which was a fucking teenager. Well, maybe he had not exactly killed them, as they were already dead, but he had laid to rest two vampires — he preferred that term, it sounded less violent — and he was now sitting in his car waiting to hunt down another.

'Don't panic, Ben,' he told himself. 'Breathe deeply.' Hellen wasn't here to see him afraid, and he wouldn't have wanted to push his fears onto her, she had enough worries. He breathed deeply, and smiled. He might not be a real warrior, and had next to no experience in fighting — the rugby field didn't really count, he guessed — but he had one thing that he clung onto, one thing that was his driving force: Hellen loved him, he could tell. He pushed the thought of what would happen if she turned into a vampire to the back of his mind. He couldn't cope with that thought. He knew that there was no way that he would be able to put a stake into her. He knew himself too well, and that was beyond him. He brushed away a tear that was forming at the side of his eye and turned his mind back to simpler things: normality, love, the future. The sparkle in Hellen's eyes as they had made love, the gentle way that she rubbed his hand, the way her hips swayed as she walked, the jingle of her laugh. There had to be a chance for the future for them, and he would try and do anything to make that happen; she was counting on him.

The time passed slowly, and his mind kept drifting to the night he had spent with Hellen, but at eleven he heard a click and looked up to see the door of 'The Ivy' click shut and a tall dark shape head down the road. He waited a few minutes until it vanished from sight and was just going to open his door to get out when he saw a woman standing in front of his car, just looking at him. His heart missed a beat. She was dressed in white and

287

was looking straight at him. He blinked, and when he looked again, she was gone. He blinked again: maybe he had been seeing things, a trick of the light?

'*Let me in. It's cold out here, Ben, let me in.*'

Ben jumped, hitting his head on the car's roof, and saw that the woman was now by his car's passenger door, and looking in. Her eyes were burning pits and he was sure that this must be Jasmine.

'*Let me in, Ben... Warm me up...*'

'*I'm so cold, Ben...*'

He felt his hand moving to the door handle. He tried to stop himself, but all he could see was her eyes, and they burned into his mind.

'*Let me in... Say I can come in.*'

His lips moved without his control, and his hand kept reaching out. 'Come... in...' he whispered,' and he knew his mistake, a terrible mistake that could bring about the end of him, and Hellen's chances of freedom. The door opened and she got in next to him. Jasmine reached out and began stroking his hair and exposing his neck. Static crackled and the hairs on his chest began to stand up, along with his nipples and cock. Shit, was this the horror that Hellen went through every night? He closed his eyes and all at once she seemed to be staring at him with her piercing green eyes, saying, 'Fight it, Ben, fight!' It was at that precise moment that the cross Hellen had put around his neck fell into Jasmine's gaze, and she halted like a statue, quickly pulling back, knocking her head on the cross hanging from the mirror and releasing a hiss.

'*Remove the chain, Ben, my dear. Remove the chain.*'

She seemed to release a hiss at the end of each of the words. Her face was still close to him and he could see every detail and imperfection, but especially her enlarged canine teeth.

It was the time Ben needed and he turned to face the vampire, lifting the cross Hellen had given him from his chest and moving it into her full view. She grabbed his wrist in a vice-like grip, knocked the cross from his hand, and, slipping her free hand behind his head, she tried to pull him closer, her mouth open, with those horrible teeth getting closer and closer.

Outside, a passer-by walked past the rocking car, steam building up on the inside of the windows, and shouted angrily, 'Get a room, you fucking perverts; children live round here, you know?'

Inside, Ben was reaching towards his UV torch, as his face edged closer and closer towards Jasmine's teeth. He couldn't quite reach the torch enough to unclip it from his belt, and resorted to punching the vampire in the face with his left hand. There was a crack from his hand and lightning shots of pain shot up his arm. Ben felt he had broken several bones in his good hand, but he punched again and again, trying to ignore the pain. The woman loosened her grip slightly, not much; it was like striking a brick wall, but it gave him enough space to unhook the torch, despite the shooting pains through his knuckles he placed it right in front of her face and turned it on. The results were rather more spectacular than he thought possible. She released a high-pitched scream, as her face started to blister and smoke. She scrambled to get away, to shift further from him and away from the burning light, but luck for once was on Ben's side, and the dodgy lock that he had been meaning to repair but the part hadn't arrived from America yet, failed, and the door wouldn't open. The vampire couldn't get out, but was instead trapped inside with him. She lashed out at him in pain and desperation, leaving cuts across his face and torso, but he kept the torch focused on her face, which was when Jasmine caught fire, burning all over and screaming, her dress going up in bright orange flames, spewing black smoke into the car, making him cough. He searched in the haze and pulled a stake from the door's storage container and swung it as hard as he could with his bad right hand, and it hit its mark, but the result was different from before — the creature seemed to explode in a cloud of dust, leaving him on his own, trying to put out the fire on his passenger seat with a small fire extinguisher, which added to the choking atmosphere of the smoke. Having put out the fire, he opened the window and shifted the gear lever into drive and drove off with a squeal of burning rubber, and smoke bellowing out of the window. He had drawn too much attention with the fight to stay there and he could see faces at the windows of the residents looking out at the scene. He would have to come back for Adam tomorrow, if it wasn't too late.

'*Hellen...*'

    '*Open the door, Hellen...*'

    '*Let me in.*' [No... I mustn't]

    '*You cannot resist me, Hellen... End this impossible resistance and let me in...*' [I said NO!]

    '*You cannot resist forever, Hellen... You want me... I feel your desire... Your need...*' [No]

    '*Your body craves me... It aches for me...*' [No]

    '*Look how it longs for my touch...*' [Please no]

    '*It aches for me... It wants me...*' [I... Please... No... Help me...]

* * *

Sophie was woken by Hellen's shouting and sat up quickly. Her friend was arching and writhing on the bed, trying to free herself from the restraints, while moaning and screaming, 'No... no... Daddy, help me... Ben...' There came a scraping on the window, and the door buzzer began to ring continually, sounding above the crows tapping on the glass. Hellen screamed, or perhaps howled like a wolf might have been closer to the animalistic sound that she made, and with a massive pull she managed to wrench free her left hand, breaking the metal links of the handcuffs' chain, and she began to use the jagged edge of the metal to cut her other arm, its sharp edge slicing deeply into her flesh.

'It feels so good,' she muttered as she interspersed the cutting with licking up the blood that flowed down her arm. Her eyes were now open and burning with an uncontrollable fire.

'Hellen, stop!' Sophie pleaded, as her friend began to cut through her nightie and across her chest. 'For God's sake stop!'

'Oh, Sophie, come… Come and taste heaven,' she said, ripping her nightie open and revealing the blood running down her body from the fresh deep red welts, and flowing between her breasts. 'Come and be with me,' she said, and she opened her legs and started gyrating on the bed as the flowing blood began to stain the waist elastic of her white panties.

'Fight it, Hellen, you've got to fight it. Think about Ben, your love for him; think, Hellen.'

For a moment indecision flashed across her eyes, and the brightness dimmed, revealing the green beneath.

'I'm… trying… It's just so strong this time… I can't… resist it. I'm… trying… I'm…' Her eyes began to burn again, and she pulled free from the other restraint, a crack coming from her thumb as she pulled her hand through the cuff, ripping off her crucifix and leaping at Sophie, teeth bared. Sophie managed to side step and trip Hellen, but in doing so broke the salt circle, allowing her to go beyond the bed. She fought off a tirade of clubbing blows from her bleeding friend, managing to deflect a few of them, but many landed with a crushing force, leaving her face and arms cut and badly bruised.

'Hellen, please fight it, I don't want to hurt you!' She raised her cross, stopping her friend in her tracks, and Hellen took a few steps back, hissing, anger on her face. Then the green broke through, and her face wrinkled as if in pain.

'Run, Sophie, I can't... stop him... Just run... Please... run.' With this, she picked up the door phone and said the words, 'Come... in...'

'My God, Hellen, what have you done?' Sophie went to step towards Hellen but was knocked to the side by her friend's sweeping arm. Stunned, she lay in a heap on the floor, blood pouring from her nose and moaning in pain.

A dark shape entered the room and stood in front of Hellen. It was Adam, dressed in a long red frock coat, black trousers and a frilled Romantics shirt. He swept back his cape and pulled his shirt open to the waist, revealing a pale, muscular chest, and with one long nail made a deep cut across his chest. The burn mark on his face had completely vanished.

'*Drink, my dear, drink of my blood and you will become mine forever. I give you the same offer that was once put to me. Drink.*'

She sank to her knees before him, and her head began to approach the tall figure and his flowing blood. Sophie watched the scene from behind Adam, and it appeared that was why he hadn't seen her yet. She raised her rifle and shot him in the back three times, jerking him forward as the shots penetrated his skin. Hellen's eyes cleared to green, and she punched Adam in the face with her rosary that had somehow wound itself around her fist like a knuckle-duster. He screamed in pain as smoke issued from the wounds on his back and face, and he spun around to face Sophie as Hellen jumped onto his back, stabbing at him with her small cross. His eyes burnt as his gaze fixed on her, and Sophie reached up instinctively with fear, pulling the UV light from the window frame. In desperation of those hateful eyes focused on her and approaching, she pointed it at the vampire and turned it on. Both Adam and Hellen screamed. The noise of it seemed to penetrate her very brain with its pitch, and she fell down, clutching her ears. Adam's shape shimmered and vanished as a shadow towards the door. Hellen, however, crumpled to the floor and rolled into a ball, trying to shield her face as her skin began to smoke and blister. Seeing this, Sophie switched the light off quickly and approached her friend with caution, rifle at the ready, but Hellen seemed to be back in control for the moment and was sobbing uncontrollably, clutching her torn nightie around her protectively and grimacing in pain.

As Sophie approached, she screamed, 'No, don't come near me. I... I can't control myself. I... I...' She staggered up, almost falling over, colliding with the mirror on the door, breaking it, and ran out of the flat, tears streaming down her face and without any idea of direction — she just ran and ran.

Sophie grabbed her rucksack and a long blouse, as Hellen was next to naked, and ran after her. She knew that they shouldn't be outside. Adam had not been permanently hurt, and could come after either of them again, and the flat was now no longer safe. Looking at her watch, it was only nearing midnight, and there was a lot of night left.

'Hellen, wait!' she called out as she followed her up the road towards Waterlooville. But Hellen kept herself fit and was getting a greater lead on Sophie in the dark with a supernatural strength, and was now far off, becoming the occasional gleam of ginger hair with her white panties flashing in Sophie's torchlight, like a deer running from a car's headlights.

When Sophie finally caught up with Hellen, she was standing shivering in front of the church door, dripping blood from all over her body. The sight of her vulnerability made Sophie cry, the way her friend kept shifting her weight as if to move forward, but was being held back by an invisible force, which Sophie guessed was kind of true. Tears and snot dripped from her face, and Hellen looked imploringly at her sobbing, breaking her friend's heart.

'I… can't… go… in… Sophie… After all these years… of not wanting… to go in… When I really… really need to… I can't.' She collapsed to the frosty ground, shaking. Sophie pulled Hellen's phone out of her bag and texted Ben, 'Get to church NOW', and then wrapped the blouse around her shoulders and held her tightly.

'I'm here, Hellen, I'm here. Ben's coming as well,' she whispered. 'He's on his way'. She gently rocked with her as if comforting a small child. She felt so frail and bony, Sophie feared that she might break.

It was only five minutes until Ben's car came roaring into view and pulled up. A bloody and bruised Ben ran over to them and picked Hellen up, ignoring the pain that shot through his broken fingers, and she held onto him tightly, leaving blood all over the front of his already dirty and smoke-stained shirt.

'We have to go,' he said. 'I had just arrived at the flat when you called; it's no longer safe by the look of it. Those damn birds are everywhere, and I couldn't get out of the car as there were dogs roaming the car park. They attacked the car.'

'We can't hold up here, Ben. Hellen can't go in.'

A wolf-like howl rung out in the background.

'Shit!' he cursed and looked up as a crow landed on the wall opposite and looked straight at them. Its eyes focused on Hellen, and squawked 'Mine… Mine.'

'We have to go,' Ben said, and he laid Hellen on the back seat and jumped in.

'What the fuck's on my seat?' Sophie's nose wrinkled at the smell.

'That,' smiled Ben, 'is Jasmine, or what's left of her. She exploded in a most spectacular fashion. Now get in.'

Ben hit the gas and the car shot up the road, just as a mist began to gather by the crows.

'Where are we going to go?' Sophie asked as Ben pulled onto the A3.

'It's not long until light, but it's still a few hours away yet. If we can lose him for a bit, we can go after him during daylight. I saw a hotel around here, somewhere! It will be enough to keep us safe tonight... I hope.'

'I'm sorry, Ben, I couldn't hold him off,' a weak voice said from the back seat. He glanced up to the rear-view mirror and saw that Hellen was sitting up, holding the now bloody shirt together, in a failed attempt to hide her modesty.

'You didn't drink his blood, did you?' Sophie asked, turning around and sounding worried. 'I must have lost consciousness for a few seconds once you'd hit me.'

'I'm so sorry, Soph.' She looked up at her friend's bruised and cut face. 'Oh my God, I'm so sorry. No, I didn't, you saved me from that. I can't thank you enough.'

'We'll stop here,' Ben interrupted, and pulled the car sharply into a small and rather tatty hotel just off the motorway. 'I'll get the room and we'll head up together,' and he wiped the blood off his face, went to the boot and pulled out a clean jacket and, slipping it on, he disappeared inside. He returned a nerve-wracking fifteen minutes later and carried Hellen in through the side entrance, whilst Sophie brought their equipment. He couldn't use the front door, as even the inattentive assistant might ask questions about a man carrying a bloody and mostly naked woman up to his room.

Chapter 19
Blood of the Innocent, the Phone Call, The End

'For whether we live unto the Lord;
and whether we die, we die unto the Lord;
whether we live therefore, or die,
we are the Lord's'
Romans 14:8
(King James version)

Hellen sat in the hotel bath with her knees tucked up and hugged closer to her body by her arms wrapped around them, as the steam from the hot water covered the mirrors.

'Are you feeling better?' asked Ben, who was sitting, partly collapsed on the loo, trying to tape up his broken fingers, but his bad hand kept shaking too much, and he couldn't get it to lay flat. His face was wrinkled and pale, reflecting his pain.

'Come over, Ben' she said. 'I'll do it for you, sweetie.'

'But you've been through so much tonight, I can't ask you to.'

'I'm not a delicate flower, Ben, I'll survive. Come over and let me do it,' she said defiantly.

He knelt down by the bath looking embarrassed. She was covered in cuts, deep purple bruises and blisters from where the UV light had burnt her. Her own hand had been tightly bound in tape by Sophie, who had declared her thumb was probably dislocated and not broken, and in a cringeworthy crack had pulled it back into place, making Hellen grip his hand so hard he had screamed, bringing back the memory of her belly button piercing at MetalFest. He hesitantly offered her his left hand, which she took gently, looking at the growing swelling around his index and middle fingers, and kissed them gently before taping them up tightly.

'I'm afraid I think these are broken,' she said, frowning. 'If we get through tomorrow you will have to get them set properly. You must have one hand that doesn't shake.'

'I'll worry about that then. Compared to our other problems, it seems small for now.'

'I know, I can't believe you killed another one,' she said. 'At least Jasmine is at rest now if the legends are correct, which, given everything else we have seen, I tend to believe.'

He turned to face her and started to clean the cuts on her chest with the bottle of antiseptic he had brought into the room with him, his hand shaking badly, this time with nerves.

'I should have been with you, Hellen. I shouldn't have… I mean, it was wrong of me to leave you.'

'Don't blame yourself, Ben. We are still alive and taken out another one. There's only Adam left now and I'll be free. Ouch.' She flinched as he dabbed more of the liquid onto her breasts. 'I hope these don't scar,' she said optimistically, examining herself; they looked awfully deep. He glanced once more at the network of scars that covered her entire body and lifted her chin up to face him, and they just looked at each other, locked into a dream world of their own, which was interrupted by Sophie calling out.

'Hope you're behaving yourself in there, I'm coming in!' and she threw the door open and started squirting holy water around the windows and placing garlic bulbs at the corners. 'That's the last of it; it's only got to cover us until morning.' Then she disappeared out of the door again. They both laughed, and Ben held a towel open for her and she painfully stood up and let him wrap her in its folds, enjoying the hug, and she went and sat on the comfy chair in the bedroom, waiting for him to sit opposite. Ben followed after her rather stiffly, as his muscles began to tighten from his fight earlier.

His neck in particular was throbbing, and the bruises were now spreading down as far as his breastbone and up to his jaw. *'Why did they always grab the throat?'* he thought, trying to rub his stiff shoulder muscles. *'I have bruises on top of bruises.'*

'What now then?' Hellen stated to the room, and no one in particular. Ben was pleased that she was now more her normal self. He sat down on the floor in front of her, and she began to rub his shoulders, seeing his discomfort.

'We have to go to the house and confront him,' Sophie said, sitting down on the end of the bed and subconsciously rubbing the huge purple bruises that now engulfed most of her arms. 'What choice do we have?'

'You're right,' said Ben. 'He can't have had time to move out already. I've destroyed his London bolt-hole and he can't cross the river without being taken anyway, so he would have to get people to do it, and that must take time to arrange; and after you shot him, he will need to rest. If the books are right, though, if he feeds the wounds will heal.'

'There's no indication that he has anywhere else, is there?' Hellen asked.

'Not that I could find, but he's a sneaky bastard and I wouldn't put it past him. I can't see him wishing to exist in condemned buildings, so he must have a main place to exist in somewhere. We'll just have to hope he doesn't, or can't get to it.'

Hellen made her way over to Ben's bag, and without embarrassment dropped her towel and put on a pair of his jeans and his checked shirt. They were far too big and she had to make a new hole in the belt to hold them up, but there was no way she was going to her flat until Adam was dead, and for some reason the smell of Ben's clothes made her feel safe, and if she was honest, a little excited. She felt closer to him.

'No point sleeping,' she said. 'It's almost light and we will need to move quickly.'

'You're not coming with me,' Ben said, terrified.

'You try and fucking stop me. He can't control me during the day yet, and all three of us stand a better chance than one.' She looked at him, her eyes piercing his with determination. He smiled and walked over to her.

'I wouldn't expect anything else… I just worry… I shouldn't, but… Maybe I'm jumping the gun… but I couldn't lose you… I…'

'Thank you, Ben, I just have to be there. Besides, if I'm going to die there's no better place than with my oldest friends.' She cast a knowing glance at Sophie, one that said, '*You remember your promise?*', and Sophie nodded silently and looked away as Hellen kissed Ben. '*I love you,*' she thought. '*You'd never be able to kill me if it came to it, and I couldn't ask you.*'

* * *

The sun was almost breaking through the mist when Hellen's mobile rang, causing her to jump and drop it on the floor, cracking the screen. She picked it up as if it might bite her and answered.

'Hello?'

'Hello, Dr Oswold, it's John here, John Harker. I've been working all night on this, I just couldn't stop.

And I just can't understand your blood. I'm sorry, but it's darn well scuppered me.'

'Oh,' was all Hellen could think to say.

'There is nothing that would indicate a virus, no additional molecules, it's fascinating. But when I tried putting a drop of holy water on it, it actually parted for a second as if trying to escape it, and then broke down. The blood cells actually broke down... And when I exposed the blood to UV, the slide caught fire. It's truly fascinating, but I have nothing to help you, I'm afraid. It could take years of research to make any headway. It must alter the DNA itself, or perhaps rewrite it somehow, or something like that, but it's too complicated to come up with anything so quickly. I'm so, so sorry.'

'That's all right, I didn't expect it to show much really. Thanks anyway for all your effort. Hopefully by tonight it will all be over.'

'Give me the phone,' Sophie mouthed at Hellen. 'I may not get another chance.' Hellen passed the phone over.

'Er, hello, John, it's Sophie here.'

'Oh, hello, my dear, how might I help you?'

Hellen was smiling at her, blowing kisses, making her stutter.

'Well... I've never asked an older guy out before, but what the hell, would you like to go out with me? I've been thinking about you since we met, and, well, I, you know, I'd like to get to know you better.'

It was now Professor Harker's turn to stutter. 'Em, I... er...'

'Well, do you want to or not?' Sophie sounded a bit peeved and embarrassed.

'Well, of course I would, but you must be more than fifteen years younger than me. I wouldn't have dreamt of making a fool of myself and asking, but yes, of course, if, you're sure? I'll sort us out a table somewhere nice for the weekend, if that's OK?'

'Excellent!' She gave a few hops of excitement. 'Eight o'clock then, and book us a hotel room,' and she turned the phone off. She looked at Ben and Hellen's smiling faces. 'Hey, why not? If I'm dead I won't have to go, and if not, it might be great fun. I just love his moustache! Now let's go do this.' With that, she picked up the bags and headed out to the car, hoping that they hadn't noticed her flushed face — she wasn't used to blushing and wasn't sure why she was doing it now. Hellen looked at Ben, gave his ass a cheeky squeeze and followed Sophie outside, leading Ben by the hand.

For the first time, they drove in silence towards the ivy-laced house. Each had their own thoughts, most of them particularly gloomy. Hellen kept a constant hold of Ben's arm, who in turn slowly clenched and unclenched his hand, trying to get some strength back into it, and Sophie sat on the back seat, carving crosses into her air gun pellets, in the hope of increasing their potency, given the success of the added holy water.

It hurt. And it hurt badly. He had been forced to dig his claws into his wounds and pull the pellets out himself, for they would not stop burning, as Jasmine had failed to return by daylight, and was therefore most likely permanently dead. His face burnt from where the cross had marked him and the blisters on his skin from the light were also bad. However, they would heal, but he had run out of time to find fresh blood before dawn and he had to move that night. He would have to head back up to York, where his manor house was, and his final coffin, among other things. London was no longer viable as news had reached him but an hour ago about the death of his girls. They were all girls to him at his age, but there was something about the sweetness of young blood: it had stronger restorative powers and seemed to appease the burning hunger more than anything else. But no one had come close to Rebecca. His Rebecca, soulmate for over two hundred years, who had so cruelly been hunted down over a hundred years ago, and Hellen had been the first one in all that time that had the potential to come close, her defiance was admirable. Sometimes the loneliness was more painful than the hunger. For now, there was nothing he could do other than return to his coffin in Cosham and rest after the attack. If the day was dark, he might be able to resist the pain of the light and go out to make arrangements, but it hurt so badly... He closed his eyes, trying to suppress his anger, hunger and pain...

The Firebird pulled up in the neighbouring Knowsley Road, and the engine went silent, as all three friends got out, looking the worse for wear. Sophie opened the boot, as Ben's fingers couldn't twist the handle properly, and he lifted out the bag, and they walked up the road, crossed the railway tracks via the rickety metal walkway as the barriers were down, and within minutes they were standing outside the house. Sophie gripped her rifle, Hellen had a stake through her belt, her bottle of holy water in one hand and a crowbar in the other, and Ben had opted for the trusty spade he had killed the vampires in London with, and he also had the bag of stakes over his shoulder. They made a grim sight, but the street was empty, and they entered the building as quietly as forcing the door would allow them to. Ben lifted his torch and looked around, following the footprints into the next room, which seemed to have been a kitchen, and they spread out, searching the vandalised room.

'Over here,' Hellen said, and they noticed that she was pointing towards a shabby metal door, which she pulled but seemed to be locked. 'I'll use the crowbar,' she whispered, but Sophie signalled 'no'.

'It will make too much noise; that metal will squeal when forced. Let me do it.' She knelt down and set about the lock with a small screwdriver.

'Where did you learn to pick locks?' Hellen whispered, and there was a click, which seemed to echo around the empty room.

'Don't ask, and I won't lie,' she said, and they descended down the wooden stairs into the darkness.

At the bottom, as in the London building, the floor was earth, and there were two coffins on the floor, one open and empty, which must have been Jasmine's, and the other had the lid shut.

'We all ready?' Ben asked in a hushed voice as he approached the casket.

'As ever,' said Sophie, lifting her gun.

They crept closer, and Ben reached out to lift the lid, but just as his fingers were about to touch the handle, the lid flew open and Adam sat up, grabbing Ben by the throat. He stood to his full height and threw him across the room as if he was a toy, where he collided with the wall, producing a horrid crack, where he collapsed groaning. Sophie fired several times, the shots hitting Adam in the chest, but he ignored the small flames that came from the wounds and he pulled the gun from her hands and tossed it away. He then started to approach her as she backed away, pointing at Hellen and saying, '*Stay.*'

Hellen tried to move, but it was like wading through treacle. She closed her eyes and kept fighting his command, and step by step she edged forward.

'Fuck you!' Sophie shouted at him and jumped, gripping her legs around his waist and twisting around him, converting her hold to a headlock, as she had done with Hellen. But he was so much stronger, and he reached up, grabbing her arm in a vice-like grip and twisting, breaking the bones of her left arm with a snap. Sophie howled in pain and with her remaining hand slipped her cross around his neck, before being thrown away like a rag doll. But he started to stagger around, the cross burning his skin. Hellen found that she could move again, as his attention was diverted, and she broke into a run towards him, just at the same time Ben hit Adam in the back of the knees with a rugby tackle, knocking him to the ground, but he brought his elbow down on the side of Ben's head, knocking him out. Adam shifted around, grabbing the unconscious man's head, and was just about to twist and break his neck, when Hellen smashed into him with her small body, but now part-vampire strength, and he was knocked over and she brought her rosary cross down into his eye, sinking it as deep as she could with a sickly squelching noise, the type made when a jelly flops out of its mould onto a plate. The scream was deafening, but she resisted, turning over as he lashed out at her, catching her hard in the stomach, doubling her over, but her eyes now burnt with determination, not red but green, looking at her fallen friend and lover, and she rammed her stake into Adam's leg, pinning him to the coffin. As he reached down to pull it out, she pulled his head back and poured the holy water down his throat, and he made a terrible gasping sound as his throat burnt, smoke emanating into the air, and he knocked her to the floor, causing her head to hit the side of the coffin hard, and everything went black.

Sophie, cradling her arm, recovered her rifle and started shooting Adam one-handed, resting the barrel on her elbow as pain raced through her, each shot leaving a bright burning flame on his body. Just as she ran out of ammo, Ben staggered up and rammed the stake into Adam's chest, but it didn't fully pierce his heart and his one good eye locked on Ben, and his hand again found his throat, squeezing the life from him. Hellen, the world spinning around her, blood gushing from her temple, grabbed her lover's fallen spade and swung it hard at the head of the stake, driving it deep, and Adam suddenly froze like a statue right where he stood, dropping Ben, who crumpled to the floor, gasping for air. She looked the vampire straight in the eyes and swung again, decapitating him with the sharp edge of the spade, and the head dropped to the floor with a look of peace on its face. She then dropped to her knees, searching for Ben. She reached his hand, gripped it tight and passed out. Sophie watched as the vampire's body collapsed into dust, and she could no longer hold herself up, and fell to her knees, gripping her arm, and let the flashing lights take her.

* * *

Ben awoke, wondering where he was as everything was dark. As he moved, stabbing pains shot through his hands and shoulder and he remembered. He scrambled to find his torch, and grunted in pain to the realisation

310

that his shoulder was dislocated. He used his other hand and switched the torch on, casting a weak beam of light around the room. Hellen was crumpled on the floor like a discarded paper doll, blood flowing from her head, and he crawled over to her, placing her head on his lap, and he began stroking her hair, pulling the bloody strands away from her face. She looked so peaceful as he traced the outline of her face with his broken fingers, but he had to know, was she still alive? With a heavy weight on his heart and tears in his eyes, he lifted her upper lip, and to his shock her teeth had shrunk back to normal. Feeling a surge of hope, he slid his hand into her shirt and found that he could feel the rise and fall of her warm chest, and the steady thump of her heart. He gripped her tightly to him and sobbed with relief: she was still alive and it seemed that the curse was lifted.

'Yep, don't worry about me, I'm OK,' came Sophie's voice from behind him, as she limped towards them. 'Let's get out of this shithole, shall we?'

They each took one of Hellen's arms and despite their own wounds, managed to painfully drag her up the stairs and into the light outside, where the fresh air seemed to start bringing her around.

'It's over,' she said, gasping the fresh air, and she gripped Ben tightly and wouldn't let go of him despite his winces of pain — but no pain could remove the smile on his face.

Chapter 20
Life After the Night

'Cause me to hear thy loving kindness
In the morning; for in thee do I trust:
Cause me to know the way wherein I
Should walk; for I lift up my soul unto thee.'
Psalm 143:8
(King James version)

'Bless me, Father, for I have sinned. It has been over twenty years since my last confession.'

'Go on, my child, please, when you are ready.'

'I lost my faith, Father, and I let my pride and work get in the way and used it as an excuse not to return.' She chose her words carefully and outlined her recent experiences, expecting interruptions and disbelief. But if Father Daulton had any, he didn't say. He listened carefully and provided encouragement whenever she choked up.

'May the merciful Lord have pity on thee and forgive thee thy faults. In the virtue of my priestly power, by the authority and command of God expressed in these words, I absolve you from your sins in the name of the Father, and the Son, and of the Holy Spirit, Amen.'

'Amen.'

Hellen left the confession booth feeling lighter in her heart, and Father Daulton joined her.

'My dear, my condolences on the passing of Father Thomas. I know that you knew him as a child, as did your mother. I spoke to him the day before he died, you know. I will speak no more of it, other than to say that I agreed with him, and believe you. If ever you need help, come and see me.' And with that, he left her at the door, looking confused. Had he known?

She left the church and headed down to the waiting Pontiac, and Ben. He was sitting on the bonnet, and turned as she approached. Ever since the events in Portsmouth, Hellen had been unable to bring herself to return home, and she had relied on Ben and Sophie to pack up her possessions for her, and put the property up for sale, which had sold quickly, and she was now just waiting for the transfer of funds, for which she was not in a rush as her mother's estate had finally been settled. She wondered if it had been too soon, but had taken the chance and moved up to Nottingham to live with Ben after they had been discharged from the QA Hospital. It had all happened so quickly that she couldn't help laughing, thinking back on it.

They had gone to tidy up her flat, but she just couldn't go through the door. She knew it was silly, but the memories were too bad. She just kept seeing Adam, and had refused to go in. Ben had taken her to dinner in the local greasy spoon cafe, and that was where her world had seriously changed. As they had sat at a table, he had held her hands and asked what she wanted to do.

'Look, Hellen, move up to Nottingham with me, right now. Your job starts soon, just a few months, and you will need to be there anyway.'

'Ben, I'll never find anywhere to rent that quickly. Oh, I don't know, for once I just don't know what to do.'

He looked down at his shoes, and back up at her, his bad hand beginning to twitch from the nerve's random signals induced by stress.

'Come and stay with me,' he had said very quietly. 'My place is big enough... I mean, you wouldn't have to share a bed with me, or anything... I don't mean anything wrong... I don't expect... I...' and he broke off, fumbling with a small box in his pocket.

'Oh, I couldn't, Ben, it would be an imposition. I...'

And that was when he got down on one knee, produced a ring and proposed, in his rather clumsy and endearing way, and wow, that was a lovely ring.

'I wouldn't ask so soon... and you've been through so much... but, marry me, Hellen, please... Don't think badly of me for asking. I know it's only a short time since we met again, but... I love you... I always have... Let's just give it a try... Let me try to make you happy. I want to look after you, and be there for you... I want to do this properly… I don't want you to feel uncomfortable, or conflict with your faith, so marry me.'

She didn't know what to say for a minute, and just sat there stammering. She had always planned everything, except timings, and had been sensible, done the right thing, but she had been so lonely, and 'why not?' kept crossing her mind. So many emotions in a short time left her in complete turmoil. The look of rejection that came across Ben's face with her silence was unbearable to see, and she started to cry, and just had to get out of the café, and she ran into the street and back to where the car was parked. When he caught up to her, he was apologising profusely; he had always been very sensitive, and his eyes were filled with pain. She held her hand across his mouth to stop him talking and looked him in the eyes, her dark green irises penetrating into his pale blue ones, and she leant forward and kissed him.

'Yes,' she whispered in his ear. 'Fuck traditions! And fuck my tick lists. Yes, of course I will. We left this far, far too long as it is; we were meant to be together and we're already in our forties, so let's do it. I want to be with you so badly, I just didn't expect… I don't know…' They kissed again, and Hellen jumped up, locking her legs around his waist, which he wasn't expecting and they both fell over in a heap on the verge, still kissing. He then, with her sitting on top of him, slid the ring on her finger. 'I'll always be willing to share a bed with you,' she whispered. 'It's not against my faith to love someone as much as I do you,' and she squeezed him tighter. 'Let's marry as soon as possible. I'm done with waiting, we've been through too much of that. Let's walk to the jewellers now and buy the wedding bands. I can't wait any more.' She climbed off him and helped him up, and she grabbed his hand, pulling him in the direction of the jewellers.

After that day, time had blurred and seemed to pass so quickly. Hellen had driven up to Nottingham with Ben the next day and moved straight in, immediately beginning to redesign the interior; but she wouldn't hear of him selling the car, that had good memories for her, but the passenger seat definitely needed to go — besides, they had her Golf as well, but that was too small for, well, fun. Sophie had come up by train a few days later, as her cast wasn't off yet and she couldn't drive, and to their surprise she brought John Harker with her, and she proudly announced that they were an item. Their hastily arranged first date had gone really well, and their relationship was progressing extremely quickly.

The following week, Hellen and Ben were married. Father Daulton had been delighted to call in several favours to clear room for a small event, and he wanted to keep his promise to his dear friend Father Thomas. Hellen decided a small gathering was the most appropriate anyway as both of her parents were dead, and the guests only included Ben's parents, his sister

Beth and her husband Jamie, Sophie and John and Tim and Becca. Both were pleased that Detective Dick had accepted his invite and actually managed to clear his diary and turn up. Sophie had been bridesmaid as requested, Jamie was Ben's best man and John stepped in to give Hellen away, a tender offer which had caused Hellen to cry profusely, which had held up events so that she could tidy up her make-up so she didn't spoil the photos. They chose to put their honeymoon off until later, as Ben's fingers were still setting and his shoulder — although it had only been dislocated and put back — was still causing him pain, and she had planning to do in preparation for starting her new job. Despite his pain, he had insisted on carrying her over the threshold, and once inside his hand had given way and they had collapsed in a heap in the hall, giggling like teenagers. She had been pleased to start thinking about academia again and whilst in a quiet moment waiting for Ben to come upstairs for their first night of passion as a married couple, she had sat there in her wedding dress and started working on her first new research paper. *'Could life get any better than this?'* she thought, as Ben hugged her from behind and kissed her gently on the neck.

Two months later, Sophie and John came up again with both Hellen and Ben surprised to hear that Sophie was already pregnant, and had taken a job in a university library in London to be near to John, who she was now living with. She had been so excited, she had spilt the news as soon as they had met, hopping up and down whilst gripping John's arm hard as if to prevent his escape.

'I'm pregnant!' she had said on first catching sight of Hellen. 'I'm not supposed to tell anyone yet, but I'm not superstitious. I'm going to have a child at last.'

Hellen had congratulated them both and hugged Sophie especially hard, as she could see that her friend was so excited.

'Oh, Sophie, I'm so pleased for you,' she said, and she led her aside as Ben talked with John, who both seemed to be getting on very well. 'Soph, that's so quick...'

'I know, but it happened on the first date, you see. We had such a good time, and hit it off straightaway, and well, neither of us were expecting it, and well... I've been so careful in the past that I'm embarrassed to say... well... we threw caution to the wind. But I'm going to have a little girl!' Then the excitement became too much for her and she started hopping again. It was good to see her so happy, especially after she had helped Hellen so much with the vampire problem.

'How did your mum take it?' Hellen asked carefully. 'Have you told her yet?'

'Yes, I bit the bullet, so to speak, and told her as soon as we knew. She actually surprised me, Hellen — she was pleased. They both hit it off straightaway with John, who promised them that he would make an honest woman of me. He's such a smoothie is my John, he even asked my dad's permission, as if they could stop me. But he was really pleased with the gesture and Mum's ecstatic that she will actually see a grand-daughter from me. I think that they had both given up on the idea given my age!' Then she looked worried and said, 'I'm sorry, Hellen, I didn't mean any offence. I know you're a little older than me...'

'Don't be, Soph, I'm so pleased for you, I really am.' And they both hugged again. 'I have approached the issue with Ben. I know he'd make an excellent dad, and...' She looked around as if revealing a massive secret, and she turned red. 'We've started trying, and you never know, maybe someday soon...' And she stopped, very embarrassed with revealing that she was having sex, and went quiet, starting to fan her face with her hand to try and remove the flush in her cheeks.

'That's excellent, Hellen,' Sophie said excitedly. 'If you get a move on, they could be similar ages, even the same year in school...' She was getting excited now.

'Sophie!' Hellen said, her voice a mixture of surprise at her friend's directness and that of excitement. She dropped her voice low to a whisper. 'We're working on it as quickly as possible!' And they both broke down into giggles again, causing Ben and John to look over at them, both of them wondering why their ears were burning.

Hellen blinked away the great memories and after they had driven back to the house from the church, they had to get ready for an evening meal that was booked for seven, as John and Sophie were coming back up to celebrate before her first day in her new job. Hellen stood in the shower, letting the warm water flow over her, wondering if everything had been just a dream. And she looked down at her body to remind herself of what she had been through by looking at the cuts across her body, which although still visible, were beginning to fade, but she doubted now that they would ever completely disappear. Ben stepped in behind her and drew his arms around her in a tender hug.

'Well, Mrs Harwood,' he said, smiling, 'looking forward to tonight?'

She turned around and hugged him, placing her head on his chest.

'Thank God it's over, Ben. I can't wait until the summer and our belated honeymoon,' she said.

He smiled at her. 'You are OK, aren't you?'

'Yes, I'm fine, Ben, more than fine, I've never been better.' She leaned forward and kissed him, and they shared a knowing look, both thinking back to the day they had first met and stood there clasping each other tightly.